THE NIGHT IS ENDLESS

M. R. PRITCHARD

This book is a work of fiction. Names, characters, places, and incidents are the product of the author's imagination or are used fictitiously. Any resemblance to actual events, locales, or persons, living or dead, is coincidental.

The Night is Endless Copyright © 2025 by M. R. Pritchard

Excerpt from *The Shadows are Darkest* Copyright © 2025 by M. R. Pritchard

Veil of Shadows Copyright © 2014-2025 by M. R. Pritchard.

All rights reserved.

No part of this book may be reproduced in any form or by any electronic or mechanical means, including information storage and retrieval systems, without written permission from the author, except for the use of brief quotations in a book review.

Cover Art and Interior Art: Stockphotos from DepositPhotos. Elements, Filters, Fonts and digital manipulations with Canva.
Photographs by M. R. Pritchard.
Edited by: Kristy Ellsworth

Midnight Ledger
Publishing
14391 Spring Hill Dr. Suite 203
Spring Hill, FL 34609
MidnightLedger.com

First Edition July 2025

ISBNs: 9781957709727 (ebook)
9781957709765 (Paperback)
9781957709772(Hardcover)

Printed in the United States of America

About 'The Night is Endless'

This is a new chapter of darkness, desire, and destiny.

The Night is Endless ushers in the next generation of the *Veil of Shadows* saga, following Evelyn—a human marked by blood and sacrifice—as she's pulled into the treacherous underworld of Hell. Surrounded by monsters, princes, and forbidden magic, Evelyn's journey is one of survival, discovery, and a love that could damn or save them all.

While Evelyn's story stands on its own, it pulses with the echoes of those who came before her. The setting is after *The Sky is Starless*. For the most reading enjoyment, read *The Sky is Starless* first. For maximum reading enjoyment, read *Veil of Shadows Series* first.

For readers eager to uncover the blood-soaked history that shaped this world—the ancient curses, the sacrifice stones, and the war between Heaven and Hell—look no further than the *Veil of Shadows* series.

There, you'll witness the epic origins of Rue's lineage

through the love story of Meg and Sparrow, as they defy prophecies, celestial war, and the weight of fate itself. Angels, demons, and half-blood heirs collide as the foundations of this dark world are carved in shadow.

Now, the legacy continues—with Evelyn, with Remington, with blood that won't stay buried... and with monsters that refuse to be forgotten.

Blood was spilled.
A sacrifice was made.
And now, Hell is the only place she belongs.

Evelyn never believed in fate—until a drop of her blood awakened an ancient sacrifice stone, marking her as a prize for the creatures of Hell. Hunted by half-lings and demons, she is thrust into a world of darkness, danger, and forbidden power.

She's his sister's best friend. She's off-limits. He's breaking every rule to keep her.

Remington has spent years resisting the pull of his monstrous nature. But when Evelyn is dragged into his world, the darkness inside him awakens. The prince of Hell is no savior—but he *will* spill blood to protect what is his.

Blood calls to blood.
Power demands a price.
And in Hell, nothing is ever freely given.

The Night is Endless is a dark fantasy romance perfect for readers who crave blood-stained love, forbidden temptation, and dangerously seductive monsters who refuse to let go.

The prince of Hell is no
savior—but he will spill blood
to protect what is his.

THE NIGHT IS
ENDLESS

M. R. PRITCHARD

ONE

Evelyn brushed her gloved hands over the ancient stone surface, her heart racing with anticipation. The symbols carved into the rock were faint, eroded by time and weather, but unmistakable: a giant towering over an angel with outstretched wings. She leaned closer, her breath fogging the crisp mountain air as she traced the delicate lines with the wooden tip of the brush she'd been using to discover the carvings.

A drop of red hit the stone.

"Shit," Evelyn pressed her sleeve to her nose. The altitude of the mountains sometimes made her nose bleed. "Goddamn it." Evelyn was searching for something to wipe it away, but when she turned back to the runes, the drop of blood was gone.

Evelyn moved her sleeve away from her nose and saw a bright red smear. No, she definitely had a nosebleed. And she was sure she'd seen it drip on the stone. She blinked a few times. "That's weird."

"Find anything?" Rue's voice cut through the quiet, startling her.

Evelyn turned to see her friend approaching, her dark hair tied back and a smudge of dirt streaked across her cheek. Rue carried a tablet, its screen glowing faintly as she recorded notes.

"Oh, another nosebleed?" Rue's eyes went wide with concern.

"I'm fine. It's just a few drops. Probably the altitude. I think I found something," Evelyn said, stepping aside to let Rue inspect the discovery. "The carvings are consistent with the ones we found last week. Giants and angels. Ancient runes on half buried stones. Do you think this is what we've been searching for?"

Rue crouched, her sharp eyes scanning the markings. "It's possible. These look similar to what we've seen at Dr. Malcom's cave."

Dr. Malcolm Royce was working on a similar project at an old mountain cave dig site nearby. Like Rue, his project focused on finding a link between local myths, long-forgotten lore, giants, and angels.

"We're not that far from his cave." Evelyn gazed over the ridge and pointed. "A creature this size could make it over that ridge in a day. Probably less."

Rue tracked Evelyn's gaze and nodded in agreement. "I think you're right."

Rue had been working on her doctorate project for the past year in these mountains; she'd come to know them like the back of her hand. And she'd been thrilled when her best friend Evelyn applied to join her team. Although, she'd expected Evelyn to join her *in* the doctorate program, but she'd confided in Rue that she couldn't pay for more college.

Evelyn smiled, a flicker of pride warming her despite the chilly air. This dig site, high in the mountains, was like a dream come true. She'd spent years studying artifacts and ruins in textbooks, but now she was uncovering pieces of a forgotten history with her own hands. And her best friend.

"There's something about these symbols," Evelyn said softly, her gaze drifting back to the carving. "They feel... important. Like they're trying to tell us something." Evelyn rubbed her face, a strange feeling of ache and warming growing in her stomach.

Evelyn cleared her throat. "Wait... that sounds kinda weird." She glanced at Rue. "Maybe I'm coming down with something."

Rue's expression grew thoughtful. "You might be." She turned back to the stones. "We'll have to cross-reference with the texts back at campus. For now, let's get some photos before the light fades."

As Rue moved to set up the camera, Evelyn's attention was drawn to a faint hum in the air, so low she almost didn't notice it. Her brow furrowed and she glanced around, the hairs on the back of her neck standing on end.

"Do you hear that?" she asked.

Rue looked up from her camera, frowning. "I was hoping you couldn't."

Evelyn hesitated. The sound was gone. Shaking her head, she forced a smile. "Probably just the wind."

A memory of Rue's first visit to Malcom's cave discoveries came to the forefront of her mind:

. . .

"These figures," Malcolm said, gesturing to the largest carving, "are what initially drew us here. They're believed to depict Nephilim—half-human, half-angel hybrids. The detail is extraordinary, considering the estimated age of these carvings." His head tipped curiously. "They've changed color. Hm." He glanced at Rue. "Maybe it's the angle of the sunlight."

Rue stepped closer, her fingers itching to trace the outlines. "And the symbols? Do you know what they mean?"

Malcolm shook his head. "Not yet. Some of them resemble ancient Sumerian cuneiform, but others are completely unique. It's possible they were a local adaptation, influenced by a mixture of cultures."

Rue pressed fingers to her mouth, remembering the blood ritual she'd come across at Malcom's cave. Dacre, her bodyguard and mate, had encouraged her to perform the ritual and it had brought out her fangs and had helped her complete the half-formed blood bond she'd created between her and Dacre years before.

"Are you okay?" Evelyn asked. "You look pale."

Rue nodded. "I'm fine."

"Is hot-bodyguard still out of town?" Evelyn looked Rue up and down. "I've noticed you get that way when you're apart for more than a few days.

"He comes home tonight." Rue smiled and wiped at a smudge of dirt on her face. She was hungry.

Evelyn knew about Rue's heritage since the night

before graduation when they were at a costume party and her brother Remington had shown up to surprise Rue. But the real surprise was the demons that infiltrated the party, drawn by auras of Rue and Remington being on the Earthen plane together. They'd barely escaped without a fight, but Evelyn was there and saw everything. She knew Rue and Remington were twins and that their parents were a King of Heaven and the Queen of Hell–a secret war waged between bloodlines in their veins. Rue drank blood and could see the future, a gift she'd only recently discovered and was still learning to control. And Evelyn was one of the few humans who knew.

Most days, Evelyn tried not to think about what she'd seen that night. Mostly because it brought about memories of Remington. His sharp eyes, same proud tilt of the chin– just like his sister–he was all swagger and cryptic smiles. Dark, dangerous, and totally hot.

Evelyn shook her head. "Down girl. You haven't got a chance in hell," she muttered to herself.

"What was that?" Rue asked as she crouched to snap more pictures.

"Nothing," Evelyn was quick to hide her thoughts. Rue was the one who told Remington to stay away. She didn't want Rue to know she spend too much of her free time reminiscing over her hot brother.

Rue straightened, her brow furrowed in concern. "Okay, it's back." The faint hum had returned. She set the camera down and scanned the surroundings, her hand instinctively moving to the small dagger strapped to her belt.

The air around them thickened, the temperature dropping noticeably. Evelyn shivered, clutching her jacket tightly as the humming grew louder, resonating in her chest like the deep toll of a bell.

A sudden gust of wind whipped through the clearing, scattering loose papers and sending a chill down Evelyn's spine. Then, just as abruptly as it had started, the sound stopped.

Rue exchanged a worried glance with Evelyn. "We should head out. Now."

Evelyn nodded, her heart pounding. As they packed up their gear, she couldn't shake the feeling that they'd just stumbled onto something far bigger–and far more dangerous–than they'd ever anticipated.

Two

When Remington's parents returned to their summer home for holiday and left him in charge of Hell, they never mentioned he'd be thrust into the middle of a disagreement between the demon families of the Adirondack mountains and their distaste for the Basilisk breeding program his mother had started.

"The Black River is teeming with beasts!" A man with horns curled at his temples shouted. "We can't even bathe! My goats were eaten yesterday afternoon. All fifteen of them."

"Fifteen?" Remington raised his eyebrows. "That seems like a lot." He glanced to the Hellions flanking him.

Hellions were giant creatures of the Royal Guard. With black leathery wings and massive size, any creature of Hell would think twice before approaching one.

"Why does the Queen of Hell desire so many Basilisk?" the demon asked.

Remington searched his brain for a logical answer. "Darkness is never far. The war with Lucifer was not that long ago, and I'll remind you my mother's Basilisk played a key role in defeating his army. Lucifer killed the rest. They were extinct."

"Lucifer is dead." The Demon argued. "I was there."

"And whose side did you fight for?" Remington challenged as he stood to his full height, pressing his knuckles to the desk instead of into the guy's face.

"You know, prince, that we did not have a choice. When Lucifer rules, things like free will are gone."

Remington lowered his gaze. "Then I will remind you that my mother is very invested in the protection of Hell and its people. The Basilisk are a key element."

"Could they be moved to a different river?" the demon asked, sounding defeated. "There are plenty of waterways in Hell."

Remington sighed. "I will replace your goats. Stay away from the Black River."

The demon opened his mouth but a Hellion grumbled.

The demon swallowed his arguments and bowed. "Thank you for your generosity, Prince."

Remington waited for the demon to walk away then said, "Lock the doors. I can't handle another moment of this."

The Hellions obeyed.

Remington paced to a nearby window and gazed out, suddenly missing his childhood of obscurity. He missed those days of freedom, of running around unknown, creating chaos with his cousin Thrush while his sister took the brunt of the attention. But her being known as a princess didn't help, and his thoughts drifted to Rue's kidnapping at fifteen. She had recovered from the experience, and was finding her own path on the Earthen plane. His mother had warned him that he'd be dead if anyone figured out who he was before he was old enough to defend himself. He was the Shadow Heir, an unexpected twin who was hidden from the public until the age of fifteen, when his real heritage became known just before the war.

He gripped the blade at his belt. He could definitely defend himself these days. Standing taller than his father at six foot ten, Remington was an intimidating height, and the only thing he lacked these days was the wings. Everyone told him that they'd appear when he earned them and to have faith. He itched the runes tattooed on his shoulder; waiting was for the birds.

"Remm," a familiar voice called.

He turned as Chel walked into the room. Chel was mysterious, quiet, and when he walked toward Remington, it looked like he only moved in the shadows; a skip and a ripple of movement. Remington had known the Hellion his whole life and behind the scenes the guy was goofy, but he put on a good show when he was working.

"What's up?" Remington asked.

Chel thumbed toward the door. "I heard about the goat guy."

Remington shrugged. "Yea–"

"Did you promise him fifteen goats?" Chel's eyes were wide like he couldn't believe it.

"I thought it was necessary, the basilisk ate the rest of them." Remington walked toward a ledger on the table and wrote down the transaction.

"Are you sure the basilisk ate them?" Chel pressed. "Some of these demons are very good liars. Don't forget you are in Hell right now. Your father's side of the family can't lie but these demons thrive on it. Lying is a way of life."

"He seemed sincere." Remington wrote in the ledger.

"What would your mother have done?" Chel challenged.

Remington stood up straight. Shit. She'd have flashed her teeth and demanded a carcass or a picture. When he looked up again, Chel was waiting.

"I didn't ask for this," Remington said. "I wanted a summer of fun."

"You wanted to run off to the Earthen plane and smash." Chel crossed his arms, a smirk spreading across his lips.

Remington shrugged. "You're not wrong."

Chel slammed his hands down on the table. "Your sister forbids it. Get your head straight, man."

His sister Rue's words echoed in his mind for the thousandth time: *Stay away from her, Remington. Evelyn's not part of our world.* Yet no matter how hard he tried, Evelyn was always there, lingering in his thoughts like a forbidden melody.

She wasn't just any human. Evelyn was Rue's classmate from college, the one who had smiled at him like she wasn't terrified of the shadows clinging to his presence. They'd graduated over a year ago but the memory of their meeting at that costume party still burned bright in his mind. He'd been brooding in a dark corner, uncomfortable and out of place among the humans, until Evelyn waltzed into his orbit, her infectious laugh cutting through the haze of alcohol and chatter and smoke.

She'd been dressed as a red devil, complete with little horns on a headband holding back her long, golden hair. He'd pretended to be unimpressed, but her confidence and easy grace had disarmed him. They'd danced–or rather, she'd dragged him onto the dance floor–and he could still feel the warmth of her body pressed against his as she moved to the music, her laughter bubbling in his ear. For the first time in years, he'd felt freedom.

A sharp snort from Chel brought him back.

"What?" Remington threw up his hands.

"Stop thinking about her, she's human," Chel growled, his voice gravelly but tinged with exasperation.

Remington frowned, turning his gaze to the window where the ochre sky of Hell stretched endlessly. *Human.* The word felt like a curse, but Evelyn was so much more than that. Everything about her was etched into his mind like a brand. He could almost feel her small hands on his shoulders as they danced, her breath against his ear as she whispered to him.

Chel smacked him on the shoulder. "Pull yourself out of it, Princeling. You've got goats to deliver."

Remington scowled but couldn't hold back a faint smirk. Chel had a talent for snapping him out of his brooding.

He pushed off the edge of the desk, adjusting his jacket. "Fine. Goats it is." A long drive to the mountains sounded perfect. Maybe he'd stop by the Black River and see if the demon had been lying.

Chel chuckled as he made his way to the door. "A nice long drive to the mountains will do you some good. Clear your head. Maybe even knock some sense into it if we get to fight."

Remington ignored the jab and glanced out the window again, his mind shifting to the Black river; anything to distract him from the persistent ache of wanting someone he could never have.

But as he stepped outside and the scent of brimstone and pine hit his lungs, one thought lingered stubbornly: *What if I saw her again?*

THREE

THE SUV'S HATCH CREAKED AS EVELYN HEAVED the last of the equipment into the back. The cases of excavation tools rattled as she shoved them into place, her hands raw from the cold mountain air. She brushed a strand of blond hair from her face and leaned against the bumper, her breath fogging the air.

"Hey, hurry up! We're losing daylight" Evelyn called over her shoulder as she watched the sun dip closer to the mountain peak in the distance.

Rue didn't answer.

Evelyn sighed, turning to glance toward the rune-covered stone where Rue was crouched with tablet in hand. The wind had teased a few strands of her dark hair loose, whipping them across her face as she focused on getting pictures of the rune and stones.

"What's taking so long?" Evelyn started toward her, brushing her palms against her jeans, wishing she'd brought gloves. "We've got what we need–"

A low hum rippled through the air, stopping her mid-step.

It was faint at first, just a vibration she could feel in her chest, like the mountain itself was waking up. Evelyn froze, her eyes darting to Rue. Her friend had gone completely still.

"Rue?" Evelyn's voice was barely above a whisper.

"I hear it," Rue murmured, not looking away from the runes. Her brow furrowed, and she took a cautious step back. "It's... getting faster."

"And louder," Evelyn said.

The hum deepened, resonating like a heartbeat. A slow, deliberate thrum grew quicker with each passing second. The air felt heavy, charged with a strange electricity that made Evelyn's skin prickle.

"My nosebleed dripped on it. Is it the blood?" Evelyn asked, her voice rising as panic crept in.

Rue's gaze was fixed on the stone where the faint carvings of the runes now glowed a soft, pulsing red. With each beat of the hum the glow brightened, spreading like veins of fire across the surface. A chill climbed up Rue's back. This didn't feel like the light from the runes in Malcom's cave. This felt darker. Demanding. Dread started to rise in her chest.

"Evelyn, get back to the car." Rue's voice was sharp now, breaking through the growing noise.

"I'm waiting for you, Tink—"

"Go!" Rue shouted, finally snapping out of her trance. She shoved the tablet into her bag and sprinted toward the SUV, grabbing Evelyn's arm as she passed. For a short girl, Rue moved fast.

Evelyn stumbled after her, glancing over her shoulder. The runes were blazing now, the hum no longer a hum but a deafening roar, like the mountain was alive and furious. The ground trembled beneath her feet, loose stones rattling as if warning them to leave.

They reached the SUV just as the air around the runes seemed to ripple, a wave of force rushing outward. Rue yanked the driver's side door open, slid across the seat, and fumbled with the keys.

"Hurry! Get in!" Rue shouted.

Evelyn didn't need to be told twice. She dove into the passenger seat, slamming the door behind her as Rue turned the key. The engine roared to life, and Rue didn't wait to let it warm up—she threw the SUV into gear, the tires spinning on the loose gravel before catching traction.

As they sped down the winding mountain road Evelyn twisted in her seat, her heart pounding as she stared out the back window. The glow of the runes was still visible, even from this distance; a red beacon against the darkening sky.

"What the hell was that?" Evelyn demanded, her voice shaking.

"I don't know," Rue said, her knuckles white on the steering wheel. Her eyes stayed locked on the road ahead, but there was a tightness in her jaw, a tension Evelyn hadn't seen before.

Evelyn swallowed hard, her pulse racing as she stared back at the distant glow. Evelyn had seen some shit hanging out with Rue and her people, but there was always some sort of protection hanging around; a massive Hellion or Dacre. This was the first time Evelyn had sensed danger and they'd been alone.

"Did you get any pictures?" Evelyn asked.

Rue smiled. "Yeah. I got some good ones."

Evelyn exhaled a breathy laugh. "Oh Christ, Tink. You didn't warn me crap like this would happen when I signed up for this job."

Evelyn frequently called Rue the nickname Tink because she was so short at just five foot two.

The SUV bumped along the dirt road and the wheels kicked up dust as they descended the mountain. The air inside was thick with silence, except for the hum of the engine and the occasional scrape of a loose rock pinging the undercarriage.

Evelyn sat with her knees pulled up to her chest, her arms wrapped tightly around them as she tried to get warm. Her head leaned back against the seat but her eyes were wide, still shining with the remnants of adrenaline.

"I can't believe we made it out of there," she finally said, her voice breathless. "That was insane."

Rue glanced at her from the driver's seat, a wry smile tugging at the corner of her lips. "You mean the part where the mountain decided to hum like a death drum or the part where you finally found a rune?"

"All of it," Evelyn said, shaking her head. Her soft laugh was the sound of a mix of nerves and relief. "I mean, I knew your life wasn't normal, but this is the first time it's actually felt really dangerous. It's weird. I'm... exhilarated."

Rue's smile widened. "Adrenaline's a hell of a drug."

Evelyn turned to her, expression growing serious. "Wait. What if your family hears about this? If they send more bodyguards, we could lose access to the site. They'd tear everything apart trying to 'protect' you. Or that bumbling giant Chel will show up and step on everything."

Rue tightened her grip on the wheel, her jaw tensing. "They won't find out. I won't tell them. I don't want my parents intervening and ruining our research."

Evelyn stared at her. "Rue, if something had gone really wrong—"

"But it didn't," Rue cut in. "We're fine. And no one's going to learn about this unless you plan on writing my mom a letter."

Evelyn huffed, leaning back against the seat again. "Never. Gosh, she's scary. That site is too important, I'm not telling a soul. You saw those runes—whatever they are, they're ancient. Unique. If your family shows up, do you think they'll see it as a threat?"

"I don't think so," Rue said, softer this time. She glanced at Evelyn again, her expression gentler. "My parents have always said they support my research and hope to learn more about our lineage from it. I won't let anything happen. I promise."

"Good. Cause I can't afford to lose my job." Evelyn warmed her hands on the dash vent.

The conversation settled, replaced by the quiet hum of the car. Until Rue's stomach growled.

The sound broke through the silence like a thunderclap, startling both of them. Evelyn blinked then burst out laughing, the tension from earlier dissolving in an instant.

"Are you serious right now?" she said, clutching her stomach as she laughed. "We've been running on adrenaline and near-death experiences, and now you're hungry?"

Rue shrugged, grinning. "What can I say? Near-death experiences work up an appetite."

Evelyn wiped a tear from her eye, shaking her head as her laughter faded. "Let's stop at Doggo's Diner when we get to town. You're buying."

"Deal," Rue said, chuckling. "I could really go for some pancakes."

Rue slowed around a curve and a spattering of rocks bounced across the roadway. Evelyn sat up and leaned across the middle of the seat, looping up the mountain. "That was weird."

Rue gripped the steering wheel. She didn't like driving fast at night along these winding mountain roads, but the dread spreading up her spine wouldn't let up.

The bell above the diner door jingled as Rue and Evelyn stepped inside, the smell of frying bacon and strong coffee hitting them like a warm embrace. The Doggo's Diner was small, with a row of vinyl booths along the windows and a counter where a few locals nursed cups of coffee. It wasn't much but it was cozy for a mountain retreat for a meal, and at that moment, it felt like the safest place on Earth.

They slid into a booth by the window, and Evelyn grabbed a laminated menu from the holder on the table. She flipped through it, glancing up at Rue with a grin.

"So, pancakes or burgers?"

"Both," Rue said without hesitation, her eyes scanning the menu as well. "And coffee. Lots of coffee."

Evelyn snorted. "You sound like you haven't eaten in weeks."

"Feels like it," Rue said, her stomach growling again for emphasis.

"Is it because Dacre has been gone?" Evelyn lowered her voice.

Rue nodded and looked away, embarrassed. Evelyn got that a lot from her friend. She'd hid her lineage for nearly six years from her best friend. The fact that Rue was a princess of the underworld didn't bother her. The fact that Rue drank blood from her hot-bodyguard/ boyfriend didn't bother her. The only thing that really bothered Evelyn was when Rue didn't take care of herself properly.

A waitress appeared, her notepad ready. She had a tired smile; the kind of friendliness that came from years of small-town hospitality. She recognized the girls.

"Ladies, you're becoming regulars." The waitress's name was Anne, and she had red curly hair.

"We can't help it," Rue said. "You've got the best coffee on this mountainside."

Anne snapped her gum. "True story. Now, what'll I get you?"

Rue rattled off their order—pancakes, burgers, fries, and two coffees—while Evelyn added a side of pie, "just because."

As the waitress walked away, Evelyn leaned back in the booth, propping her elbows on the table. "So, what's Dacre up to? I've never seen him gone this long."

Rue counted the sugar packets on the table, her expression casual. "He had to go check on some investment property in New Jersey."

"New Jersey?" Evelyn raised an eyebrow and frowned. "Why not Florida? At least it's warm there."

Rue hesitated, her fingers stilling over a sugar packet. "We... already have a family house in Florida. In the panhandle."

Evelyn blinked, sitting up straighter. "Wait. You have a *family house* in Florida, and you've never mentioned this? You're holding out on me!"

"It's not exactly a vacation spot," Rue said, her tone uneasy. She shrugged. "Well, I guess it used to be."

"Not a vacation spot?" Evelyn looked appalled. "It's Florida. Sunshine, beaches, and—okay, yeah, hurricanes, but come on. How have you been sitting on this and not taken me there?"

Rue looked out the window, her fingers twitching on the edge of the table. "It's... complicated. That house isn't just a house. It's got memories."

Evelyn crossed her arms, undeterred. "I don't care if it's haunted by a hundred demons. I want palm trees and piña coladas. You owe me a vacation, Rue."

Rue finally cracked a smile, shaking her head. "You're impossible."

"Thank you," Evelyn said with a grin, just as the waitress returned with their coffees.

The food arrived not long after, piled high on plates that barely fit on the table. They dug in, the tension from earlier melting away as they joked and swapped stories about previous digs and odd encounters.

Evelyn was in the middle of recounting a particularly disastrous date when the bell above the door jingled again. She glanced up, mid-laugh, and her smile faltered.

A man stepped inside, tall and broad-shouldered, with dark eyes that seemed to scan the room in an unnervingly deliberate way. His clothes were unremarkable—a plain black jacket and jeans—but something about him felt *off*. He looked like he belonged in a suit.

Rue followed Evelyn's gaze, her fork pausing halfway to her mouth. The man's eyes landed on their booth, lingering for a moment too long before he moved to sit at a nearby table. He didn't order; just sat barely out of their periphery, his posture stiff, not much more than a looming shadow.

Evelyn leaned in, lowering her voice. "Okay, is it just me, or is that guy... weird?"

Rue didn't answer right away. Her gaze stayed fixed on the man, her expression carefully blank. Finally, she forced a smile and picked up her coffee. "It's probably nothing."

Evelyn wasn't convinced. She glanced at the man again, then back at Rue. "Probably?" Her eyes bugged exaggeratedly.

"Let's get the bill," Rue said as she pulled out her cell phone and checked to see if she had service.

Evelyn frowned and did the same and frowned when she saw one bar. Service was shoddy in the mountains.

Evelyn picked at the last of her pie and glanced at the man occasionally. His stillness was unsettling, like he was waiting for something or someone.

"I swear he's not even blinking," Evelyn muttered under her breath, leaning toward Rue.

Rue sipped her coffee as she prepared a message to send to her mother. "Don't stare. We don't want to give him a reason to come over."

Evelyn pushed the pie away and waved at Anne.

"You want the check?" Anne asked loudly.

Evelyn tore her hand out of the air and cringed. She smiled quickly and gave Anne a thumbs up.

"So much for discreet." Rue rubbed her face.

Evelyn glanced back at the man again, just for a second, and something caught her attention. Around the man's neck, barely visible beneath the collar of his jacket, was a pendant. It was small and made of dark metal, etched with a design that looked familiar.

Evelyn froze, her mind racing. She'd seen that symbol on one of the stones of the dig site, right next to the runes.

"Rue," she whispered.

"What?"

"That guy is wearing something like a pendant that I swear is the same symbol I saw at the dig site."

Rue shifted in her seat, her coffee cup lowering to the table. "Are you sure?"

Evelyn nodded, her heart pounding. "Positive."

Rue's jaw tightened and she leaned back, pretending to stretch as she stole a look at the man. Her gaze lingered on the pendant for just a moment before she turned back to Evelyn, her voice calm but firm.

"We need to leave. Now."

Rue tossed a few large bills onto the table, grabbed her bag, and slid out of the booth. Evelyn followed her lead, her movements stiff with unease.

The man's head tilted as they stood, his gaze following them without subtlety.

"Don't look back," Rue murmured as they headed for the door.

"Goodnight, ladies." Anne waved. "See you next time."

Evelyn swallowed hard, her pulse racing as she pushed the door open and stepped into the cool mountain air. The SUV was parked just a few feet away, and they made a beeline for it through the dark parking lot. Both wished for a streetlight out here. Rue unlocked the doors with a quick press of her key fob.

They climbed in, thumping the doors shut in unison. Each slammed down the door lock. Rue started the engine, and the SUV rumbled to life.

Evelyn risked a glance back at the diner. The man was standing in the window now, watching them with an unsettling intensity.

"Okay, officially creeped out," Evelyn muttered.

Rue threw the car into gear and pulled out onto the road, her hands gripping the wheel tightly. "I hope Anne is okay."

"I think she keeps at least one shotgun behind the counter." Evelyn checked her phone. "I got two bars. I'm calling the sheriff."

"I don't want them involved," Rue's voice was worried.

"For Anne. I want them to go check on her," Evelyn clarified. "That guy gave me the creeps."

Rue breathed out a breath of frustration. "Sorry. That's a good idea."

For a moment, the tension in the SUV eased as the diner faded into the distance. But when Evelyn glanced at the rearview mirror, her stomach dropped.

"Shit. He's following us," she said, her voice barely above a whisper.

Rue glanced at the mirror, her expression unreadable. Behind them a dark sedan had pulled out of the diner parking lot, its headlights cutting through the gathering dusk.

"Hold on," Rue said, her voice steady.

She pressed down on the accelerator, the SUV picking up speed as it wound through the narrow mountain road. The sedan kept pace, looming like a shadow.

"Who is he?" Evelyn asked, her voice trembling.

"I don't know," Rue admitted, her eyes flicking between the road and the mirror. "But he's not here by accident. He's tied to the runes. He has to be."

Evelyn's mind raced. "What if he's not alone? What if —" She turned toward her friend. "You've got no bodyguards tonight. And that guy was big."

"Evelyn," Rue said sharply, cutting her off. "Don't panic. We'll lose him."

But the road ahead wasn't making it easy. The twists and turns of the mountain route were treacherous, and the headlights of the sedan never wavered. Traffic cones and uneven lanes blurred in Rue's periphery as her heart beat faster and faster.

"This damn construction is never done," Evelyn complained.

Blue and red lights lit up the night.

"Oh thank god," Evelyn said, gripping her seatbelt.

The trooper pulled onto the road and behind the vehicle following them.

The sedan slowed and pulled over.

"We have got to be the luckiest bitches alive right now." Evelyn turned in her seat. "The cop is getting out. I hope that guy gets arrested."

Rue gripped the wheel tighter. "Hold on to something."

Rue spotted a fork in the road ahead, one path leading toward town and the other veering off into a wooded area. Without hesitation, she took the second path, the SUV bouncing over uneven terrain as they left the main road.

Evelyn clung to the door handle, her heart in her throat. "Are you sure about this?"

"Nope." Rue's voice was tight as she turned off the lights and cast them into darkness.

The trees closed in around them, the path narrowing until it was barely wide enough for the SUV. The moon and the stars were the only light.

Rue slowed the SUV to a stop, cutting the engine. They sat in silence for a moment, the only sound was the ticking of the cooling engine.

Evelyn exhaled shakily. "Do you think he'll catch up to us?"

"I think so," Rue said, though her tone was far from reassuring. She glanced at Evelyn, her expression grim.

Evelyn leaned back in her seat, her heart still racing. "What the hell is going on, Rue? Who was that?"

Rue stared out the windshield. "I don't know. But we need to find out before they come back."

FOUR

The Black River twisted through the dense Adirondack forest, its surface dark and inky under the cloudy sky. Shadows clung to the water's edge, where jagged rocks and tangled roots protruded like skeletal hands.

Remington stood on the riverbank, his sharp gaze sweeping over the churning current. The air was thick with the scent of damp earth, river mud, and rotting. Bones were scattered across the riverbank. He could feel the teeming of the creatures in the water, their presence making his skin crawl.

Beside him Chel crouched, his dark eyes gleaming with amusement. He held a thin blade in one hand, twirling it idly.

"Looks like your mother's little breeding program is a roaring success," Chel said, his voice tinged with sarcasm.

Remington ignored the Hellion, his attention fixed on the river. Beneath the surface, he could make out the shifting forms of basilisks—serpentine creatures with gleaming scales and eyes that glowed faintly even underwater. They twisted and coiled, their movements synchronized like a sinister dance.

"There's plenty more than I expected," he admitted. "They're multiplying faster than my mother anticipated."

Chel smirked, rising to his feet. "Careful, boss. You're starting to sound worried. You're telling me the Queen left you in charge with a rapidly growing Basilisk population and no plan to claim or train them?"

"I'm not worried," Remington said, his voice flat. "I'm annoyed. If this gets out of hand, it's my head on the line. And no, she didn't tell me anything other than they were breeding."

Chel stepped closer to the water, his boots skimming the edge. "Well, you might as well get your hands dirty. Catch one. Show me you've still got it."

Remington shot him a withering look. "This is not a game I wish to partake in."

"It could be," he quipped, tossing his blade into the air and catching it effortlessly. "Unless you're scared."

Remington sighed, slipping off his jacket, and handing it to him. "You're insufferable."

"I try," Chel said with a grin. "Your parents would be so proud."

Without another word, Remington stepped into the river. The icy water surged around his legs, soaking his boots and jeans as he waded deeper. The basilisks sensed his presence immediately, their movements becoming more frantic. One broke the surface briefly, its head crowned with bony ridges, before vanishing again.

Remington focused, his green eyes narrowing. With a sudden, fluid motion, he plunged his arm deep into the water, his hand closing around something slick and power-ful. The basilisk thrashed, splashing dark river water like a faucet and soaking him before its body coiled around his arm like a whip. Remington held firm, his muscles straining as he hauled it out of the river.

The creature was nearly six feet long, its scales shim-mering with an iridescent sheen. It hissed, its forked tongue flicking as its glowing eyes fixed on him.

"Happy now?" Remington said, turning toward Chel.

Chel clapped slowly, his grin widening. "I'll give you an eight out of ten. You're getting rusty."

"What a crock of shit," Remington said as he stepped away from the river and tossed the baby Basilisk back.

Chel tipped to the side and glanced behind Remington. "I think you've got a friend."

Remington turned and noticed the basilisk he'd captured then freed was close behind him.

"Go away," Remington told the beast.

"It doesn't work like that," Chel said.

Remington took off his wet shirt and twisted the cold river water out of it.

"You've claimed it. You're it's master now."

Remington paled. "I don't want a basilisk."

Chel crossed his arms. "Your mother had a whole bunch of them ages ago. They're good to have around, like a guard dog."

"A slimy guard dog." He sighed, watching the writhing of bodies in the water. "There's a hell of a lot of them." Remington put his damp shirt back on and walked toward the SUV they'd drove.

"Sure are." Chel shivered in disgust as the basilisk slithered back into the water.

Later that afternoon, Remington stood at the edge of a barren field, his SUV parked nearby. Behind him, a livestock trailer rattled softly, the bleats of fifteen goats filling the air.

Across from him a demon with gray, leathery skin and curling horns paced back and forth, his clawed hands wringing together. His name was Barok, and he looked deeply unimpressed.

"These are replacements," Remington said, gesturing toward the trailer. "Fifteen goats, as promised. That should cover the ones you lost."

Barok stopped pacing, his yellow eyes narrowing. "You're lucky I don't demand compensation for the trauma, Shadow Heir. Those basilisks were *your* problem, not mine."

Remington crossed his arms. "And now your problem is *solved*. You have your goats. Don't push your luck, Barok."

The demon muttered something under his breath but waved a clawed hand. Two imps scurried forward to open the trailer, guiding the goats out one by one.

Barok inspected the animals with a critical eye, then finally nodded. "Fine. This will do."

Remington turned to leave, but Barok's voice stopped him.

"You might want to keep a closer eye on that river," the demon said, his tone smug. "I hear whispers. People are starting to notice things. Strange things. Someone is controlling those beasts and it's not your mother."

Remington didn't turn around. "The river is none of your concern."

As he climbed back into his SUV, Chel leaned over from the passenger seat, his smirk firmly in place. "Fifteen goats and a lecture. You're really living the dream."

Remington shot the Hellion a look but said nothing, revving the engine as they left the field behind.

FIVE

It was close to midnight when Rue pulled the SUV into the gravel driveway of the secluded cabin. The headlights illuminated a familiar silhouette of Dacre standing on the front porch, hands resting casually in his pockets, his sharp gaze softening as the car came to a stop.

Evelyn leaned forward, peering through the windshield. "Wow, your personal bodyguard is waiting. Does he ever take a break?"

Rue smirked, cutting the engine. "I'm surprised he didn't come looking for us on the road."

Dacre stepped down from the porch as Rue got out, his expression warm as his eyes scanned her for any signs of trouble. "Long day?"

"Something like that," Rue replied, her voice light as she closed the door.

His gaze swept over both of them, lingering just a moment longer on Rue. "You're later than I expected," he said, his voice calm but mildly curious.

"We stopped for dinner," Rue replied smoothly,

brushing her hands off on her jeans. She didn't mention waiting in the dark roadway for nearly two hours praying that strange man didn't find them.

Evelyn chimed in, slinging her bag over her shoulder. "Yeah, you know how it is—rocks, runes, endless note-taking. Absolutely riveting stuff." She patted her bag. "I'm gonna look those pictures over with a fine-toothed comb."

Dacre chuckled softly, his attention flicking between the two. "You found something new. Everything went well, I assume?"

"Like clockwork," Rue said quickly, her tone light. "Nothing out of the ordinary. Unless you count Evelyn tripping over her own feet," she added with a sly grin.

"Hey!" Evelyn protested, laughing. "That's called inspecting the ground for clues, thank you very much."

Dacre shook his head with a faint smile. "As long as you're both in one piece, that's what matters."

Evelyn wandered over to her old BMW, unlocking the door. "Well, I'll leave you two to your evening. Rue, don't forget to text me the pics you took on the tablet."

"Sure," Rue said, giving a casual wave.

Evelyn paused, leaning against the car door with a sly grin. "Oh, and Dacre? We really missed having you around these past few days."

Dacre's smile deepened, though his tone remained soft. "I'm back now. No more missing out on all your fun."

Evelyn laughed, sliding into the driver's seat. "See you, Rue!"

Rue watched as Evelyn backed out of the drive, her tail-lights disappearing down the road. As the sound of the car faded, she turned toward Dacre, who was studying her carefully.

"Long day?" he asked again, his voice gentle.

Rue nodded, stepping toward the house. "Yeah, but productive. I'll fill you in tomorrow. Right now, I just need to get out of these clothes and crash."

Dacre's eyes lingered on her for a moment, but he nodded. "Perfect."

"Maybe you can make me a pot of coffee," Rue said, offering him a faint smile before disappearing inside.

Dacre sighed. "But it's been two days why do you need coffee first?"

Rue was laughing to herself for teasing him.

Dacre caught on and ran after her, lifting her from behind and kissing her neck until she squealed.

The winding mountain road was quiet, the faint hum of Evelyn's old BMW blending with the rustle of trees in the night breeze. Her headlights cast long shadows across the uneven terrain, illuminating the dense forest that flanked either side of the road. Normally Evelyn found solace in the solitude of these drives, but tonight an unsettling feeling clung to her like a second skin. She couldn't shake the hum they'd heard; the beat of it was stuck in her head like a song.

She tightened her grip on the steering wheel, her eyes flicking to the rearview mirror every few moments. *Why am I being so jumpy?* she thought, shaking her head.

The strange events at the site and the man in the diner lingered in her mind. They had two more days at the dig site, then they'd head back to campus to analyze everything more thoroughly. Rue's lab had better computers than Evelyn's old laptop. She had wanted to buy a new one but the bills were piling up.

Evelyn reached up to rub her temple, her hand brushing under her nose. She froze, feeling wetness, then glanced down at her fingers.

Blood.

"Damn it," she muttered, pulling the car to a stop on the side of the road. She grabbed a tissue from the center console and pressed it to her nose, tilting her head back. Her heartbeat quickened, and the silence outside the car felt louder than it should.

A soft rustling came from the forest to her left. Evelyn snapped her head toward the sound, her breath catching. The trees swayed gently in the wind—nothing out of the ordinary—but her chest tightened all the same. She stayed like that for a few moments, listening, before shaking her head.

"You're losing it," she muttered, starting the car again and driving the last stretch to her cabin.

When she pulled into the small gravel clearing, the cabin's familiar silhouette came into view. She had really wanted the cabin closer to Rue and Dacre but it had been closed for plumbing issues. This one was a few miles down the road. It was simple but cozy, with a wraparound porch and soft amber light glowing from the motion-activated bulb above the front door.

She stepped out of the car, the crunch of gravel beneath her boots sounding unnaturally loud. The air was crisp and cool, carrying the faint scent of pine. Evelyn adjusted the strap of her bag on her shoulder, her eyes darting to the dark line of trees bordering her property. She pressed the tissue to her nose again and checked the bleeding. It had slowed at least.

A shadow shifted.

Evelyn froze, her breath hitching. Her eyes locked on the spot where she thought she'd seen movement, but the shadows held steady now, the trees swaying innocently in the wind.

Her throat tightened. "Hello?" she called, her voice sounding smaller than she intended.

No response.

"Probably just a damn trash panda," she muttered to herself.

Forcing her feet to move, Evelyn hurried up the porch steps and fumbled with her keys. Her hands trembled slightly as she unlocked the door and stepped inside, flipping the light switch. She locked the door behind her and slid the chain into place.

Dropping her bag by the door, she walked to the window, her gaze darting toward the forest. She squinted, scanning the shadows for any sign of movement. There was nothing.

"Get a grip," she whispered to herself, pulling the curtains closed.

But even as she tried to shake the feeling, Evelyn couldn't ignore the small voice in the back of her mind whispering that she wasn't alone out here tonight.

Evelyn moved through the small cabin, checking the locks on every last window. She pulled her jacked tighter around her shoulders and made her way to the bathroom.

The fluorescent light buzzed softly as it flickered on. She caught her reflection in the mirror; the year had changed her. In the years before graduation she had never ending energy, she was never tired. Now she had weary eyes, wind-blown hair, and a faint red streak near her nostril.

With a sigh Evelyn grabbed a washcloth, running it under warm water before wiping her face clean. "You need to sleep," she muttered to herself. But even as she said it, her mind raced.

Back in her bedroom, she swapped her jeans for a pair of flannel pajama pants and sat cross-legged on the edge of the bed, her laptop balanced on her knees. She opened it, intending to distract herself with some light reading or a documentary, but the moment her inbox loaded, her stomach dropped.

At the top of her unread emails was a subject line in bold:

Reminder: MRI Appointment – Friday, 10:30 AM.

Evelyn stared at it for a moment, her fingers hovering over the trackpad. The nosebleeds had started as a minor incon-venience a few months ago, but lately they'd become harder to ignore. At first she chalked it up to the suckhole of adult-hood and the high altitude of the dig site. But after the third instance of waking up to blood-streaked pillows, Rue had insisted Evelyn see a doctor.

She opened the email, scanning the details. The message was routine and polite, but it felt accusatory to her now as if it were reminding her she couldn't keep brushing this off. She made a mental note to print off the instructions Monday.

"It's probably nothing," she whispered, as though saying it aloud would make it true.

Still, her hand moved to touch her nose, half-expecting to feel the telltale warmth of blood again. The memory of her earlier nosebleed at the dig site resurfaced, along with the way the drop of blood had vanished from the rune stone.

She closed the laptop with a quiet snap, her pulse quickening. Her rational side told her the MRI was just a precaution, but the way her life had been unraveling with strange occurrences lately made her doubts grow.

Pushing the thoughts aside, she stood and turned off the light, sliding under the covers. The cabin was dark now, illuminated only by the soft glow of the moon filtering through the curtains. Evelyn closed her eyes, willing herself to sleep.

Suddenly, the steady hum from the rune site invaded her mind again. The steady beat was slow and... soothing. So unlike before. She drifted off to sleep.

Six

The first light of dawn painted the sky over the mountains in soft hues of gold and lavender as Evelyn pulled her jacket tighter against the chill. The air was crisp, and the forest surrounding the dig site was eerily quiet. Too quiet. No birdsong, no rustling leaves—just an unsettling stillness that clung to the morning. Evelyn watched the sunrise between the mountains in the distance for a few more minutes before getting to work.

She busied herself unpacking equipment, the repetitive motions a welcome distraction from the unease gnawing at her. She knelt by a metal case, pulling out brushes, chisels, and a handheld scanner, arranging them methodically on a folding table. Rue would be there soon in a flurry of activity, no doubt with Dacre at her side. The bodyguard had a knack for sensing when something was off. So Evelyn was going to ensure her setup was perfect and avoid questions.

Her gaze drifted to the stone where the runes were etched. The early sunlight caught the faint grooves, highlighting the patterns. She walked over, crouching to inspect them closer. The marks looked to be carved by a steady hand. Evelyn ran her fingers just above the surface, hesitant to touch it again. The memory of her blood disappearing into the stone played on repeat in her mind. She dabbed her nose just to make sure it hadn't started bleeding again. It was nearly every day now.

"It's fine," she muttered to herself, though the words felt hollow. "It's nothing."

The tension in her chest refused to dissipate. The hum repeated in her head, she couldn't seem to get rid of it. Evelyn stood and glanced toward the treeline. She half-expected to see movement, a shadow shifting where it shouldn't be like last night at the cabin, but the forest remained still. A shiver ran down her spine and she turned back to the stone, pulling out her notebook to map the stones.

She looked everywhere for the drop of blood from yesterday. On the edge of the stones, the grass, a stick that was nearby.

It took my blood. She shook her head and scribbled furiously in the notebook, trying to drown out the intrusive idea.

The wind picked up suddenly, rustling the pages of her notebook. Evelyn pressed her arm to the cover, cursing under her breath as a page tore.

The hum. She was sure it wasn't just in her head this time.

It was faint, almost imperceptible, but it was there; a low, rhythmic vibration that seemed to come from everywhere and nowhere at once. Her pulse quickened as she glanced back at the rune stone that had absorbed her drop of blood. The sound was coming from beneath her feet.

Evelyn backed away from the stone instinctively, her breath shallow. The hum faded just as quickly as it had begun.

She forced herself to take a deep breath. "Get a grip, Evelyn," she whispered. But her voice wavered. She'd hoped Rue and Dacre would be there soon; she suddenly regretted her decision to get a head start on the day. She should have waited for her friends, especially after the incident with that creepy guy at the diner.

The faint crunch of gravel startled her, and she spun around. A dark SUV was pulling up the narrow path toward the dig site. Her heart leapt into her throat. That wasn't Rue's.

Her stomach tightened as she watched the dark SUV cutting through the trees. A wave of unease washed over her, her mind snapping back to the strange man in the diner. She set down the brush she'd been using to clear debris and moved toward the table, her eyes fixed on the vehicle as it rolled to a stop. There weren't many options for a weapon. Her boot nudged a large rock. She could throw that sucker.

Evelyn's breath hitched as the door opened, but the figure that stepped out wasn't who she had ever expected. She hadn't seen him in nearly a year but he didn't look any different. Still just as handsome. Something like hope surged in her chest. God, the guy was a sight for sore eyes. Evelyn licked her lips and tried not to look desperate but it was *so* hard.

"Remington?" she blurted, her voice sharper than she intended.

He closed the door behind him, the movement fluid. His dark jacket and boots gave him an air of effortless authority, the kind that didn't need to be announced. The tension in her shoulders eased slightly, but her stomach churned with a different kind of apprehension.

"Morning," he said, his tone low and measured.

"What are you doing here?" she asked, crossing her arms to disguise the mix of relief and irritation bubbling inside her.

"Someone flagged this location," he said, his gaze already drifting toward the rune stone. "I thought I'd check it out."

Flagged? Rue had promised not to tell her family about the discovery. Had she lied? Evelyn's thoughts raced, piecing together Rue's reassurances from the previous night and weighing them against Remington's calm demeanor.

Evelyn forced herself to keep her tone even. "I didn't think our research would be on your radar. Rue didn't mention anything to you?"

Remington's lips curved into a faint, humorless smile as he stepped closer. "She didn't. Someone else did." He looked her up and down.

"Someone else?" she echoed, trying to keep her voice steady. Her hands clenched into fists at her sides. She didn't want this project to get shut down or ruined by Rue's family. It was the only paying job she had, and with excellent health insurance. She couldn't afford to lose this.

Remington tilted his head slightly, studying her. "Does that surprise you?"

She forced a shrug, though her heart was pounding. "I just figured Rue would've mentioned it, that's all."

"She's protective of her world and her friends," he said, his tone almost kind. "Sometimes to a fault."

Evelyn bristled. Was that his way of calling her a liability? The idea made her stomach twist. She glanced at the rune stone, the strange hum from yesterday echoing faintly in her memory. If Remington knew about that, would he shut the whole site down? Or worse, send more of his lumbering Hellions who'd destroy the site with their big, stupid feet?

She swallowed hard and tried to focus on the present. "So... who flagged it?"

Remington didn't answer immediately. Instead, he stepped closer to the rune stone, his expression shifting to something more focused, more calculating. "The question isn't who," he said finally. "It's why."

His cryptic response made her blood boil. "Well, you're the one who showed up unannounced. Care to fill me in?"

He looked at her. "I'm here to make sure you're safe."

Her stomach sank. "Safe from what?"

Remington's silence spoke volumes. He wasn't here to explain. He was here to observe, to assess. And suddenly, the air between them felt heavier. Evelyn was thinking about that first night she'd met him and the sinking feeling in her stomach when Rue had forbidden Remington from seeing her.

Evelyn crossed her arms again, this time to steady herself. "Look, we've been fine out here for months. No need for the cavalry."

"Fine, have you?" he asked, arching a brow. His tone

wasn't mocking, but it carried enough weight to make her falter. He sounded authoritative. Damn, Rue's brother had really embraced his dark prince roots. Authority looked good on him. But that stare was enough to melt her where she stood.

Evelyn opened her mouth to retort but the memory of the hum, the blood disappearing, and the strange man's piercing gaze stopped her short. *Fine* wasn't the right word for any of this, but she wasn't about to admit that to Remington.

"Well, nothing we can't handle," she said, forcing a confident tone.

Remington studied her for a moment longer before nodding toward the rune stone. "Mind if I take a look?"

Evelyn stepped aside, her heart pounding. "Be my guest. Just don't step on anything, we're still excavating."

"Still?" Remington's lip quirked in amusement. "You've been up here for six months. How long does it take?" he teased.

"There's a cave across the valley and that project has been ongoing for years." Evelyn rested her fists on her hips.

As he moved closer, she watched him warily. When his fingers brushed over the grooves in the stone, a faint flicker of light sparked along the runes. It was so brief she almost thought she'd imagined it.

Remington's jaw tightened. He straightened, sliding his hands into his jacket pockets. "If anything changes, you'll let me know." The words weren't a suggestion—they were a command.

Evelyn nodded, though every instinct screamed at her

to push back. Instead, she asked the question she didn't really want the answer to. "Do you think we're in danger?"

Remington's gaze met hers, unflinching. "I think you should be careful." He looked her up and down. "Are you feeling well?"

Evelyn blinked and stepped back. "I... I'm fine."

Remington smiled. "I know you're *fine*. You look pale. Did something happen?"

"I don't know what you mean." Evelyn took another step back. It was the way he said she was fine that made something deep in her belly flip flop.

The quiet hung between them. Evelyn's fingers tightened around her notebook, the pages crinkling slightly under her grip. Remington stood a few feet away, his presence imposing but strangely calm, waiting.

"So," he finally said, his voice low and steady, "what's been uncovered at the site?"

Evelyn glanced at him, her lips pressing together in hesitation. How much should she tell him? She shifted uncomfortably, debating whether to bring up the strange man, the hum from the runes, or the blood that had disappeared. But something warned her to keep those details to herself.

She forced a shrug, trying to sound nonchalant. "We've made progress with the runes. The carvings are... complex. But nothing we haven't seen before. Rue has been able to read most of them. What we've discovered so far hints at some type of healing location here. Almost like an ancient medical facility of some kind or even directions to one." She sighed, flustered, and not ready to discuss their findings without a thorough analysis.

Remington's dark eyes narrowed slightly, as though he could see through her words. "Healing, how?"

"We aren't sure yet," she added. "There's probably a cave opening nearby with more, we just haven't been able to find it yet."

His gaze lingered on her for a moment before he continued. "And have you noticed anything... unusual? Strange creatures? Any disturbances? Anything out of place?"

Evelyn's heart quickened at the question. She swallowed, her mind flashing back to yesterday—the strange man at the diner, the hum from the rune stone, and the way her blood had disappeared before her eyes. The memory sent a chill through her. But could she trust him with that?

"I..." she began, then faltered. She glanced at the rune stone, debating whether to say something or keep it to herself. Her eyes flicked back to Remington, trying to gauge whether he was genuinely concerned—or just there to gather intel.

"I did notice something," she admitted carefully. "There was... a strange vibration yesterday. Like a low hum, but it only lasted for a few seconds."

Remington's expression didn't shift much, but his eyes darkened slightly. "A vibration?"

"It was faint. Almost like it was coming from the ground beneath the stone," Evelyn explained, recalling the eerie feeling of the sound. "But it stopped before I could figure out what it was."

He frowned slightly. "Anything else?"

Evelyn hesitated again, the memory of the blood disappearing flashing through her mind. She could tell him about the blood, or she could keep that to herself. She didn't know what his reaction would be.

"No," she said at last, masking her hesitation. "That was the only thing."

Remington studied her for a long moment, then finally nodded. "Okay. Let Rue know if anything else strange happens. I know this project is important to you both but you understand that when our worlds mingle, all hell breaks loose."

Evelyn felt his gaze linger on her a little longer, as though he was waiting for something more. But she wasn't ready to give him anything else—not until she could figure out exactly what was happening.

"Is that all?" she asked after a tense beat.

"For now." His tone was clipped, his eyes sharp as if he were measuring every word she gave him. "But you'll let me know if anything else comes up?"

Evelyn hesitated, then nodded slowly. "Of course. I'll just text you." She rolled her eyes.

He gave her a brief nod before stepping away from the rune stone, his eyes still flicking toward the trees, as though he was already thinking ahead, calculating.

"Good," he said finally. "I have to go before my sister gets here."

"Things do tend to get weird when you show up," Evelyn said with a smile. "And, I don't have your number to text you, fyi."

He stopped, hand on the doorhandle of the truck. "You saw what happened last time we were in the same room together."

How could Evelyn forget anything about that night?

She'd seen the most handsome man she'd ever laid eyes on and when she dragged him onto the dancefloor he'd said yes. He was easy to kiss, easy to touch, easy to laugh with. Evelyn looked into his eyes...

His cheeks flashed pink and he sucked in a stuttered breath. "I gotta go," Remington suddenly said as he ripped open the door to the SUV and climbed inside.

"Buh-bye, Rue's hot-brother," Evelyn muttered to herself as she watching his vehicle drive away. Weird that he went up the mountain instead of down it.

Sucks that he didn't give up his number.

Damn.

SEVEN

It was probably more than coincidence that at the peak of the mountain Remington had found an old portal with a stone cabin half sunk in the dirt.

He'd been woken in the dead of night by a humming noise that had drawn him out of the castle.

Even more strange was that the portal was big enough for him to drive the whole SUV through the portal from Hell to Earth. It was huge, almost... giant sized. Chel was waiting on the other side. the Hellion had given the dark prince forty-five minutes to investigate before he'd be going through with a handful of Hellions ready to battle whatever noise was calling Remington.

Remington drove through the portal back into Hell, the air shifting instantly from the crisp coolness of the mountain to the heavy, woodsmoke-laden heat of his domain. The hum that had drawn him out was quieter now, retreating to the back of his mind, but it left behind a lingering tension, a feeling that something had been set into motion. Something had yet to be answered.

Chel was waiting for him as he exited the portal. He straightened as Remington drove closer, the faint hint of a smirk tugging at the corner of his mouth. He waved to the other Hellions to carry on with their day, opened the passenger side of the truck, and climbed in.

"Back in one piece, I see," Chel said. "Did you find what you were looking for?"

Remington shrugged off his jacket, tossing it onto the backseat. "Found more questions than answers," he muttered. His thoughts were still tangled with the memory of Evelyn—her hesitant smile, the way her hands had trembled slightly as she organized the equipment at the dig site. She looked different. Tired. Fragile in a way that tugged at something deep inside him. He'd missed her smile and usual loudness.

"You look like you've seen a ghost," Chel said.

Remington shot him a glance. "Not a ghost. Just someone I didn't expect to see."

Chel tilted his head, clearly curious but knowing better than to pry. "You want the rundown on the Black River chaos?" he offered to take Remington's mind off whatever he'd encountered on the other side of the portal as they drove back to the castle.

Remington nodded, grateful for the distraction. Chel launched into a report about the basilisk situation near the Black River, the escalating disagreements between rival demon houses, and a new issue with the infernal supply lines being tampered with by opportunistic lower-level demons.

Remington listened, his expression carefully neutral, but his mind kept drifting back to Evelyn. What was she doing there, at that dig site? And why had the hum—so similar to the one that had woken him—been centered around the runes she was studying?

Chel paused, frowning. "You're not even listening, are you?"

"I'm listening," Remington said. He sighed and rubbed a hand over his face. "It's just... complicated."

Chel raised an eyebrow. "When is it not?"

Remington smirked faintly but didn't respond. He slowed as he pulled into the royal grounds and parked the truck.

"Princeling," a tall demon shouted from the forest shadows. "A moment?"

"No," Chel stopped Remington. "They must approach you formally. We'll deal with that guy."

Remington nodded and made his way inside. He went straight to the kitchen to get blood from the fridge.

Chel wasn't far behind. "Are you feeling okay?"

Remington swallowed, his throat dry. "I'm fine. Just... hungry." He drank a bag of blood. Ice cold.

Chel maintained his composure. He'd never seen the dark prince do such a thing in his entire life.

Remington began pacing, his boots echoing against the obsidian floor. "Something's happening, Chel. That portal led to the Earthen plane. It wasn't far from my sister's dig site. The runes at that dig site—they're tied to... something. I can feel it. And Evelyn... she's caught up in it somehow."

"Evelyn?" Chel repeated, his tone unreadable. "The human girl? Rue's friend? The one you've been beating off to for the past year?"

Remington stopped pacing, his jaw tightening. "Yes.

Her. She was at the site, and I'm certain the humming sound that woke me might have had something to do with her."

Chel frowned, crossing his arms over his broad chest. "Humans aren't built for this world."

Remington frowned.

A sharp knock on the kitchen door caused them both to turn.

"Sir, there's a visitor who has information for you." The guard looked between the two. "He was the one calling you outside."

Remington sighed.

The office was quiet when Remington entered, except for the crackle of the ever-burning torches lining the wall. Remington sat on the obsidian chair behind a matching desk as the demon approached. The creature was small, more of a dwarf of sorts.

The demon bowed, its smoky voice carrying through the chamber. "Princeling, I bring you news of a disturbance in the mountains."

Remington's gaze sharpened. Twice now mountain demons have mentioned something out of the ordinary.

"A series of strange sightings," the demon said, its voice quivering slightly. "Figures moving in the shadows, sounds that don't belong to the winds, and..." The demon hesitated, glancing nervously at Chel, who stood nearby with his arms crossed like a silent sentinel.

"And?" Remington's tone cut through the room. "Finish." He motioned for the demon to spit it out.

The demon swallowed hard, forcing the words out.

"There have been whispers... of the princeling named Thrush."

The room fell deathly silent. Even the torches seemed to dim, their flames flickering as if cowed by the weight of the name. Chel's expression darkened and his stance shifted subtly, as if bracing for an outburst.

"When was the last time you saw your cousin, Princeling?" the demon asked, its words teetering on the edge of insolence as it failed at hiding a smirk of darkness.

Remington's jaw tightened. "It's been years," he said evenly, though the tension in his voice betrayed the storm brewing beneath his calm facade.

The demon took a step back, sensing the shift in the room's atmosphere. "He... he was seen near the Black River. At least, that's what the rumors say. I thought you should know."

Remington stood, his imposing figure casting a shadow over the trembling demon. He towered over the creature by feet. "You'd best be certain before you bring me a name like that again," he said, his voice a low growl.

The demon nodded hastily, backing away before turning and scurrying out of the room. "I tell truth. I tell truth." His voice echoed.

When the doors slammed shut, Chel broke the silence. "Thrush," he said, his voice heavy. "You think it's true? We've been searching for so long."

Remington ran a hand through his hair, his usually composed demeanor cracking for a moment. "I don't know. But if someone has seen him... we can't afford to ignore it."

Remington turned to another Hellion in the room and motioned for the guard to follow the demon. "Don't let that guy out of your sight."

Chel grunted. "He's been missing since shortly after the war. No word, no trace. If he's still alive—"

"He's alive," Remington interrupted, his tone clipped. He sighed and sank back into his chair, his mind racing. "You know what happens if he doesn't return to fulfill his time as a Hellion. The curse will claim him." Remington was tapping his finger on the desk. They'd both worried about the royal requirement to train in the Hellion guard. They both knew that to rule they needed to know light and dark. It hadn't been that bad, Remington thought. The worst part was doing it alone; he'd always thought Thrush would have the experience with him.

Chel nodded grimly. "And if the curse has already started?" The old Hellion had seen what ignoring the call to Hellion duty had done to Remington's family. Decades earlier, his grandfather had refused, thrusting his father, Sparrow, and his aunt Nightingale into a future of chaos and madness.

Remington's eyes darkened. Thrush had been more than a cousin—he'd been like a brother. They had grown up together, fought side by side during the war, their bond unbreakable until the conflict ended. But the Thrush who emerged from those battles had been consumed by a shadow of the young man he once was. Something had changed him.

Remington had worried it was something about spending time in Heaven that had made him change. Heck, the time in Heaven had bleached Thrush's hair white. The guy couldn't stand the months he'd stayed there; he could barely stand the time he spent with the Angel Legion who'd been assigned to train him as a teenager. Being surrounded by angels, even though it was half his lineage, had done something damaging to him.

"I've been searching for years," Remington said quietly. "Every lead's been a dead end."

Chel crossed his arms. "If the rumors are true and he's near the mountains, it might explain the disturbances we've been hearing about. Strange activity near the Black River, the basilisk, and goats going missing."

Remington's head snapped up at the mention of the basilisk. "You think it's connected?"

Chel shrugged. "I think it's worth looking into. But if Thrush has gone mad, it won't be a family reunion. It'll be a fight."

Remington's expression hardened. "If it comes to that, I'll do what I must. But I won't give up on him. Not yet."

Chel nodded, his usual levity absent. "What's the plan?"

Remington stood, his mind already forming a strategy. "We go to the mountains. I need to see for myself if there's any truth to these rumors. And if Thrush is there... I'll bring him home. One way or another."

"And if he's already claimed a basilisk to help defend whatever he's doing in those mountains?" Chel asked.

"Then I'll bring my own."

Chel smirked. "Dark prince is going to claim a monster?"

The humming sound started again in the back of his head. He rubbed his neck until it went away, then tapped the desk. "I'm not waiting on this. I'm not bringing anymore goats up there."

EIGHT

THE HUM OF FLUORESCENT LIGHTS BUZZED softly above as Evelyn rearranged a stack of notebooks on the long table in front of her. The archaeology department's lab was quieter than usual, save for the occasional rustle of paper or the tapping of Rue's fingers on her laptop. The room smelled faintly of dust and old books, a scent Evelyn usually found comforting. Today, it did little to calm the unease that lingered after the dig site drama.

Rue sat cross-legged in a chair, her dark hair tied back in a messy bun, a stack of thick tomes surrounding her like a fortress. She thumbed through one, her expression focused, lips moving silently as she read.

Evelyn glanced over at her and smiled faintly. "How's it going over there? Found the meaning of life yet?"

"Give me another hour," Rue replied dryly, not looking up. "Though I'm starting to think these runes were just ancient grocery lists." She paused, tilting the book to show Evelyn an intricate spiral design. "But seriously, look at this.

Doesn't it remind you of the patterns on the southern ridge stone we cataloged?"

Evelyn leaned closer, her brow furrowing as she traced the shape with her eyes. "It does. Maybe there's a connection we missed." She pulled out their sketches from the dig site, laying them next to Rue's book.

Before Evelyn could comment further, the lab door creaked open. Dr. Malcolm stepped inside, carrying a slim folder and a USB drive. His sharp gray eyes scanned the room as he gave them a brief nod. "Ladies, I think you'll want to see this."

Rue sat up straighter, closing her book with a soft thud. "What is it?"

Dr. Malcolm crossed the room and set the folder on the table, sliding it toward them. "New runes. My team uncovered these deeper in the mountain at our site. They're... unusual."

Evelyn and Rue exchanged a glance, intrigue sparking between them. Evelyn opened the folder, revealing a series of crisp, high-resolution photos. The runes were etched into a smooth cave wall, their lines more refined than anything they'd found so far.

Rue reached out, tracing the image with her finger. "These are... incredible. Look at the precision."

"They haven't been worn down by the elements, is what I'm thinking," Malcom said.

Evelyn's eyes narrowed as she examined another photo. Something about the arrangement of symbols tugged at her memory. She flipped through their sketches again, stopping at one of the stones from their dig. Her heart skipped a beat.

"Wait," she said, pointing to the paper. "This symbol—it's the same as the one here." She tapped one of the photos. "See? The grooves match perfectly."

Dr. Malcolm leaned in, his brow furrowing as he studied the comparison.

Evelyn said, her voice firm, "It's identical."

Rue's eyes lit up with excitement. "If the symbols match, that means the sites could be connected. And if they're connected..." She trailed off, her mind racing. "There's more to this. There has to be."

Dr. Malcolm straightened, crossing his arms. "We've suspected as much, but this confirms it. There's something significant about these locations. And you're right—these aren't isolated finds."

Evelyn hesitated, her unease from the dig site resurfacing. She didn't want to dampen the moment, but the memory of the strange man at the diner and the eerie events near the runes lingered in the back of her mind. Still, she kept those thoughts to herself, forcing a smile. "So, what's the next step?"

Dr. Malcolm's expression turned serious. "We map out everything. Compare the coordinates and see if we can narrow down any patterns. If these runes are pointing to something, I want to know what."

Rue smirked, her excitement overriding any apprehension. "Sounds like a plan. Let's find out what these symbols are hiding."

Evelyn looked at Rue. "Do you think we're chasing something we shouldn't be? Remember that humming sound and that man?"

Rue paused, "I don't want to stop searching for answers."

Evelyn smiled. "I don't want to either. And we have your bodyguard if things get too dangerous."

A message pinged on Evelyn's phone. It felt like a stone singing in her gut. "Oh, I forgot to tell you, Friday I have to leave early."

Rue was moving two pictures together and measuring the rune markings between them. "Whatever you need."

"Thanks."

The afternoon sun cast long shadows across the sidewalk as Evelyn stepped out of the clinic, her mind still replaying the MRI technician's clipped instructions and the distant hum of the machine. She shivered, remembering the cold room and the thin paper gown she had to wear. Even more concerning was the technician evading eye contact and half-smile. It gave her a bad feeling.

Evelyn adjusted the strap of her bag on her shoulder and sighed, her thoughts spinning. The results wouldn't be ready for a few days. She wasn't looking forward to stewing and worrying and had planned to bury herself in work, hoping to occupy her mind. She hadn't had a nosebleed in days and she was beginning to think that maybe she was just a hypochondriac. Evelyn thought of the medical bill she was about to get. The office had wanted five hundred dollars up front. That was a big chunk of her savings and she expected a second bill to arrive in a few weeks after the radiologist read the MRI. She thought about getting a second job, but that would limit the trips to the dig site.

Evelyn took a deep breath and pushed the thoughts away.

The smell of freshly brewed coffee wafted through the air. Up ahead, the Coffee Connection café came into view, a warm glow spilling from its windows. A moment of normalcy, she thought. Coffee was always a good option, and maybe she'd get a muffin for dinner.

Inside, the café bustled with quiet conversation and the clinking of mugs. Evelyn stepped into line, scanning the chalkboard menu even though she already knew her order. She fished a few bills from her wallet.

"Caramel latte, please," she said when it was her turn, her voice almost drowned out by the sound of steaming milk.

As she moved to the side to wait, a deep voice spoke behind her. "Make that two. I'll cover hers as well."

Startled, Evelyn turned to see a man standing just a step away. He was tall, broad-shouldered, and impeccably dressed in a dark suit that looked custom-tailored. His hair was jet black, slicked back in a way that highlighted his sharp jawline and piercing, dark eyes. A faint, disarming smile played on his lips. The guy looked completely out of place in a college town. Evelyn figured he'd look more at home in New York City or Chicago. Not Loyola campus.

"You don't have to—" Evelyn began, but he waved her off with a casual gesture.

"Please, I insist," he said smoothly. "It's not every day I get to treat a pretty stranger."

Evelyn felt a flush rise to her cheeks. She wasn't sure if it was the compliment or the intensity of his gaze that threw her off balance. "Thank you," she murmured, unsure of what else to say.

The barista handed them their drinks and the man stepped aside, gesturing for her to follow him at a nearby table.

"Would you join me?" He flashed a smile.

Evelyn hesitated but found herself nodding. She followed him to the corner of the café, where the noise of the room seemed to fade into the background.

"I'm Al," he said, offering his hand. His grip was firm, his skin cool to the touch.

"Evelyn," she replied, feeling a bit like she was floating outside herself. "Thanks again for the coffee. You didn't have to do that."

"You looked like you could use it." Al said with a shrug, his smile widening just enough to be charming.

Evelyn took a sip of her drink, the caramel sweetness grounding her slightly. "Rough day, I guess."

"Anything you'd like to share?" he asked, tilting his head in curiosity. "Sometimes it helps to talk to someone who's not involved."

Evelyn hesitated. There was something about him—an air of confidence, a magnetic pull that made it hard to look away. Still, she wasn't about to pour her heart out to a stranger. Even a really good looking one. Remington flashed through her mind and she felt a sense a guilt. She pushed it away immediately. He was forbidden. She couldn't wait for him. For nothing.

"It's nothing serious," she said lightly. "Just... a lot on my mind."

He nodded, as if that answer satisfied him. "Under-standable. Life has a way of doing that. But you strike me as someone who handles it well."

Evelyn laughed softly, a bit surprised by the observation. "You don't even know me."

"Maybe not yet," Al replied, his tone warm but edged with intrigue. "But I'd like to." He took a sip of his coffee and glanced out the window.

The words hung between them, and Evelyn wasn't sure how to respond. She felt a flicker of both caution and curiosity.

"You don't look like someone who would be named Al." Evelyn rotated the cup in her hands, searching to warm her fingers.

"It's a nickname." He smiled.

"Oh? Sometimes my friends call me Ev. What's your full name?"

"Alastor." Something flashed in his eyes.

"Wow. That's a name."

"It's a family name." He shrugged. "I don't use it often."

Evelyn stared. "The formal name suites you better than Al."

"How about dinner?" he continued, leaning back slightly in his chair. "Nothing fancy, unless you'd prefer that. Just a chance to get to know each other better."

Evelyn blinked, caught off guard by the directness of his invitation. She searched his face for any signs of insincerity but found none.

"That's... very kind," she said slowly. "But I don't even know your last name."

"Fair point," Al said, his grin widening. "It's Laurent. Alastor Laurent. And now the mystery is solved."

Evelyn bit her lip, considering. She couldn't deny that he was handsome, and his charm was undeniable. But something about his presence made her stomach twist—not entirely unpleasantly, but enough to make her hesitate.

"I'll think about it," she said finally, standing with her cup in hand. "Thanks again for the coffee, Alastor."

He rose with her, his movements smooth and deliberate. "I'll hold you to that, Evelyn. After all, you're the one who called me here."

"I did?" Evelyn's expression turned confused.

He passed her a napkin. "Your nose."

Evelyn felt the cool sensation of a nosebleed starting. "Crap." She grabbed the napkin and pressed it to her nose. "Thank you."

She was suddenly flustered and embarrassed. "Thanks for the coffee. I'll see you around."

"Take care," he said softly.

As she left the café, she felt his gaze follow her. She couldn't shake the feeling that there was something different about him. Something different about the whole meeting, but it wasn't until she got a few blocks away, rethinking the conversation.

After all, you're the one who called me here.

NINE

Rue jolted upright in her bed, a strangled gasp escaping her lips. Her heart was pounding violently, her breaths shallow as the remnants of a vision lingered in her mind. Sweat beaded her skin and soaked her shirt as she clawed at the damp sheets, trying to ground herself.

"Rue," Dacre's steady voice cut through her panic. "What's wrong?" He was touching her shoulder then her neck, pressing his thumbs against her jaw and tracing light circles. "Wake up." He turned her to face him. "Wake up, princess. Come back to me."

She turned to him, her wide eyes glistening with unshed tears. She blinked and focused on him.

"Did you see something?" Dacre was searching her face.

"It's Evelyn," she whispered, her voice trembling. "I saw her... She's hurt, Dacre. Someone's hurting her."

"Right now?"

"I–I'm not sure when." Her chin trembled. "They're going to hurt her really bad. I can't..."

Dacre's brows furrowed, his voice clouded with concern. "Tell me what you saw."

Rue took a shaky breath, recounting the vision in disjointed fragments...

Rue's hand went to her throat. "She was covered in bruises here." Her fingers lingered under her ear. "There were bite marks here." Tears fell from Rue's eyes. "She was trying to hide it. She was so pale and sad. There was no light in her eyes. She was thin, gaunt." Rue's fingers drifted to her forehead. "There's something else wrong. I think she's sick." Rue squeezed her eyes closed. "No. There's something... whoever is hurting her is giving her blood to make her heal but only a small amount. She gets sick all over again. I can't... I can't figure it out." Rue squeezed her head between her hands. "I have a terrible feeling. She looked so sickly. The bruises... the bite marks..."

By the time Rue finished, her hands were trembling, and she clenched her fists tightly to still them.

Dacre listened intently, his dark eyes studying her every move. When she fell silent, he spoke. "You need to tell Remington." He took her hands. "If this means you're in danger again..."

"No. I'm fine. The danger is all to Ev."

"Call Remm."

Rue shook her head. "I can't. I told him to stay away from her. He's got too much to deal with back home."

"Maybe," Dacre agreed. "But you're not the only one who cares about Evelyn. He's been obsessed with her since the moment they met. Call him, Rue. You'll regret it if you don't."

Rue hesitated, teeth worrying her bottom lip. She knew. She'd seen the way Remm and Evelyn connected before graduation. They asked Rue about each other and tried to hide their interest. Truthfully, Rue felt terrible that she'd told them to stay away from each other. She watched Dacre and remembered a time when they were kept apart. It wasn't right. But there was plenty not right with the world they lived in.

Finally, Rue grabbed her phone and dialed.

Remington answered on the second ring, his voice groggy but instantly alert. "Rue?"

"Remm. I need your help. It's Evelyn," Rue blurted, her fear spilling out. "I saw her. In a vision. She's in danger, Remm. Someone's using her—draining her blood. She's barely standing, and if we don't do something…" Her voice cracked, and she fought to steady herself. "I know I told you to stay away, but I was wrong. You have to help her."

The line went silent, and Rue could hear the faint sound of his breathing. "Right now? I just saw her Sunday and she looked fine."

"You what?" Rue was shocked for a moment then remembered Evelyn had told her about his brief visit to the dig site.

"Is someone hurting her now?" Remington asked.

"I'm not sure. I just woke from a vision. If we can help her before it gets bad, we need to intervene now."

Finally, Remington spoke, his voice heavy. "I'll try, but… this could not have come at a worse time."

"Why?" Rue demanded. "What's going on there."

"I think someone's seen Thrush," Remington said quietly.

Rue's breath caught. "Thrush?"

"A demon came to me yesterday," Remington explained. "There's been a disturbance in the mountains, and he asked when I'd last seen Thrush. I've been chasing rumors for years, Rue. This is the first real lead I've had."

Rue's grip tightened on her phone. "Thrush is overdue for his time as a Hellion. If the curse takes him..."

"I know," Remington said. "That's why I have to find him. But Evelyn... If someone's targeting her, it's not random. There's a reason, and it's probably because of *us*. Introducing her to our world was dangerous."

His words were calm, measured, but beneath them a storm churned. Remington's hand clenched the edge of his desk, the wood groaning under the pressure. He could feel it—a pull, deep and insistent, tugging him toward the Earthen plane. Toward *her*. The humming had never stopped since that first night it woke him.

Ever since he'd seen Evelyn at the dig site, he hadn't been able to shake the feeling that something else was at work. But Thrush... Thrush was family. The thought of losing him to the curse was unbearable.

"Rue," he said finally, his voice softening, "I can't be in two places at once. You need to stay close to Evelyn. Watch her. If anything else happens, call me immediately."

"I will," Rue said, her voice barely above a whisper.

"Good," he said, ending the call.

Remington leaned back in his chair, staring at the ceiling. The hum of the stones still echoed faintly in his mind, only seeming to get louder with resistance. His chest tightened as his thoughts drifted to Evelyn; her smile, the way she'd felt under his hands, her softness. Remington sighed. She was human and off limits.

He closed his eyes, exhaling slowly. "I'll protect you," he murmured. "Can't promise I'll keep my hands to myself though."

TEN

THE WARM GLOW OF THE EVENING SUN FILTERED through the large windows of the university library as Rue packed the last of her books into her bag. Evelyn sat cross-legged on the nearby couch, flipping through a worn notebook filled with sketches of runes. Next to her was a pile of high resolution photographs from the dig site.

"So, we're still on for the dig this weekend, right?" Rue asked, glancing up.

"Of course!" Evelyn said with a bright smile. "But I'll be a few hours late. I've got a dinner date."

Rue paused mid-movement, her brows furrowing. "A date?"

Evelyn nodded, her excitement bubbling over. "Yes! I met him at the café after my MRI. He's... amazing. Handsome, charming, the whole package. You'll love him! I want to introduce you and Dacre to him soon."

Rue exchanged a quick glance with Dacre, who was leaning casually against a nearby bookshelf. His expression didn't shift, but Rue could sense his unease.

"Evelyn..." Rue started, choosing her words carefully. "That sounds great, but just... be careful, okay?"

Evelyn's smile faltered, her brow knitting in confusion. "Careful? What do you mean?"

"I just mean," Rue said, hesitating slightly, "you've been working so hard lately. And, you know, there's been a lot going on. It wouldn't hurt to slow down a little. That's all."

Evelyn tilted her head, studying Rue. "Are you worried about me? Did you see something?"

"I'm worried," Rue said. "You've been pushing yourself so much between the dig, school, and... everything else. Are you really okay?"

Evelyn's grin returned, wider this time. "I'm wonderful, Rue. Never better, actually. The dig is going great, work is manageable, and now this date? Things are finally falling into place. I'm excited!"

Rue forced a smile, but her stomach twisted. "All right," she said softly. "Just... promise you'll call me if anything feels off?"

Evelyn laughed lightly. "I promise. But seriously, you don't have to worry. I'm fine."

From his place by the bookshelf, Dacre finally spoke, his deep voice calm and measured. "Have fun, Evelyn. But keep your guard up. First impressions can be deceiving."

Evelyn rolled her eyes, playfully dramatic. "You two are acting like I'm walking into a dragon's lair. It's just dinner. I haven't gone on a date in so long. I think I deserve it." She stood, grabbing her bag. "I'll see you at the dig tomorrow, and I'll bring good news about my amazing date. You'll see. He's perfect."

Rue watched her leave, her unease lingering like a

shadow. As the door closed behind Evelyn, she turned to Dacre. "You feel it too, don't you?"

Dacre nodded, his gaze fixed on the door. "Something's not right."

Rue sighed, gripping the edge of the table. "I just hope I'm wrong."

ELEVEN

THE COZY ITALIAN RESTAURANT BUZZED WITH the quiet hum of conversation and the clinking of silverware on porcelain. Evelyn sat across from the man she had met at the café, her hands wrapped around a half-empty glass of wine. The low light made his sharp features seem even more striking, his dark eyes catching the faint glow of the candle between them.

"So, Evelyn," Alastor said, leaning forward with an easy smile. "Do you always work yourself to death over old rocks, or is this a special phase?"

Evelyn laughed, setting her glass down. "You mean the dig? It's not just rocks, you know. These are pieces of history. Each one tells a story. I majored in Archaeology. I really enjoy the work."

"And you're the storyteller of the rocks?" he teased, his voice warm. "What do the rocks say to you?"

"Something like that," she admitted, though her smile faltered. "They don't really talk back. There's a lot of research that goes into it."

There was something about the way he looked at her—too focused, too intent. As if he wasn't just interested but studying her. It was like he cared, like he wanted her. Evelyn hadn't had this kind of attention in months.

Alastor noticed her hesitation and leaned back, his charm effortless. "You're fascinating, you know that? I don't think I've met anyone quite like you."

Evelyn flushed at the compliment, but her stomach twisted. He was handsome, and his conversation was smooth, but there was an edge to him she couldn't place. She wondered if he was a little bit dangerous. She liked that. A strong man who could take care of her and compliment her. And look handsome while doing it.

"Thank you," she said softly, her voice almost drowned by the noise of the restaurant.

Evelyn ordered Chicken Alfredo and Alastor ordered a steak, rare with a side of shrimp. Evelyn had another glass of wine. Alastor had bourbon on the rocks and the waitress stared a little too long at him as she took the order.

"Do you want dessert?" Alastor asked.

"No thank you," Evelyn replied.

"Just the check then," Alastor said to the waitress.

As they walked out into the cool night air, Evelyn shivered and enjoyed the sound her heels made on the cold cement. Alastor matched her pace, his hands tucked casually into the pockets of his tailored coat.

"Can I walk you home?" he asked, his voice low and inviting. "I didn't see you arrive in a car."

Evelyn hesitated. She had refused to let him pick her up at her apartment. It was only about ten minutes away and close enough to walk. Her instincts screamed at her to be wary, but she didn't want to any longer. She'd been a good girl for long enough. It was time to live again.

"Sure," Evelyn said, forcing a smile.

They strolled down the quiet street, the dim glow of streetlights casting long shadows. Evelyn hugged her coat tighter around herself, her mind a whirl of conflicting thoughts. She'd been hoping to feel a spark tonight—something to help her move on from the ever-present ache that was Remington. The one guy she could never have.

Remington. His name alone sent a pang through her chest. She wanted him desperately, but he was untouchable. A prince of Hell, weighed down by responsibilities she couldn't begin to understand. And yet...

"You seem quiet," Alastor said, pulling her from her thoughts.

"Sorry," Evelyn replied quickly. "It's the wine. Makes me ruminate." She smiled.

Alastor nodded, though his gaze lingered on her face for a moment too long. "I get it. You're a busy woman."

They reached the gate to her building. Evelyn stopped, turning to face him. "Thanks for dinner. It was nice." She sighed. "The best, actually. It's been a while since I was on a date."

His smile returned, but there was something in his eyes —something dark and unreadable. "I enjoyed it too. I'd like to see you again, Evelyn."

She hesitated, the unease clawing at her. "Maybe," she said softly, biting her lip.

"Goodnight," he said, reaching out to gently take her hand. His touch was cold, and it sent a shiver down her spine. He brought her hand to his mouth and kissed it. When he looked up, his eyes were half-lidded, his lips upturned, dark hair fell over his face. And then... he licked the back of her hand.

Evelyn sucked in a breath as something flip-flopped in her belly.

"Ev." His voice was seductive. "Ev, you called me here. Remember that." He was watching her like she was his next meal.

"I... I don't understand."

He turned her hand in his and pushed the sleeve of her coat up, revealing the soft skin of her wrist.

"Little human, do you not know what you've done? Do you not know who you've called?"

Evelyn's mouth was hanging open, her legs were trembling. Alastor was rubbing her wrist and it was totally erotic. Evelyn blamed the wine as she bit her lip again and closed her eyes. She felt his mouth again, then his tongue, then... something sharp like he nipped her skin with his teeth. Evelyn moaned, then slapped her free hand over her mouth.

"I... I don't know what's wrong with me." She gripped the gate to steady herself. Whatever was happening, it felt equal parts right and wrong. She wanted to run and fall into his arms at the same time.

Alastor stood and stepped closer. Evelyn's back hit the gate and she tipped her chin up to look into his eyes.

"Do you even know what you've called?"

"I didn't call you." Evelyn's voice was soft. Her eyes wide.

"You most certainly did. And I must say, I was thrilled to see you that first time. You're very pretty, not like the other ones."

"Th–Thank you... I think." She swallowed hard. "You should go."

Alastor's body was flush against hers, pressing upon her in all the right places. His hand moved to touch her hair. "I've never had one with hair like this." He smelled it.

"Please stop."

He took half a step back.

Evelyn side-stepped and rushed through the gate, hurrying toward the entrance to her building. Evelyn felt her chest tighten. She glanced over her shoulder. He was still there, standing on the sidewalk, watching her.

Evelyn slipped inside, bolting the door behind her. Her hands shook as she leaned against it, her heart pounding. She wanted to forget the way his eyes seemed to pierce through her, but she couldn't shake the feeling that she'd just walked into something far more dangerous than she realized.

Her thoughts drifted back to Remington. She couldn't help but wonder if he'd been here, would he have told her to stay far away from this man? Or had she already gone too far? She should call Rue and Dacre, they'd know what to do. Her hands shook as she searched her pockets for her phone.

There was a strange noise from the kitchen. Footsteps. She looked up.

Alastor was inside her apartment.

Then he was in front of her in a heartbeat. Evelyn

opened her mouth to scream but he pressed his large hand over her lips.

He tsk'd. "No, little human, you called me, you don't get to deny me. You. Called. Me." He flashed sharp teeth.

Evelyn's eyes widened as she recognized the pendant hanging around his neck. He was at the diner. He'd been following her.

TWELVE

RUE PACED IN FRONT OF THE SUV, HER BOOTS grinding against the gravel with each step. Her arms were crossed tightly over her chest, and her phone was clutched in one hand. Every few seconds she glanced at it, her thumb hovering over Evelyn's contact.

"She's late," Rue said, breaking the tense silence. Her voice was sharper than she intended, betraying the knot of anxiety in her chest. "Evelyn is never late. She's always punctual."

Dacre leaned against the side of the SUV, arms folded and brow furrowed. "We've only been waiting twenty minutes," he said, though his tone lacked the calm assurance it usually carried. He was watching Rue closely, picking up on her unease.

Rue stopped pacing and shot him a glare. "I told you about the vision. She wasn't fine in it. She was hurt—bruised, sick, and someone was... hurting her." Rue's voice cracked slightly, and she shook her head to clear the rising panic.

"I know," Dacre said quietly, his jaw tightening. "But we don't know if that vision is something that will happen or just something that could happen."

Rue exhaled sharply, running a hand through her hair. She wanted to believe Dacre's logic, but the image of Evelyn—injured and in pain—was seared into her mind. Rue was just learning how to use her gift and didn't fully understand everything she saw. She rubbed her jaw, wishing she were better at this.

"Ev said she'd be here by 7:30," Rue muttered, glancing at her watch. It was nearing 8:15. "She's always early, Dacre. *Always*." She stared down at her phone, thumb tapping the screen to call Evelyn again. "I'm calling her."

It rang. And rang. And rang.

"Voicemail," Rue said through gritted teeth as she hung up. She shoved the phone into her jacket pocket, frustration bubbling over. "I shouldn't have let her go on that stupid date. I should have insisted—"

"You warned her," Dacre interrupted. He stepped closer, his large frame blocking Rue's pacing. "You told her to be careful. Evelyn's not reckless—she listens to you. But, step into her shoes, it has to be strange being half-caught up in our world. Humans don't see the kind of danger we do. She has no idea what monsters truly lurk in the shadows."

Rue looked up at him, her jaw clenched. "That doesn't make me feel better right now. It actually makes me feel awful."

Dacre's gaze softened, but there was a flicker of worry in his dark eyes. "I don't like this either," he admitted. "What do you want to do, Rue?" He asked. "It's your call. I don't want to leave you unprotected if something evil is lurking on this plane." He searched her eyes. "If we go together and your life is threatened... I won't keep this form. We'll have to leave this life. Do you want to risk that?"

Rue nodded reluctantly, her hand gripping the edge of the SUV for support. She hated feeling powerless, and that's exactly what this moment felt like.

"No," she said, though her voice wavered. "I'm going to her place. If she's not here and I don't call in an hour, we'll figure out our next move."

"Oh no. I'm coming with you," Dacre said, already moving to grab the keys. "With whatever is going on, I'm not letting you out of my sight for one minute."

She hesitated, her throat tightening. "If she's not fine, I'll need you ready."

Ready had a hidden meaning. Dacre was kind of a monster himself. A kind of shape shifter that Hell hadn't seen in ages, the last of his kind. His beast could alter every-one's perspective.

Dacre hesitated, his protective instincts warring with his trust in Rue's judgment. Finally he nodded, repeating his earlier warning. "If anyone sees me, we are done here," he warned. "All of this is over. We will have to leave and start over somewhere else."

Rue nodded in understanding before she climbed into the SUV, her hands gripping the door handle tightly. Dacre got behind the wheel, his body tense with Rue's warning. He'd do anything for Rue, even if that meant ruining the peace they'd found on the Earthen plane.

As Dacre pulled out of the gravel lot and onto the main road, the sense of urgency gnawed at them both.

Thirteen

The crisp mountain air of Hell stung Remington's face as he sprinted through the uneven terrain, his boots pounding against the rocky ground. His pulse roared in his ears, but it wasn't enough to drown out the faint but insistent crunch of footsteps ahead. Remington was on the hunt.

A shadow darted between the jagged cliffs, just out of reach. It moved with unnatural speed and precision, slipping through the terrain like smoke. A flash of white hair caught the moonlight.

"Thrush!" Remington's voice echoed through the mountains, but the figure didn't slow. "Stop!"

He pushed harder, his muscles burning as he leapt over a fallen log and landed in a crouch. For the first time in years, he felt the thrill of the chase, the primal rush of hunting something—or someone—that mattered. His cousin. His brother in all but blood. Close enough to blood.

The figure ahead slowed, pausing at the edge of a steep

incline. For a fleeting moment, moonlight illuminated the figure's profile, and Remington's breath caught. It was Thrush. It had to be. The bastard was big.

"Stop running!" Remington shouted, his voice rough with desperation. "I want to help you!"

The figure hesitated, turning slightly as if considering. But then it bolted again, disappearing into the shadows.

Remington pushed himself harder, his lungs heaving. Every ounce of him was focused on catching up. He was so close now, his instincts screaming to keep going—until the humming began.

At first, it was faint, like the low buzz of bees on a distant breeze. But with every step, the sound grew louder, deeper, until it was a demanding force vibrating through the air. It resonated in his bones, throwing his balance.

"Damn it," Remington hissed, stumbling to a halt. He pressed his hands over his ears, but it was no use. The hum wasn't coming from the outside—it was inside him, reverberating through his skull, demanding attention.

He dropped to one knee, panting as the noise intensified, drowning out everything else. The mountains blurred, the edges of his vision narrowing until there was nothing but the sound. It was maddening, relentless. Just like the night it woke him and led him to...

Evelyn.

The thought surged through him with startling clarity, cutting through the haze.

He forced himself to his feet, wobbling slightly as the humming began to subside. The chase was over—Thrush was gone, the moment lost.

"Fuck," Remington muttered to himself. He ran a

hand through his hair damp with sweat. "Thrush!" he shouted into the forest.

There was no reply.

Chel appeared at his side, his imposing figure stepping out from the shadows. "You lost him." The Hellion was breathing heavy from the run.

Remington clenched his fists, frustration bubbling beneath the surface. "I know. It's not like you had a lead on him." Remington glanced at Chels wings.

Chel tilted his head, his dark eyes narrowing. "Are you hurt?"

"No." Remington shook his head, his voice sharper than he intended. He drew in a deep breath, forcing himself to steady. "But something else is happening. Something I can't ignore."

Chel folded his arms, his expression skeptical. "Thrush is more important. We've been searching for him for years. We were so close just now. I saw him on the ridge." Chel pointed to where he was running.

"I know that," Remington snapped, his temper flaring. "But I can't stop this noise in my head." Remington was rubbing his temples. "I can't focus. It's driving me insane."

Chel's lips pressed into a thin line, but he didn't argue. "What do you want me to do?"

"Stay here," Remington said, his voice resolute. "Keep searching. If you find anything—anything—you send word immediately."

Chel nodded, his gaze unwavering. "And you?"

"I'm going home." Remington's voice was quieter now, but no less determined. "I need to prepare. I have to talk to Rue. I'm going to the Earthen plane."

Chel's eyebrows rose. "The annoying and loud human?"

Remington nodded.

"She's pretty. Tired of fighting fate?" Chel smirked. "She was smitten with you. Probably broke her heart already."

"Shut up," Remington muttered as he walked away.

The air in the castle was cool and still, a stark contrast to the frigid mountain winds. Remington entered through the side gate, brushing snow from his dark jacket, his steps echoing in the empty corridors. The humming had faded to a faint vibration in his chest, like a heartbeat that wasn't his own.

The castle was quiet at this hour, most of its inhabitants either on patrols or buried in administrative duties that kept the underworld's delicate balance intact. With his parents gone, the realm was running relatively well. During the day, the place thrummed with an energy that was both comforting and oppressive. There was still the issue of the basilisk in the Black River, and more goats had gone missing. Remington stretched his arms and headed straight for his chambers. As he entered, the flames in the hearth roared to life, casting a warm glow over the room. The high ceilings and dark stone walls were lined with bookshelves, basilisk skeleton weapons from the war—a stark reminder of the responsibilities he now carried.

He shrugged his jacket off and tossed it onto a chair, revealing the fitted black shirt beneath. His fingers brushed against the blade at his hip. The faint glyphs etched into it glowed softly in response; a protective charm—one of the few things he trusted completely.

Remington moved to a chest at the foot of his bed, unlocking it with a quick incantation. Inside were carefully arranged tools and weapons: a silver-bladed dagger, enchanted restraints, vials of dark elixirs. He selected each item methodically, strapping them into place with practiced ease.

A knock sounded at the door.

"Enter," he said without looking up.

The door creaked open, and one of his attendants stepped inside, a young demon with sharp features and an anxious expression. "Prince Remington, shall I summon the Queen for your departure?"

"No," Remington replied, sliding a small blade into his boot. "Don't bother my parents. I'm handling it alone for now."

The attendant hesitated, then nodded. "Shall I ..."

"Three packs of blood," Remington said, his tone leaving no room for argument.

The running had brought a hunger he couldn't ignore. He licked his lips, wishing for a pretty neck instead of a bag of blood. Remington squeezed his eyes together. No. No, he wouldn't risk it. The bagged blood would do, it had been doing just fine all of these years.

The attendant disappeared, and Remington returned to his preparations. His thoughts drifted as he changed his clothing, the memory of the humming sound sharp in his mind.

Her face surfaced in his thoughts—sharp blue eyes, an

easy laugh that could light up even the darkest of rooms. She had always been a source of brightness in his otherwise grim world, a reminder of what could be. And yet, he had stayed away for Rue's sake. He couldn't lie to himself, the memories of her the night before her graduation were frequently brought to the forefront of his mind.

Now, it seemed fate wasn't giving him a choice.

The attendant returned with a tray loaded with a glass and three bags of blood.

"Thank you," Remington said, tugging on a leather jacket. He picked up his basilisk dagger, sliding it into its sheath with a finality that settled over him.

He drank. Thirst lingered. He thought to get more before leaving, but the humming in the back of his head was more insistent as each minute passed. He had to go.

He stepped into the hallway, his boots thudding against the stone floor. He jogged down the spiral stairwell and walked faster toward end of the corridor. He passed the door that led to the courtyard, the portal not far. It shimmered like oil on water.

Chel's words echoed in his mind: *Tired of fighting fate?*

He knew the Hellion was right, but something deep inside told him that this detour wasn't a mistake. He would find Thrush but first, he had to find Evelyn.

With a steadying breath, Remington stepped into the portal, the swirling darkness swallowing him whole.

The portal spit Remington out onto the Earthen plane, depositing him in a narrow alley not far from the Loyola campus. He glanced up at the abandoned Peabody Library. The cold, damp air carried the scent of asphalt and car exhaust, a jarring contrast to the crisp, ancient chill of the mountains. He zipped his jacket, shivered, and knowing he didn't belong in the mortal world, he stepped out onto the street.

Rue and Dacre were waiting for him near a row of parked cars, their faces taut with worry. Rue's arms were crossed tightly over her chest, and Dacre stood close beside her, his massive frame radiating tension.

"Remington," Rue said, relief washing over her features as he approached. "Thank God you're here."

"What's happened?" he asked, his tone sharp as he scanned their surroundings.

"It's Evelyn," Rue said, her voice trembling. "She's missing. She was supposed to meet us this morning, but she never showed. She's not answering her phone, and Dacre tried tracking her—"

"But there's nothing," Dacre interrupted, his deep voice edged with frustration. "No trail, no scent. It's like she vanished into thin air."

Remington's jaw tightened. "When was the last time either of you saw her?"

"Yesterday," Rue said. "She had a date last night. I told her to be careful, but she seemed so... happy. She was excited about it. Said she wanted to introduce him to us." Rue's voice cracked, and she looked away. "God, I should have stopped her."

"Do you know who she was with?" Remington pressed, holding back a gnawing need to slam the guy's face in once he figured out who dared to touch her.

"No," Rue admitted. "She didn't give a name. Just said she met him at a café."

Dacre placed a reassuring hand on Rue's shoulder. "We thought maybe she'd gone back to her apartment, so we were about to check there."

"Then let's not waste time," Remington said, his voice low and dangerous.

They piled into a black SUV, Dacre driving with a precision that belied his size. Rue sat in the back alone, her hands clenched into fists. She kept stealing glances at her brother, as if searching for answers in his expression but Remington's face was a mask of cold determination.

When they arrived at Evelyn's apartment, unease settled over the group like a shroud. The porch light was off and the windows were dark.

"Looks like no one is home," Dacre said, his tone grim.

Rue reached for the door handle, but Dacre turned in his seat. "No," he said firmly. "You're staying here."

"What?" Rue protested, her voice rising. "I'm not just sitting in the car while—"

"I won't let you put yourself in danger," Dacre said, cutting her off. "You saw what happens in your visions. I'm not risking you too."

"Dacre's right," Remington said, already moving toward the house. "Stay here. Both of you."

Dacre gave a curt nod and positioned himself protectively by the car as Remington approached the front door. He knocked once, hard enough to make the wood creak on its hinges.

Nothing. He listened, nearly pressing his ear to the door. There were no sounds.

Without hesitation, he stepped back and kicked the door in. The wood splintered under the force, and the door swung inward with a crash.

Inside, the apartment was eerily quiet. The air was thick and stale, carrying a faint metallic tang that made his stomach churn. The living room was undisturbed—blankets neatly folded, a book resting on the arm of the couch.

"Evelyn?" Remington called, his voice echoing through the empty space.

He moved deeper into the apartment, his sharp eyes scanning every corner. The kitchen was empty, as was the small dining area. But when he reached her bedroom, his breath caught.

The bed was unmade, the sheets twisted and stained with drops of dark red. A shattered mug lay on the floor by the nightstand, the remnants of its contents soaked into the carpet.

He knelt, running his fingers over the dried stain. Blood.

"Damn it," he muttered, his fist clenching.

He forced himself to stand and keep searching, moving to the bathroom. The sink was dry, but the mirror above it bore faint smudges, as if someone had wiped it hastily.

His chest tightened. Someone had taken her. The humming in the back of his head intensified. His hand slammed against the wall as he tried to focus.

"Remington?" Rue's voice called from outside, strained and anxious.

He turned on his heel and strode back to the door, his expression grim. Dacre was standing guard, his sharp eyes scanning the surrounding forest while Rue hovered by the porch, her worry etched into every line of her face.

"She's gone," Remington said.

Rue paled, her hand flying to her mouth. "We have to find her."

Remington's jaw set. "Do you have any idea where she might have been taken?" He walked closer to his sister. "Think, Rue."

Rue rubbed her neck and thought back to the runes they'd found in the mountain. There was the man at the diner who'd followed them. Rue told them everything.

Dacre's expression hardened. "You kept all this from me?"

"I'm sorry," Rue said. "We were just trying to protect our research. It's important. There's so much we don't know about our heritage." Rue looked to her brother. "There is so much that has been buried and forgotten."

Remington was watching her closely. "You didn't like it when we lied to you. You absolutely hated it when we kept information from you even though it meant you'd be safe." He stepped closer, knew that his height was intimidating to his sister. She was so much shorter than him. "In the future, I'd expect you to tell us if you'd been followed after digging up ruins covered in runes."

"Okay," Rue nodded as she said, "I'm sorry. Jeeze, you look like dad before he goes postal."

Remington stepped back. "Sorry. I didn't mean to scare you."

Rue huffed out a small laugh. "You don't scare me, little brother. Much."

Remington shrugged before glancing at Dacre. Neither

knew how to effectively deal with Rue; she was small and sweet but lived in a bubble where she only answered to morals she thought were valuable. Remington sighed. Dacre had it worse when it came to dealing with her. Rue had bitten the guy when she was fifteen; she didn't know any better at the time but she'd created a blood bond between them. It took nearly ten years for them to get to a place in life where they could be together.

"We have to find Evelyn," Rue said.

Remington nodded, his expression hardening. "I think I know where she is." He knew that the humming in his head would lead him to Ev. "But you two are staying here."

He held out his hand.

"Give me your keys."

Fourteen

EVELYN STIRRED AWAKE, HER HEAD POUNDING and her body trembling. She blinked rapidly, the dim light making it hard to focus on her surroundings. The air was damp and cold, and the scent of earth and wet stone surrounded her. Slowly, the fog in her mind began to clear.

She was at the dig site.

The faint outlines of the stones covered in runes glimmered dimly in Alastor's presence. Rue had said something similar happened when she'd been in Dr. Malcom's caves. It seemed beings from other realms activated the stones somehow.

Alastor stood a few feet away, his tall frame bent over one of the stone slabs. He muttered to himself in a language she didn't understand, his fingers tracing the lines and grooves of the runes with a mixture of fascination and frustration.

Evelyn tried to move, but her arms felt like lead. A sharp ache flared in her neck, and her hand slowly rose to touch the tender spot. There, beneath her fingers, she felt the faint indentations left behind from Alastor's fangs. Her stomach twisted in fear and anger.

"You're awake," Alastor said without looking at her, his deep voice laced with amusement. "Good. I thought I might have taken too much."

She glared at him, though it took all her strength just to lift her head. "Why...why are you doing this?" Her voice was barely a whisper, hoarse and dry.

Alastor straightened, turning to face her with a predatory smile. "Because, little human, you called me. You sacrificed yourself. I'm only doing what you requested." He crouched down, his piercing gaze locking onto hers. "Your blood woke the stones. They called to me."

Evelyn's breath hitched, her heart pounding. Her mind raced as her body refused to cooperate. Every part of her wanted to run, to scream, to fight—but she couldn't even muster the strength to sit up. The betrayal of her own body made her feel even more hopeless.

Her voice cracked when she finally spoke. "I didn't call you. I don't even know what you're talking about."

"Oh, but you did," he replied smoothly, reaching out to brush a stray strand of hair from her face. She flinched, and his smile widened. "When your blood touched the stone, it created a beacon. I followed that call and it led me here. To you. Good thing I was first though. I wouldn't want one of the others to claim you."

"Others?" Evelyn's eyes went wide.

He stood again, his attention shifting back to the runes. "Those of Lucifer's bloodline. Half-lings, demons, whatever he mated with."

Her stomach churned as his words sank in.

"You're wrong," she said, her voice trembling but firm. "I don't want any of that."

Alastor laughed, a low, chilling sound. "Too late..." He turned back to the stones, his expression hardening. "There's something missing here."

Evelyn's chest tightened as she watched him.

No. Focus. Think. She couldn't give in to despair, not now. Her gaze darted around the site, looking for anything she could use—a tool, a distraction, anything. Her thoughts flitted to Rue and Dacre. She missed meeting up with them, and she wasn't even sure what day it was. Did they even know she was gone? Would they know where to look?

The weakness in her body was overwhelming but Evelyn clenched her jaw, forcing herself to focus.

"What happens if you don't find what you're looking for?" she asked, trying to hold her voice steady.

Alastor glanced back at her, a flicker of amusement in his eyes. "Oh, I'll find it," he said simply. "And when I do, everything will change."

Evelyn's stomach twisted, but she masked her fear with defiance. "You sound so sure of yourself."

He chuckled darkly. "Confidence is an earned trait, little human. You'll learn that, too."

As he turned back to the stones, Evelyn's mind churned with a thousand desperate plans. She just needed one chance, one moment to act. Until then, she had to stay alive. Stay awake.

She bit her lip and glared at his back. *Hang on, Evelyn,* she told herself. *Someone's coming. They have to be.*

She heard footsteps and turned to find Alastor in her personal space. He licked his lips. "Your blood tastes off.

But still good." He reached out and Evelyn jerked her arm away.

"Don't touch me."

"What are you going to do? Get up and run?"

Evelyn glanced around them. There was nowhere to go and her legs felt like they weighed a thousand pounds. Maybe a bear would bound out of the forest and interrupt Alastor. She watched him take her arm as he slid his fingers between hers. With his free hand, he reached for her neck to push her hair away and leaned in closer.

"You still smell good. I would have traded you for that steak in an instant. But I have plans for you. We can always use a pretty human like you." He looked her up and down. "Even though I'd like to keep you to myself. You're worth more if I share."

Evelyn gripped the nearby rock that she'd spotted. She swung her arm, but what she thought was fast was actually magnificently slow. Alastor laughed, shoving her arm away. The rock rolled into the grass.

"Nice try." Alastor's hand slid behind her shoulder and lifted her neck to his mouth.

Fifteen

The sound was maddening.

The hum was barely perceptible above the rumble of the SUV's engine. But as Remington drove further into the mountains the noise grew sharper, louder, clawing its way into his thoughts like a persistent, unrelenting whisper. When he turned down the wrong road it spiked and threatened to deafen him. When he made a correct turn that would bring him closer to her, it caressed his mind with only a whisper.

Remington clenched the steering wheel, his knuckles pale against the black leather, and forced his eyes to stay on the winding road. The trees on either side blurred into shadows, their skeletal branches stretching toward the early evening sky. He drove faster, much too fast for these mountain roads. But, they weren't much different than the battered roads in Hell. And many were the same, only a dark reflection of the Earthen plane. He pressed down harder on the gas pedal.

The hum seemed to pulse in time with his heartbeat; a

deep, resonant vibration that wasn't entirely physical. It pulled at him, threading through his chest and settling deep in his core.

"Where is she?" he muttered under his breath.

Evelyn flickered in his mind. Her face, pale and determined, standing in the middle of that dig site just a few days ago. She had been different. There was something in her gaze that unsettled him.

And now she was missing.

Remington's jaw tightened as he pressed his foot harder on the gas pedal. The SUV roared up the steep incline, gravel spitting out from under the tires. He could feel the hum in his chest now, vibrating against his ribs like an ancient chant he didn't understand.

He couldn't deny the truth any longer—the sound was connected to her. And he had to figure out what was going on.

The dig site wasn't far.

The sound grew deafening as he approached the final stretch. He grimaced, the vibration rattling through his bones. It was almost unbearable, yet he couldn't stop. Every instinct screamed at him to keep going, to find its source. Find her.

He slowed the SUV as he reached the edge of the dig site. The dirt parking area was empty, eerily silent except for the hum, which seemed to seep into the very air around him.

Remington stepped out of the vehicle, boots crunching against the gravel. The chill of the mountain air bit at his skin, but he barely noticed. His gaze swept over the site, scanning for any sign of movement.

Nothing.

The hum intensified as he walked toward the excavation area. It wasn't coming from the stones themselves, but from something deeper, something beneath the surface.

He paused at the edge of the largest trench, staring down at the runes carved into the ancient stones. They seemed to shimmer. The sight was deeply unsettling.

"Evelyn," he muttered, the name slipping from his lips like a prayer.

The hum shifted suddenly, becoming a low, resonant growl. It felt...angry. The ground beneath his feet seemed to tremble, just slightly, as if the earth itself was warning him.

Remington straightened, his senses on high alert. He scanned the shadows, searching for anything—anyone— out of place. The pull of the hum was almost unbearable now, an overwhelming force that demanded his attention.

He didn't notice the figure behind him until it was too late.

A sharp, resonant laugh echoed through the site.

"So the Shadow Heir comes to play," a voice drawled, cold and mocking.

Remington spun around, his eyes narrowing as he took in the figure emerging from the shadows. The man was tall, his sharp features illuminated by the faint glow of the moon. His eyes glinted with a predatory light, and his smirk was one of pure malice. He knew this demon, would never forget him after all he'd done.

Alastor.

Alastor's smug confidence faltered the moment his eyes met Remington's. Recognition flickered in the demon's sharp features, and his smirk dissolved into something more cautious—something closer to fear.

"You..." Alastor took a step back, his bravado cracking. His gaze darted briefly to the runes before returning to Remington, and for the first time, he looked unsure of himself. "You're Sparrow's whelp."

Remington took a slow, deliberate step forward, his boots crunching against the dirt. His expression remained composed, but the fire in his eyes betrayed the storm brewing beneath the surface.

"My father's name is Sparrow." He smirked darkly.

Alastor's lips twisted into a sneer. "You think your father scares me? I've walked through fire and shadow. Sparrow's name means nothing—"

"Does it?" Remington's voice was low and steady, his tongue a blade wrapped in velvet. He stepped closer, forcing Alastor to retreat another step. "Then why do you look like you've seen a ghost?"

Alastor's jaw clenched, but he said nothing.

"Do you remember what you did to my mother?" Remington continued, his tone calm but laced with venom. "How you cut off her wings before the war?"

Alastor's composure cracked further, a flicker of panic flashing in his eyes.

"Because I do." Remington's fists tightened at his sides, the memory igniting a fury so deep it burned cold. But he held himself in check, his voice remaining measured. "And I've spent every day since imagining what it would feel like to tear you apart. Slowly."

Alastor's fear was palpable now, the confident facade

gone. "You wouldn't dare," he hissed, though the tremor in his voice betrayed him.

Remington's lips curved into a cold, dangerous smile. "Wouldn't I? My parents would love to see your head on a spike. They'd call it a gift. A long overdue one."

The demon had once stormed the castle, having been possessed by Lucifer, and ejected Remington's mother from the throne. The weeks that followed were pure chaos. And once Alastor had been successful in resurrecting Lucifer, he disappeared just as quickly as he'd made his entrance.

"Where is she?" Remington demanded, his voice low and deadly.

Alastor tilted his head, feigning innocence. "She?" he asked. "You'll have to be more specific."

Rage flared in Remington's chest. "Don't play games with me, Alastor. I know she's here. I can feel it."

Alastor's smile widened, and he spread his arms in a mock gesture of welcome. "Feel free to look, then. But I think you'll find she's...occupied."

The hum rose to a crescendo, a deafening roar that drowned out everything else. Remington staggered, clutching his head as the vibration tore through him.

Alastor laughed again, his voice cutting through the noise. "You're too late, Remington. She's already mine."

Remington gripped his blade. "I beg to differ."

For a moment, it seemed as though Alastor might stand his ground. But then, with a snarl of frustration, he turned on his heel and disappeared into the shadows.

"Run, Alastor," Remington called after him, his voice ringing with quiet menace. "But don't think you're safe.

You'll slip up eventually and when you do, I'll be there, ready to send you to your grave."

Alastor didn't respond, his retreat marked only by the fading sound of his footsteps.

The air was still now, the oppressive hum gone. But the tension in Remington's chest didn't ease. He turned back toward the dig site, scanning the area with sharp, focused eyes.

A faint sound caught his attention—a weak, ragged breath. He moved quickly, rounding a small mound of rocks.

There she was.

Evelyn lay crumpled on the ground, her skin pale, and her breathing shallow. Blood smeared her arms and neck, stark against the soft fabric of her clothes. She looked fragile, like a porcelain doll, as if the smallest touch might break her.

"Evelyn." Remington dropped to his knees beside her, his heart twisting painfully in his chest. He brushed her hair back from her face, his fingers trembling slightly. "I've got you," he murmured. "You're safe now."

Her eyes fluttered open briefly, her gaze unfocused. She tried to speak, but the words didn't come.

"Don't," he said softly. "Save your strength."

Carefully, he slid an arm beneath her shoulders, lifting her into his embrace. She was too light, too cold. The anger he'd felt toward Alastor flared again, but he pushed it down. Right now, all that mattered was getting her to safety.

Remington rose to his feet, cradling Evelyn against his chest. He cast one last glance toward the shadows where Alastor had disappeared, his jaw tightening.

"You'll pay for this," he muttered under his breath before turning toward the SUV.

The hum was gone, but its memory lingered; a reminder of how close he'd come to losing her.

And how far he'd go to protect her.

He opened the door, noticing her nose was leaking blood. Her body went limp.

"Ev…" Remington shook her. "Ev. Wake up."

Nothing.

Her heart was still beating, he could see the veins in her neck pulsing. Slow. Too slow. She looked so pale.

Sixteen

The drive to the hospital felt endless, the tension in the SUV thick and suffocating. Remington glanced at Evelyn every few seconds, her pallid face and shallow breaths gnawing at his composure. She was cradled in the passenger seat, a trickle of blood still visible beneath her nose despite his earlier attempts to wipe it away. It kept trickling and he was sure she didn't have much to spare.

"Stay with me," he murmured, his voice low but firm. His hand hovered near hers, hesitant, as if afraid she might slip away if he let her out of his sight.

He reached for his phone and called Rue.

"Remm," her hurried voice answered.

"I've got her. But there's something wrong."

"What happened?"

There was a long a pause as Remington contemplated telling his sister the truth. She'd figure it out; she hated being lied to. He couldn't. "Alastor had her."

Rue sucked in a breath.

"You remember Alastor? The demon who cut off mom's wings?"

"I remember." Rue's voice was low. "Why did he have Evelyn?"

"That stone you unearthed was a sacrifice stone, he called it. Somehow her blood got on the stone and *called* him."

"Oh." Rue sucked in a breath. "She had a nosebleed that day."

"Maybe that was it." Remington glanced in the backseat where Evelyn was still motionless.

"What happened to Alastor? Please tell me you killed him."

"The coward ran off."

"Shit," Rue cursed. "He'll be back. We can't leave her alone, she won't be safe until we figure this out."

"Well, she's unconscious now. I'm taking her to a hospital."

When they arrived at the hospital, Remington carried Evelyn inside the Emergency Room entrance. His commanding presence parted the crowds like a force of nature. Everyone turned to stare.

"She needs help," he said to the first nurse who approached them.

The nurse motioned for a stretcher as she checked Evelyn's pulse. "What happened to her?" the nurse scanned Evelyn's limp body before glancing up at Remington's face.

"Her nose keeps bleeding," he said. It wasn't the whole

truth, but he couldn't just tell the nurse that Evelyn had been kidnapped by a demon after her blood dripped onto a sacrifice stone and the demon who kidnapped her drank her blood and was trying to bind himself to her forever. Nope, the nosebleed excuse would have to be enough.

A tech rolled a stretcher closer.

"Set her here," the nurse instructed, helping him arrange Evelyn comfortably on the stretcher.

Evelyn was whisked into an exam room. Remington followed, his jaw tight, his fists clenched at his sides as he watched the flurry of medical staff surround her. There was a lot of equipment he didn't recognize, and it all made strange beeps and clicks. Then came the needles. They took her blood in small vials then attached plastic tubing to the catheter in her hand. Remington knew a little about human medicine from movies and shows and books. Sometimes a healer came to the castle and used similar methods of healing and used a little magic. He was sure these people had no magic but it appeared they were giving her fluids and after a few minutes the pallor in her skin started to improve.

Evelyn stirred, her eyes fluttering open. "Remington..." she whispered, her voice barely audible as she searched the room.

"I'm here," he said softly, stepping closer. His normally steady voice wavered.

The nurse was watching them from her computer.

Evelyn noticed. "He didn't hurt me." She told the nurse. "Is that why you're watching him?"

"It's a concern," the nurse said. "You have a lot of bruises and those marks on your neck."

"It wasn't him. I promise."

Remington looked between the two women until the nurse nodded. "Okay, Evelyn." She moved away from the computer and dragged a chair closer to Remington. "You can sit here with her."

The chair looked like a child's next to Remington. He sat and reached for Evelyn's hand. "You're going to be okay."

Evelyn nodded, her eyes on the nurse.

"You had an MRI not long ago," the nurse said.

"Yes. I'm still waiting on the results."

The nurse made a face. "Let me go speak with the doctor."

When they were alone, Evelyn turned to Remington. "I don't like the way she said that."

"Why haven't you gotten the results for your MRI?" Remington asked.

Evelyn looked away before sitting up on the gurney. "It's almost two hundred dollars for the doctor's appointment to review the results. I was going to schedule after I got paid."

Remington's brow furrowed. "You should have asked Rue for the money."

Evelyn's eyes went wide. "I... no. I don't make it a habit of asking people for money."

"But this is your health."

Evelyn just stared at him, wondering why he was getting so worked up since he didn't give a crap about her health the entire year he'd been gone.

Remington sighed and ran a hand through his hair.

"I don't even know how I'm going to pay for this emergency room visit." Evelyn was fidgeting with the hemline of her shirt. "This is going to be thousands of dollars."

"My family will pay for it," Remington said. "We got you into this mess."

"No–"

"Stop. It's settled." Remington leaned closer, elbows on his knees. "You're Rue's best friend. We take care of our friends."

"But... I'm not like you."

"It doesn't matter."

There were footsteps approaching in the hall. Remington sat up straight as someone knocked on the door.

"Yes?" Evelyn asked.

A group of medical staff entered the room. There was the nurse from earlier and a man with a "Doctor" badge.

The doctor's expression was serious. "Miss Wren," he began. "We've identified the source of your symptoms. The bruising and the nosebleeds. There's a tumor pressing against your brain."

Evelyn's breath hitched, and for a moment, the room felt like it was spinning. "A... a tumor?"

The doctor nodded, his gaze sympathetic. "It's the cause of the nosebleeds and your fainting spell you had today. We need to operate as soon as possible. It's critical. You should have had a biopsy or more testing but... you haven't made a follow up appointment."

"I was waiting for payday." Evelyn's voice was low as the medical team watched her.

"This is serious." The doctor glanced between the two of them.

"She won't miss any more appointments," Remington interrupted.

Evelyn's hand instinctively went to her head, her fingers brushing through her hair. "Will I... will I lose my hair?"

The doctor hesitated, then nodded. "Yes. For this procedure, we'll need to shave a small section so we can reach the tumor."

It felt vain, even selfish, to care about something like her hair in the face of such a dire situation, but she couldn't help it. Her hair had always been a part of her identity, a shield she hid behind when she felt insecure.

"I..." She glanced at Remington, her voice trembling. "I don't know if I can do this."

Remington scooted closer, his expression softening. He gaze level with hers. "Evelyn, this is just hair. It'll grow back."

Her eyes filled with tears, and she nodded slowly, taking a shaky breath. "Okay," she whispered. "Okay."

The nurse handed her a clipboard with consent forms the doctor started rambling about risks and benefits of the procedure, but Evelyn barely heard a word of it. Her hands trembled as she signed her name.

As she handed the clipboard back, the nurse smiled warmly as the doctors filed out of the room. "You're very brave, Miss Wren." Then, with a glance toward Remington, she added, "Is this your husband?"

Evelyn froze, her cheeks flushing despite her exhaustion. She opened her mouth to respond, but no words came out.

Remington, unperturbed, met the nurse's gaze with an even expression. "I'm here to support her," he said simply.

The nurse nodded, her smile widening. "Well, you're

lucky to have someone so devoted." She patted Evelyn's arm before leaving the room.

Evelyn looked at Remington, her emotions a storm of confusion, gratitude, and something deeper she didn't dare name. "Thank you," she whispered.

"For what?" he asked, his voice gentle.

"For... being here. For caring."

Remington's gaze softened, and for a moment, the walls she'd built around herself seemed to crumble. "You don't have to thank me, Evelyn," he said. "I'd do anything to keep you safe."

Remington stood up and moved his chair across the room as the medical team returned to prepare Evelyn for surgery.

SEVENTEEN

THE HOSPITAL SMELLED LIKE ANTISEPTIC AND something faintly metallic, a scent that set Remington's teeth on edge. He was used to the scent of blood, of fire and smoke, but this? This was different. This was the sharp, sterile tang of mortality, of fragility. And he hated it.

Evelyn looked so small in the hospital bed, wrapped in thin blankets that did nothing to warm her. The usual spark in her eyes was dimmed by exhaustion and her lips pressed into a firm line as she stared at the door, waiting for the surgeon to arrive. She hadn't said much, hadn't complained, hadn't fussed. Her asking about losing her hair fractured his heart at tiny bit. Now she just sat there quietly, waiting for fate to take the wheel.

It made him want to break something.

He had been holding in a hell of a lot of emotion, maybe even anger—anger that she hadn't taken care of herself, that she had let it get this bad, that Rue had kept them apart as if he were some sort of threat to Evelyn rather than the only one willing to protect her properly.

That was going to change.

He wouldn't see otherwise.

It was bad enough that Alastor had hurt her, but it was a double whammy knowing she'd been sick for a while. That she had known and done nothing. That no one had noticed. That she had carried this burden alone.

Remington exhaled slowly through his nose and clenched his fists against his thighs. He wanted to throttle someone—Alastor, Rue, maybe even Evelyn herself for being so damn stubborn. Maybe he'd just punch a tree. But none of that would help her now.

Instead, he gave up and dragged his chair closer to the bed again and leaned forward, forearms braced against his knees.

"You comfortable?" he asked, his voice gruffer than he meant for it to be.

Evelyn blinked, pulling her gaze from the door to look at him. A ghost of a smile curved her lips. "It's a hospital bed."

"Right." His fingers flexed. "Dumb question."

She watched him for a moment, her expression unreadable. "You don't have to stay."

His jaw locked. "Yeah, I do."

She sighed, rolling her head against the pillow to stare up at the ceiling. "Rue is going to freak out when she finds out you're here."

"I don't give a damn." He let out a slow breath, forcing himself to relax. *I care about you. And I'm done pretending otherwise.* He wanted to say it out loud but didn't want to scare her.

Evelyn's fingers twitched against the blanket, and she

hesitated before speaking. "You're just saying that because I'm in a hospital bed."

A low growl rumbled in his chest. "You really think that little of me?"

"No," she admitted, her voice quieter now. "I just... I don't know what you want from me, Remington."

He wanted everything.

He wanted to take her out of this sterile place, to keep her safe, to make sure she never had to feel this weak again.

But he couldn't say any of that.

So instead he reached out, brushing his knuckles across her wrist where the IV line curled against her skin. Her pulse fluttered beneath his touch, faint but steady.

"I just want you to be okay," he said finally.

She turned her hand palm up, and for a moment he thought she might push him away. Instead her fingers curled around his, small and warm.

They sat like that in silence, the distant beeping of machines filling the space between them.

Then the door creaked open and a nurse stepped inside, clipboard in hand. "Miss Wren? It's time."

Evelyn's grip on his hand tightened for a brief second before she let go. Remington stood as the nurse approached, his heart hammering in his chest. He hated this. Hated feeling useless.

Evelyn met his gaze as the nurse unlocked the brakes on her bed. "I'll be fine," she murmured.

He wanted to believe that.

But as he watched the nurse wheel her toward the door, he had a sinking feeling in his gut that nothing would ever be the same again. His mind was moving a mile a minute with scenarios. He didn't kill Alastor, so that meant the demon would be back. And he'd be damned if Evelyn would be left alone to face that demon again.

Eighteen

The soft hum of hospital machines filled the recovery room as Evelyn stirred awake. The harsh fluorescent lighting above her seemed dim, muted by the haze of lingering anesthesia. She blinked slowly, her vision sharpening enough to see Rue perched at her bedside, her face a mix of relief and worry.

"Hey, you," Rue said softly, offering a small smile. "You gave us a scare."

Evelyn's throat felt dry, and her voice came out as a whisper. "Did they get the tumor out?"

"Yes. You're fine now," Rue reassured her, brushing a stray hair from Evelyn's face. "They got it out. You're officially tumor-free."

Evelyn's lips twitched into a weak smile, but her hand instinctively moved toward her bandaged head. Her heart sank at the realization of what was missing. Rue caught the motion and gently placed a comforting hand over hers.

"It's just hair," Rue said. "It'll grow back." Rue held up

her own dark braid. "I'll give you some of mine. It will be very Cruella Deville."

Evelyn made a face that faltered into a smile. "I don't think that's my style. I'll take the puppies though."

Behind them the door creaked open, and Remington stepped inside. He was still in the dark jacket he had worn to the dig site but there was a tension in his stance, his usual composure fraying at the edges.

"She's awake," Rue said softly, glancing at him.

"Good," Remington replied, his voice low. He stepped closer, his sharp gaze assessing Evelyn with an intensity that made her feel simultaneously safe and exposed.

"How are you both here at the same time? Is there something you're not telling me?" Evelyn asked, her voice small but firm.

Rue and Remington exchanged a look, a silent conversation passing between them. Historically, when Rue and Remington had been on the Earthen plane together their auras lit up and drew demons and other creatures out of hiding.

Rue pointed to the lights. "It's the fluorescent lighting. Dims the aura." She glanced at her brother. "But one of us has to go."

"I'm headed out." Remington pushed his hands into his pockets.

Evelyn's jaw dropped in disappointment but she quickly closed it and swallowed. It was nice having Remm close, but she knew deep down he couldn't stay. This was only temporary. Soon he'd be gone and Evelyn would have to stop living in a fantasy world thinking they might have something together.

"I'll be back later," Remington said, his tone leaving no room for argument. "For now, you need to rest and let Rue take care of you. Promise me, Ev."

Evelyn's stomach flip-flopped at the way he said "*Ev.*"

"I promise," she said as she sank back into the pillow and closed her eyes. Her head felt heavy and the bandages were itching.

A nurse came into the room, glancing up as Remington walked out.

"He's tall," the nurse said with a smile as she greeted Rue and Evelyn. "And handsome. I brought you some pain medicine, Miss Wren."

"Thank you," Evelyn whispered.

Once Evelyn was asleep again, Rue stepped into the hallway to speak to Remington. The hospital's muted buzz surrounded them as they moved toward a quiet corner. Dacre stood nearby, his towering frame leaning against the wall, watchful as ever.

"She's not safe here," Remington said, his voice low and urgent. "Alastor won't stop. If he knows she's weak, he'll come back for her."

Rue folded her arms, her expression tense. "And what's your solution? Drag her to Hell?"

"Yes," he said without hesitation. "It's the only place I can keep her safe. Alastor wouldn't dare set foot on our lands, not with the Hellions watching."

Rue's eyes narrowed. "And you think that's the best place for her? A human? In Hell?"

"It's better than leaving her here where anyone can get to her. Including Alastor," he shot back. "And I won't risk him targeting you, Rue. You've built a life here. I'm not letting him destroy that."

Dacre's expression agreed.

Rue sighed, rubbing her temples. "If you're going to take her, you need to be sure it's the right choice. You can't just make this decision on your own."

Remington's jaw tightened. "What are you suggesting?" He motioned to Evelyn's hospital room door. "She's going to argue no matter what. Who else do I need to involve?"

"Go to the White Horse," Rue said firmly. "You must ask permission. If you take Evelyn without understanding the full implications, you could be putting her in more danger. You could be putting our entire family in danger. We can't forget all the ways the Veil between our words can thin and tear. I don't want you to be the cause of it."

Remington hesitated, the tension in his shoulders easing slightly as he nodded. "Fine. You're right. I'll consult the White Horse. But you and Dacre need to stay here and watch over her while I'm gone."

"We can do that," Dacre said, stepping forward. "But don't take too long. If Alastor returns with friends, we'll be in a world of hurt. I can protect them, but that means shattering the peace we've found here."

Remington nodded, his resolve hardening. "I'll leave now. I'll drive as fast as I can."

Rue placed a hand on his arm, her expression softening. "Be careful, Remington. This is about more than just

Evelyn. If you bring her to Hell, you're opening doors you might not be able to close."

"I know," he said quietly. "But we don't have a choice."

He turned away, his mind already racing with the journey ahead. The hum that had haunted him in the mountains was growing louder in his head, and he couldn't shake the feeling that Evelyn's fate was tied to the noise.

As he left the hospital, Remington cast one last glance back toward her room, steeling himself for what was to come. She'd stepped deeper into their world by accident, but Remington knew Hell could change a human. He thought about Shay, the last human who'd been in Hell before the war. She was injured there and demon poison was stuck in the scar; it had changed her life forever. Remington was afraid something similar could happen to Evelyn. He didn't want to see her light smudge out, she had always been so happy.

<hr>

The journey from the hospital near Loyola campus to Montana was long, but for Remington it passed in a blur with his foot pressed hard on the gas pedal of Rue's SUV. He couldn't shake the persistent hum growing louder in his head with every mile he drove further from the hospital. Further from Evelyn.

The Montana wilderness stretched before him, the snow-dusted mountains outlined against a star-drenched sky. The air was crisp, biting against his skin, but he welcomed the sharpness—it kept him grounded, focused.

Rue had warned him to bring a gift to the White Horse

with enough for Nero, the black horse. Remington checked the GPS and set it for the only grocery store in Lame Deer, Montana.

The fluorescent lights of the WinCo grocery store buzzed as Remington stepped through the automatic doors. The hum of human activity greeted him—shopping carts clattering, children whining, and the steady beep of checkout scanners. The mundanity of it all was almost jarring compared to the life he led in Hell. He wondered how his sister chose to live on the Earthen plane; a human life. He watched a young woman kiss her baby as she walked through the store. Remington blinked and looked away.

He adjusted his dark coat, blending in as much as someone of his stature and presence could. His sharp features and the air of authority he carried turned a few heads, but he ignored the glances and headed straight for the produce section.

The carrots were easy to find, their leafy green tops sticking out from a bin labeled *Organic*. He grabbed a bunch, inspecting them. Dirt clung to the roots and the carrots themselves were smaller and less uniform than the glossy, bagged ones nearby. Perfect, he thought dryly. The White Horse probably wouldn't eat anything grown without its roots in the earth. This was her realm, after all.

Carrots in hand, Remington glanced over at the small café near the store entrance. He hadn't slept and curiosity got the better of him. His sister Rue swore by the caffeinated concoctions humans seemed to love so much. Maybe it was worth a try.

A few minutes later, he stepped outside with a steaming latte in hand. The cool Montana air hit him as he took his first sip. His face contorted instantly. It was bitter and overly sweet at the same time, the foam clinging annoyingly to his upper lip.

"How does she drink this sludge?" he muttered, wiping his mouth with the back of his hand.

With a sigh, he dropped the cup into the trash can by the entrance. The bag of carrots, at least, felt like a more worthwhile purchase. He glanced at the young woman from earlier, now loading groceries into her trunk. She looked peaceful with her baby. Very human. He cursed to himself for being stupid. She was clearly human, he was surrounded by them here.

Remington gave her a curt nod before heading toward his SUV. He tossed the carrots onto the passenger seat, their green tops spilling from the bag like a bouquet.

The engine of the SUV rumbled to life as he started it and pulled out of the parking lot. The hum in his head had started to ramp up again. And he realized that the further he got from Evelyn, the worse it got.

He reached for the latte absentmindedly, only to remember it was now sitting in a trash bin outside WinCo. "Rue's addiction makes even less sense now," he muttered, shaking his head.

With a deep breath, he tightened his grip on the steering wheel. The road stretched ahead, winding toward the ranch where Jed and Shay lived with the horses, where answers—and perhaps more questions—awaited.

The Montana sky was a wide, cloudless expanse of blue as Remington pulled into the long, dusty driveway leading to Jed and Shay's ranch. The land stretched for miles, fenced pastures dotted with grazing horses. In the distance, the familiar silhouette of the White Horse stood under the shade of a tree, her head bowed as she nibbled on the sweet grass.

Remington stepped out of the SUV, brushing the dust from his dark jacket. The scent of hay and sunbaked earth filled the air, a stark contrast to the ochre skies and smell of woodsmoke and pine of Hell. Jed was the first to approach, his broad frame and easy stride exuding the calm confidence of someone who had battled angels and demons his whole life and lived to tell the tale.

"It's been a while, boy," Jed said, offering a handshake that was firm but friendly.

"It has," Remington replied. "Rue sent me. I need to discuss something with the White Horse."

Jed tilted his head toward the porch where Shay appeared, wiping her hands on a towel. She was as sharp as ever, her eyes narrowing slightly as she approached. "When the prince of Hell shows up unannounced, it's usually not a good sign," she said, her tone carrying more curiosity.

"Shay." Remington inclined his head respectfully. "It's good to see you."

"Likewise," she replied, opening her arms. "You may be a giant, but you're not too old for a hug. Come here."

Remington hesitated before stepping closer and accepting her embrace. Shay patted his back and Remington was reminded of the time he'd spent with Jed and Shay as a teenager; the time before the war, before anyone knew who he really was. His identity had been kept a secret. A shadow heir. The son his mother never anticipated but did everything to protect. That even meant waking him in the middle of the night when the castle was on fire and whisking him away to the protection of Jed and Shay. They'd taken good care of Remington and Rue. As good of care as anyone could with two royal children of Hell in hiding on the Earthen plane. Had they known of the White Horse back then, things might have been easier. It might not have taken so long to get the answers they needed to restore the balance between realms.

Glancing toward the White Horse in the distance before turning his attention back to Shay, Remington said, "I need her permission to bring someone to Hell. A human."

Shay's eyebrows rose in surprise and she exchanged a glance with Jed. "A human?" she echoed. "You realize what you're asking, right? Bringing a mortal to Hell is like dropping a lamb into a den of wolves."

"That's why I'm here," Remington said firmly. "To make sure it's the right decision. And to protect her. And… to keep the balance between realms. Rue is worried it will disrupt the Veil."

Shay stepped closer, her expression serious. "Remington, I've lived in Hell. Me and Jed were in hiding there but I was still hunted. By the new Hellions. By demons. By Alastor."

At the mention of Alastor, Remington's back straightened, his jaw tightening. "What did he do to you?"

Shay's gaze hardened, memories flashing across her face. "He took me," she said, her voice steady but cold. "He wanted revenge. I was human and he'd come after me multiple times. He wanted me for the skin trades. He wanted to use me as bait for recruiting human women. Jed nearly tore Hell apart to get me back."

Remington's hands curled into fists at his sides. "I didn't know..." he began, his voice low with restrained anger.

Shay shook her head and blowtorch blue hair shifted with the wind. "You didn't need to, Remington. You hadn't been born and it's not a story to tell children. It's about what Evelyn will face. Many Demons don't care about loyalty or love. Even the ones you trust. Most have a taste for human blood. That danger will always be there. You can't let her out of your sight. For a prince, that might be a hard task to take on." She searched his face. "I heard your parents went on holiday and left you in charge. Are you handling that okay?"

He took a deep breath, his gaze dropping to the ground for a moment before meeting Shay's eyes again. "I'm doing fine. And I'm not bringing her there lightly. Alastor has already gotten to her. She's not safe here."

Shay studied him for a long moment, then nodded slowly. "Go. Talk to the White Horse. She'll have more wisdom on this than I do. But don't forget what I've said. Hell isn't just dangerous to a human—it's cruel. And it's unforgiving. Even with the changes your mother has made. There's always darkness. Sometimes the greatest darkness lies within us."

Remington nodded, the weight of her words settling heavily on his shoulders. "Thank you, Shay."

"Don't thank me," she said, stepping back. "Just don't let her end up like me." Shay rubbed her thigh absently.

Jed clapped Remington on the shoulder, breaking the tension. "She'll be out by the tree," he said. "Go on."

As Remington started toward the White Horse, he couldn't shake Shay's words from his mind. The image of Evelyn, small and fragile on that hospital bed, flickered in his thoughts. He only hoped the White Horse would have the answers he needed.

"Ah, the shadow heir," the horse said.

Large black eyes bore into his, as if judging his soul, his intentions. It was like she already knew what he'd come here for.

"Did you bring an offering?" the horse glanced behind him. "Carrots, maybe? I don't see anything."

"Oh," Remington turned, "I left them in the car. I'll go get them."

Remington jogged back to the SUV and grabbing the bag of carrots off the back seat. He returned, opened the grocery bag, and offered the White Horse a carrot.

"Organic?" she asked.

"Yes." Remington held out another for her.

"Save a few for Nero. He's running near the mountains." The horse sighed as though it was bothersome.

Remington nodded and gazed into the horizon, hoping to get a glance of the giant black horse from his childhood.

"I need approval," Remington said, his voice steady despite the weight of the creature's gaze.

The horse inclined its head slightly. "You seek to protect the human."

"Yes. Evelyn," he replied. "She's mistakenly called a powerful demon with a sacrifice stone. Sacrificed herself, I was told. The demon Alastor is hunting her."

"Just him?" The horse's eyes gleamed with an ancient wisdom as she regarded him. "You must help her, Remington, despite your sister's fears. Evelyn's fate and yours are intertwined now. More than ever before. Rue will understand."

Remington's brow furrowed. "What do you mean?"

The horse pawed the ground, her mane rippling like liquid light. "The sacrifice stones are older than most, remnants of a forgotten era. They are tied to ancient beliefs, ancient magic. Your sister is unearthing a history long forgotten. The Veil wasn't always so heavy. An offering of blood on the sacrifice stone calls the bloodline of the *original* fallen angel. If they accept the sacrifice, the one calling can be taken to a healing well hidden in the mountains. It was once a source of life and renewal, but it has been lost for centuries. The ones who sacrifice themselves, they may live but they will always be tied to the one who accepted their sacrifice. They will be bonded to the one who claims them."

"A healing well?" Remington echoed, his mind racing.

The horse's gaze grew sharper. "Her blood awakened the stones, calling to powers long dormant. She's sick. But the well could offer her salvation. If it still exists."

"Where is it?" Remington asked, his voice edged with urgency.

"Since I have not seen a human call upon the sacrifice

stone in ages," the horse said, "perhaps the well is gone or lost. You must remember: others will be drawn to her and not all will have noble intentions."

Remington clenched his fists, his mind churning with the implications. "She's having surgery now to take out the tumor," he said with quiet determination. "The human doctors say they can heal her. I have to get her somewhere safe after. Can we reverse the sacrifice?"

The horse regarded him silently for a moment then added, "If you take her to Hell, the stones' magic will not weaken. The hum will follow, perhaps grow louder. You must prepare for what that means. For whom it may call. Someone *must* accept her sacrifice."

"I understand," Remington said, his jaw tight. "I'll protect her, no matter the cost."

"Do you realize it called you? Great-grandson to Lucifer." The horse stepped closer, its luminous presence almost overwhelming. "Human medicine can only do so much. Go, Shadow Heir. Time is slipping through your fingers. You have my permission to take the human out of her natural realm. The Veil will remain strong."

Remington swallowed hard.

"Just one thing," the White Horse stopped him as he turned to leave.

"Yeah?"

"Leave the carrots." She motioned to the base of a tree with her nose.

"Of course." Remington nearly forgot he'd been holding the bag. He emptied it out where she'd instructed then walked back to the SUV.

Remington left the valley, the hum inside him was no longer a distraction—it was a compass, guiding him back to Evelyn.

The drive back felt faster, the night giving way to the pale light of dawn. He drove faster than a bat out of hell. The hospital came into view just as the first rays of sunlight kissed the horizon.

Remington stepped out of the SUV, the cold air biting at his skin. He didn't stop to gather his thoughts or brace himself for the confrontation ahead. He had made his decision. The White Horse had agreed.

He was taking Evelyn to Hell. Whether she liked it or not.

Nineteen

Evelyn sat up gingerly in the hospital bed, her fingers brushing against the gauze wrapped around her head. She'd been recovering in the hospital for three days.

"The good news is we were able to perform the surgery minimally invasive," the doctor was saying. "The incision was small and healing time is much faster." He sat and glanced at Rue before focusing on Evelyn again. "You might have some nausea. Take it easy. Start light exercise in about two weeks. We'll prescribe you some steroids for the swelling." He pulled a pen light out of his shirt and scooted closer to check her pupils. "There's a chance of seizures with any brain surgery. Let me know right away if you experience that." He clicked the pen light and tucked it in his pocket again. "But all in all, this was very successful. We got to the tumor at the right time. And it was benign, which is even better news." He rested his hands on his thighs. "I think you're ready to go home."

"Already?" Evelyn asked.

The doctor nodded. "You're healthy and young. You don't need to be suffering with hospital food any longer." He smiled and Evelyn realized the doctor was probably not much older than her.

The doctor glanced to Rue again. "Are you going to stay with her?"

"Yes. Me and my brother are going to help her." Rue moved closer to Evelyn.

"That's good. She might have some mood changes and that's normal."

Rue was nodding along in agreement with the discharge plan.

The doctor stood and reached out to shake Evelyn's hand. His grip was strong and Evelyn thought his hand lingered on hers longer than necessary.

"Call me if you need anything," the doctor said. "My cell phone number will be on your discharge papers."

"I'll make sure she does." Rue stood and walked closer, noticing that Evelyn was becoming uncomfortable. "Thank you for saving her life."

The doctor nodded before leaving.

When the door closed, Rue turned to Ev and said, "Dude was a little handsy. I think he might ask you on a date."

"I doubt it," Evelyn's voice was low. "Would you want this hot mess express?"

She avoided looking at her reflection in the mirror opposite the bed. Half of her hair was gone, shaved away to remove the tumor that had threatened her life. Every time she thought about it, a pang of self-consciousness flared.

She'd always loved her long hair, and now she felt not herself; ugly and deformed. She was afraid of removing the bandages. She shifted in bed and a wave of dizziness hit. Evelyn grabbed the sheets and closed her eyes. The nurse had told her there would be swelling in her brain that would give her dizziness, confusion, and headaches.

The door creaked open, and Remington stepped in. His presence filled the small room–as it always did–commanding and steady. His eyes softened when they landed on her.

"You're being discharged," he said, holding up a folder of paperwork the nurse had given him. "I've already arranged for us to leave. We're going to Hell."

Evelyn blinked, clutching the blanket tighter around her. "Hell," she repeated, her voice dry. "You don't waste time, do you?"

"No," Remington replied firmly, pulling up a chair beside her bed. "You're not safe here. Not with Alastor out there. He'll come back for you."

"She has a follow up appointment with the surgeon in two weeks," Rue said. "And she'll need to pack."

Remington glanced at Rue. "I'll bring her to the apartment."

Evelyn swallowed hard, memories of Alastor's sharp bite and cold eyes flashing in her mind. "And I'll be safe in Hell?" she asked skeptically, a bitter laugh escaping her lips.

"With me, you will," he said, leaning forward, his green eyes intense. "I won't let anyone harm you. I'll bring you back for your appointment."

"I don't know if I can afford it. I might have to delay it." Evelyn rubbed the rough hospital blanket between her fingers. "I probably can't afford the surgery. Or the emergency room bill." She sighed. "And I won't have any friends in Hell." She glanced at Rue. "Who am I going to get coffee with each morning? We spend nearly every day together."

"I told you we'd take care of the money," Remington said.

Evelyn wanted to argue, but the exhaustion weighed her down. She didn't have the strength to fight him, not now. Instead she nodded weakly, muttering, "Fine." She couldn't look up at any of them. She was about to go to another realm, something unheard of. And she'd have no friends there. She couldn't call Remington a friend because their interactions were too awkward for friendship. But she couldn't stay here and risk Alastor coming back. She shivered at the thought of waking up to him in her room or outside her apartment. She'd never have a moment's rest. And she didn't want to be a burden to Rue and Dacre.

Rue touched Evelyn's arm. "I can bring work to you. The books and files and pictures. If you're feeling well enough, we can make it work."

Evelyn nodded before replying with a soft, "That sounds good. I don't want our research to fall behind."

Remington kept close, helping Evelyn get out of the wheelchair and into the back of the SUV. When he got behind the wheel, he turned around and asked her if she was comfortable before he put the vehicle in drive and slowly pulled away from the hospital exit.

It felt like too much to Evelyn. And she was exhausted

already. She touched the bandage on her head and wondered if she should get a hat to hide it.

"You look fine," Rue whispered from across the vehicle. She reached out to take Evelyn's hand. "Your hair will grow back."

Evelyn looked away.

"You need to drive by the pharmacy and pick up her medicine," Rue said to Remington. She gave him directions to the pharmacy near campus.

"Do you want anything to eat?" Rue asked.

"I don't think I can eat right now." Evelyn was watching out the window.

Rue could see old bruises and the healing bite mark under her ear.

Remington ran inside and collected Evelyn's prescriptions. He grabbed a few other items that Rue asked him to get. Then they drove to Evelyn's apartment.

The familiar scent of lavender air freshener hit Evelyn as they stepped into her apartment. It was comforting and heartbreaking all at once. Evelyn sank onto the couch, curling into herself as Remington and Rue moved through the space with purpose. They righted furniture and decorations that Alastor had knocked over and cleaned up the drops of blood that had been left behind after his attack.

"What do you need?" Remington asked over his shoulder.

"Clothes," she murmured, feeling small in the oversized hoodie she was wearing. "My brush. Toothbrush. Just the basics."

"Let me get her clothes," Rue said as she crossed the room and motioned for him to go elsewhere.

Remington nodded, disappearing into her bathroom to grab her toiletries. Evelyn stared at her hands, tracing the veins on her wrist. She couldn't stop thinking about the gauze on her head, the way she must look. She never realized she was so shallow. Maybe it was the brain swelling messing with her confidence?

Remington reappeared with a small duffle bag, already half-packed. He crouched in front of her, setting the bag down beside the couch. "Anything else?" His hand rested on her knee.

She hesitated, then whispered, "A hat. There's one on the dresser."

He left without a word, returning moments later with a knitted beanie. He handed it to her gently, his fingers brushing hers. "Here. It's spring time in Hell. The nights are still chilly."

Rue was behind him with a stack of neatly folded clothes. "I'm not sure if this will last you, but I'll bring more when I visit." She glanced at Remm.

Evelyn pulled the hat over her head, relief flooding her as the gauze bandage disappeared from view. "Thanks," she said softly.

Remington stood, scanning the room. "Let's go." He picked up Evelyn's bag and headed for the door.

Dacre was pacing the sidewalk next to the abandoned Peabody Library.

"Has it always been this close to campus?" Evelyn asked.

"Yes." Rue was holding the door open so Evelyn could get out of the SUV. Remington was hovering close in case she needed help.

When Evelyn was steady on her feet, Rue hugged her. "I'll visit soon."

Evelyn was nodding, unsure of what to say. She said the only thing that she could think of, "I love you."

Rue smiled up at her friend. "I love you too, Ev. We're going to make sure you stay safe and get well."

Evelyn was nodding with tears in her eyes. "Thanks."

Remington was beside Evelyn. "Ready?"

She sighed, feeling empty inside. It all seemed so surreal. "I guess." She waved to Dacre and Rue one last time before Remington led her down the alley between the library and an abandoned building.

The portal looked like nothing more than a garden archway. Remington whispered words that Evelyn didn't recognize and it shimmered to life. An otherworldly tear between realms appeared.

Evelyn's stomach churned as she stared at the portal, the strange energy radiating from it making her skin crawl.

"This... is going to feel weird," Remington warned, his voice steady but laced with concern. "The first time through is always rough."

"Define 'rough,'" Evelyn said, narrowing her eyes at him.

"You might feel nauseous. Dizzy. Maybe worse," he admitted.

"Great," she muttered, taking a shaky step forward.

Remington placed a reassuring hand on her back, guiding her. "It'll pass. I promise."

The moment they stepped through the portal, Evelyn felt like her entire body had been flipped inside out. Her vision blurred, her ears filled with a deafening hum, and her stomach twisted violently.

When they emerged on the other side, Evelyn dropped to her knees, clutching her stomach. "Oh God," she groaned, barely managing to turn her head before vomiting onto the rocky ground.

Remington knelt beside her, holding her steady as she trembled. "I warned you," he said softly, his tone tinged with guilt. He collected her loose hair and pulled it over her shoulder.

She wiped her mouth with the back of her hand, glaring at him weakly. "You didn't say it'd be *that* bad."

"It gets easier," he promised, helping her to her feet.

Evelyn looked around, hand over her mouth and legs shaky. The air here was heavier, thicker, carrying the faint scent of brimstone and pine. The landscape was dark and surreal. It looked exactly like her world, just... darker. The sunlight was a dimmed ochre yellow.

"So this is Hell," she whispered, her voice barely audible. "Looked very different in the movies."

Remington steadied her with an arm around her waist. "You're under my protection now," he said, his voice resolute. "No one will touch you here."

Evelyn wasn't sure if she felt reassured or terrified.

"Are you sure?" she asked, eyes widening as she took in the giant Hellions at various points around them. Her vision was blurry and they looked like giant blobish creatures.

"Absolutely." Remington adjusted her bag over his shoulder. "Can you walk?"

"I think so." She took a few shaky steps but Remington held his elbow out for support. She took it.

He led her down a cobblestone walkway, past gardens, and green grass. She noticed buildings in the distance. And... a castle.

"Jeeze," Evelyn said. "I knew Rue was a princess but I never dreamed she actually lived in a castle."

Remington chuckled beside her. "We didn't always live here. This was built about seven years ago. The original castle was destroyed during the war."

"The war?" Evelyn's voice belayed concern. "Rue didn't tell me about that."

Remington's mouth snapped shut. He instantly realized that Evelyn probably had never heard about the things they'd endured. Rue didn't discuss it on the Earthen plane. Most humans didn't know that heaven and hell were realms that existed in real time, side-by-side with the Earthen plane. Everything here would be new to her.

He felt her squeezing his arm and followed her gaze. There was an exceptionally ugly Hellion watching them.

Remington motioned to the nearest guard, a massive Hellion clad in blackened armor, and the creature stepped back without a word.

"They won't hurt you," Remington reassured her.

"They look like monsters," Evelyn's fingers gripped his arm tighter.

Remington exhaled slowly. "There are many creatures here that you've never witnessed before. They won't hurt you as long as you stay within the castle grounds."

That wasn't exactly comforting. Evelyn swallowed hard, forcing herself to look away from the Hellions and focus on the courtyard. The manicured gardens were a stark contrast to the dark fortress beyond. She glanced toward the tree line in the distance and noticed silhouettes shifting under the shadows.

"Definitely stay away from the forests." He motioned to the gardens, a stone wall, and expanse of cut grass. "Stay within the boundary of the royal grounds."

A laugh slipped past her lips before she could stop it.

Remington glanced down at her, brows furrowing. "What?"

Evelyn smirked, shifting her grip on his arm. "It's just strange hearing you speak so formally. You don't sound like the guy who threw me over his shoulder and slapped my ass the night before graduation."

Remington went still. Completely still.

For a heartbeat, he looked like he might short-circuit right there in the middle of the courtyard. His grip on her waist tightened slightly, his jaw tensing as if he was fighting off a reaction. Then, with an exhale through his nose, he muttered, "That was different."

Evelyn raised a brow. "Was it?"

He didn't answer right away. Instead he took her hand, guiding her forward with careful precision, as if touching her too roughly might break whatever fragile thing was forming between them. "That was before..."

Before everything. Before Hell. Before the sacrifice stones. Before she was tangled in a war between creatures that could destroy her with a thought. He didn't say all that though, he didn't want to scare her.

Evelyn sighed, her fingers still gripping his sleeve. "Well, I liked that version of you too."

Remington didn't respond, but she felt the tension in his body shift, something unspoken lingering between them as they crossed the threshold into the castle.

Whatever they had before... it wasn't entirely gone.

But Hell had a way of changing things.

Twenty

The halls of the castle stretched endlessly, the flickering sconces casting shifting shadows against the dark stone walls. Evelyn's steps were slow and careful, her gaze darting to every carved archway and towering doorway they passed. Power thrummed through the air, making the hair on the back of her neck stand on end.

Remington walked beside her, silent but steady, his presence grounding her even as her pulse thrummed with unease. They went up a winding stairwell and down another long hallway before he finally stopped at a heavy wooden door, its dark grain etched with intricate, unfamiliar runes.

"This is your room," he said, pushing the door open.

Evelyn stepped inside hesitantly. The space was large, far too luxurious for someone who had spent the past few years living in cramped apartments and cheap dorms. A four-poster bed stood in the center, draped in deep crimson sheets, the fabric shimmering like silk. The fireplace along the far wall had already been lit, casting a warm golden glow over the obsidian floors. Heavy velvet curtains framed a massive window where there was a balcony and a birdfeeder on the railing.

Evelyn turned to Remington, arms crossed. "This is a little much, don't you think?"

He smirked. "You would rather the dungeon?"

She huffed. "That's not what I meant."

"You're staying here, Evelyn. Get used to it."

Her lips parted, ready to argue, but then her gaze flicked past him—to the door across the hall. It was slightly ajar and, even without stepping closer, she could see inside.

A familiar dark color scheme. Heavy bookshelves filled with old tomes. Weapons mounted on the walls.

Her stomach twisted. "Is that your room?"

Remington didn't even blink. "Yes."

She swallowed. "You put me across from your room?"

"I need to keep an eye on you."

Evelyn's fingers curled into the fabric of her clothes, something fluttering in her chest that she refused to name.

Before she could say anything, a familiar presence filled the doorway.

"Well, well," a deep voice drawled.

Evelyn turned sharply, eyes widening as she took in the massive figure leaning casually against the frame.

Chel.

She knew him instantly, even without the plain clothes of the Earthen plane, even without the eerie glow of Hell's dim lighting reflecting off his bronze skin.

He was even bigger than she remembered; towering, broad-shouldered, solid muscle. His dark hair was pulled into a messy knot at the back of his head, a few loose strands falling over his sharp, angular face. His eyes—those same piercing, predatory eyes she'd seen shadowing Rue for weeks—studied her with cool amusement. He seemed sillier on the Earthen plane, but maybe that was because he felt awkward there.

"Hey, I know you," she breathed. He didn't look aloof and out of place here. The castle fit his size. He wasn't knocking holes into the walls and tipping furniture with every step.

His lips curved slightly. "I was wondering if you'd recognize me."

"You're Rue's other bodyguard. The heavy-metal cover model looking guy. But..." She moved closer to get a better look. "Do you have... wings?" Her eyes went wide. "Oh. My. God. Do you have wings like a freakin' bat?"

Chel flexed his wings tight against his back as if to hide them. "All Hellions do." He glanced at Remington. "Well, mostly all."

"You can fly?" Evelyn asked.

"Of course. You're asking strange questions." Chel frowned.

"Why didn't I see your wings when you were on the Earthen plane?" Evelyn was staring.

"Because there is balance between the realms. You can't see the wings of creatures from the other realms when we cross over. The balance tightens the Veil between realms."

"Oh." Evelyn tapped her lips. "Makes perfect sense when you say it like that. So you can fly?" She pressed.

"Yes."

"Can you take me flying? Wait-you wouldn't drop me... maybe that's a bad idea."

"Sure." Chel's face split into a huge sharp-toothed smile. "But you don't have wings."

"You can carry me," Evelyn offered.

Remington sighed. "This is a terrible idea."

Chel nodded.

Evelyn's mind reeled. She had never fully understood Rue's connection to Chel back in college.

Now she understood.

He wasn't just some bodyguard. He was a Hellion. And he was standing in her doorway, arms crossed, studying her like she was a puzzle he had yet to figure out. His eyes landed on her head. She was sure he was staring at the bandage.

"I see you've survived," Chel remarked, glancing toward Remington.

Remington shot him a warning look. "Not the time."

Chel only grinned, then returned his attention to Evelyn. "You look different."

Evelyn stiffened, instinctively reaching for her head, but Remington stepped between them smoothly. "She needs rest. If you have something to say, make it quick."

Chel's smirk remained, but his expression shifted slightly—something unreadable flickering in his gaze as he studied her once more.

Finally, he exhaled, rolling his shoulders back. "Just came to see the human causing all the trouble."

Evelyn swallowed, unsure whether to feel insulted or... something else.

Chel turned to leave but paused just outside the door, casting one last glance over his shoulder.

"You'll want to lock your door tonight," he said almost

lazily, then he winked. "Not everyone in this castle will be as welcoming as we are."

Then he was gone, leaving behind a heavy silence.

Evelyn turned to Remington, heart pounding.

He sighed, rubbing a hand down his face. "Ignore him." He was reminded of the conversation he'd had with Shay. Hellion new recruits had gone after her on these very grounds.

"Why don't you rest and settle in?" Remington was looking her over. "I'll come get you for dinner."

"Sure." Evelyn nodded. She glanced at the bed. "I am tired."

Remington stepped further into the room and set her duffle bag on the foot of the bed. "Your medicine is in here as well."

"Thanks," she replied softly.

Remington nodded and turned to leave. He paused. "Do not go flying with Chel."

Evelyn watched him go. After he closed the door behind him, she inspected the room. There was a walk-in closet and a door that led to an en suite bathroom. She took one look at the large soaking tub and huge shower and sighed. "A girl could get used to this," she muttered to herself. Evelyn had never been in a room this nice. It was nicer than a hotel. Her shoes scraped against the stone floor. She moved her bag to a side table and climbed onto the bed. Of course it was the most comfortable bed ever. She crawled in, curled up and watched the birds at the feeder on the balcony. Before she knew it, she'd fallen asleep.

TWENTY-ONE

Remington stood in the doorway, one hand braced against the frame as he watched Evelyn sleep. The dim light cast soft shadows across her face, making her look even more fragile than she already was. She was curled up on her side, breathing slow and deep, her dark lashes resting against pale skin.

She must have been exhausted—more than exhausted after brain surgery and traversing realms for the first time.

He stepped into the room, his boots barely making a sound against the stone floor. The castle walls felt colder than usual—or maybe that was just him. He didn't belong in places like this; standing over fragile human women while they slept. He belonged in war rooms, battlefields, throne rooms filled with fire and steel... and the negotiating table.

And yet...

He reached for the blanket at the foot of her bed and pulled it up, covering her gently. The soft fabric fell over her shoulder and she made a small sound in her sleep, shifting slightly but not waking.

Remington's gaze drifted to the duffle bag sitting untouched near the wardrobe. Not a single item had been unpacked.

His jaw tightened.

She hadn't settled in.

Hadn't even tried.

He exhaled slowly through his nose, shoving down the irritation curling in his gut. The dark crescents beneath her eyes were proof enough that her body needed this rest. Whatever conversations they needed to have could wait.

Turning on his heel, he stepped back toward the door and quietly pulled it closed.

The moment it latched, his phone buzzed in his pocket. He yanked it out without looking and brought it to his ear.

"What?"

"Nice greeting," Rue deadpanned on the other end. "I was calling to check in on my best friend."

Remington pinched the bridge of his nose. "Evelyn is fine, Rue. She's sleeping."

There was a pause, followed by a small exhale of relief. "Good. She needs it."

He leaned against the cool stone of the hallway, staring at the ceiling. "Yeah."

Another pause. Then, softer, "How are you?"

His fingers tightened around the phone. "I'm handling it."

Rue didn't push. She never did when he got like this. "Take care of her," she said instead. "Please."

Remington didn't answer. He just ended the call. He'd deal with getting yelled at for being rude later.

As soon as his phone slipped back into his pocket, a slow clap echoed from behind him.

Chel. The Hellion had been up his ass since he got home.

Remington didn't even turn around before the Hellion drawled, "So. You, handling princely duties and a human in the castle? With *that* human in the castle. Think you can manage both?"

Remington rolled his shoulders and started walking down the corridor. "Not your concern."

Chel followed, his footsteps easy and unhurried. "Where are you going?"

Remington growled low in his throat, teeth aching as the hunger gnawed at him. "To get blood."

Chel chuckled darkly. "Ah. Guess watching over your fragile human is making you a little restless."

Remington's steps didn't falter, but his hands curled into fists. He needed to get away before he did something reckless. Because something about Evelyn being here—something about her sleeping so soundly near his room—was making every instinct in him coil tight.

And he wasn't sure how he could ignore it.

Twenty-Two

Evelyn sat stiffly on the edge of the massive bed, hands folded in her lap. A fireplace cast flickering shadows against the carved wooden furniture. It should have been beautiful, but all she could focus on was the weight of the air; thick and wrong—like it was pressing against her skin, waiting to smother her. She wasn't sure what day it was. All she remembered was arriving and falling asleep.

She took a slow breath. Then another.

Her head ached. She wasn't sure if she'd taken the medicine. Pills rolled in the bottles held in her hand.

The air in Hell carried an unnatural heaviness, a pull in her blood, like something deep in the marrow of her bones was reacting to being here. Alastor's image flashed through her mind and a chill ran up her spine. She glanced around the room in an effort to ground herself. A hand went to her neck and she felt the tiny scabs under her ear. She shivered, remembering the way he'd made her body feel. The heat that flooded her, his hands on her hips...

"Stop," she whispered to herself, hating that she was thinking of the creature who'd kidnapped her.

Evelyn kept her hat pulled low, the soft fabric hiding the bandages wrapped around her head. The idea of seeing herself with half her hair missing made her stomach twist. The incision itched but she did her best to ignore it.

The knock at her door was sharp, but not aggressive. Evelyn sighed. She felt like she was moving underwater as she slid off the bed.

The door creaked open.

"It's me." Remington looked her over. "You need to eat." His voice was low, gruff. He stepped inside, carrying a tray of food. It smelled good—something warm and rich, but her stomach was still unsteady. There was something that looked like stew and crusty bread. It was all laid out very formally on the tray.

"I'm not hungry," she muttered, staring at the embroidered patterns on the comforter.

Remington didn't answer right away. He crossed the room and set the tray on the nightstand, then leaned against one of the carved bedposts as he watched her. His presence filled the space easily, making the large room feel warmer. Less lonely.

"Did we have dinner last night?" Evelyn was looking between Remington and the tray of food. "I can't remember."

"You were asleep."

"How long have I been sleeping?" she asked.

"Nearly a day. Are you feeling okay?"

"I was just confused when I woke up."

"It might be from traveling through the realms. Humans aren't made for that."

Evelyn stared at Remington. That's right, she was a simple human and he was a tall, handsome dark prince of Hell. Of course that was the reason for her confusion.

She licked her lips. "Okay. Maybe that's it." She looked at the food again. "I'm not sure if I can eat. I'm afraid of throwing up again."

"You need to try," he said. "The transition here is going to be hard enough. If you don't eat, you're going to get weak."

Evelyn knew he was right, but that didn't stop the frustration from bubbling up. She already felt weak. Small. Helpless. And now he was watching her like she was some fragile thing about to break apart.

She lifted her chin. "You sound like my doctor."

Remington snorted. "I'm definitely not a doctor."

Evelyn reached for a piece of bread from the tray, tearing off a small bite just to prove a point. It tasted good, but she had to force herself to swallow.

Silence settled between them, heavy but not uncomfortable. Remington didn't push her to eat more. He just stood there, arms crossed, eyes sharp. He was watching her in that way he always did these past few days—like he was taking stock of every movement and every breath as if waiting for something to go wrong.

"I'll be fine," she said, mostly just to fill the silence.

Remington gave her a look that made it clear he didn't believe her. "You're in Hell, Evelyn. No one is fine here."

She let out a dry laugh. "Great pep talk."

His lips twitched but before he could say anything else, a new voice cut in.

"This is the worst idea I've ever seen."

Evelyn looked toward the doorway, startled.

A massive figure stood in the entrance. It took her a moment to recognize Chel.

"She looks unwell." Chel's gaze flicked to Remington. "Are you sure this is the best place for her?"

"She's safer here," Remington said flatly. "She was being hunted."

Chel stepped inside. "Everyone in the castle is already talking. And I don't mean whispering—I mean preparing. They think she's leverage. They think she will bring trouble."

Evelyn's stomach twisted. "They're probably right," she joked.

Chel's eyes slid to her, assessing. Then back to Remington.

"Alastor isn't done with her." Remington leaned against the dresser closest to him. "She's not safe on the Earthen plane."

The words dropped like a stone in her gut. Evelyn's fingers clenched around the fabric of her blanket. The memory of Alastor's cold hands, his sharp teeth flashing in the dark was too fresh.

Remington's expression didn't change. If anything his shoulders just went even stiffer, his jaw tightening like he was barely holding back something dark.

"He won't get to her again," he said, voice low and dangerous. His head twitched as the humming in his mind surged at the mere mentioning of Alastor touching Evelyn. Strange.

Chel sighed. "You're not going to be able to protect her alone."

Evelyn stiffened. "I don't need protecting."

Both men turned to her, unimpressed.

"You literally slept for an entire day," Remington deadpanned.

Evelyn flushed, gripping the blanket harder. "That was from... I was tired."

"You were still very vulnerable." He didn't tell her that he'd been in her room while she slept and she didn't even wake.

Chel crossed his arms. "The moment the wrong person catches wind that you're here, it's not going to be Alastor you have to worry about. It's going to be a lot of dark creatures."

Evelyn swallowed hard. She already knew that. But hearing it out loud made it feel more real.

Remington exhaled sharply through his nose and pushed off the bedpost. "She stays within the castle walls. No exceptions."

Evelyn frowned. "That's not fair—" She wasn't even sure why she was arguing, she just didn't want rules. She was an adult and she didn't care if she was in hell.

"Not up for debate," Remington said.

Chel glanced at her again and something in his expression shifted. He knew she wasn't just some delicate human. He'd seen her with Rue. He knew there was fight in her, even if she didn't look it now.

After a long pause, Chel muttered, "If she's staying, she needs to learn how to survive."

Evelyn's pulse quickened. That was fair. It made sense. If she was going to be stuck here for an unknown amount of time, she had to be prepared.

But then, Remington's voice cut through the moment like steel. "She can't."

Evelyn turned to him, startled. "Excuse me?"

Remington's expression was unreadable, but there was tension in his jaw and his shoulders. "You're not cleared for anything strenuous yet." His eyes flicked to Chel. "She just had brain surgery."

Chel raised a brow. "So?"

"So, she can't exercise for at least two weeks."

Chel's brows lifted. "And she agreed to that?"

Remington sighed, rubbing the back of his neck. "She doesn't have a choice. She has a follow-up appointment with her surgeon in two weeks. Until then, no physical exertion. No training."

Evelyn scowled. "That's ridiculous—"

"No, it's not." Remington shot her a look. "I know you don't want to feel helpless, but pushing your body right now isn't an option. If you aggravate anything, if you get dizzy and fall, if you pass out, I'm going to have to drag your ass back to the Earthen plane for another hospital stay."

Chel huffed. "Fine. But after two weeks, she trains. At least in some basic self-defense."

Remington hesitated. His gaze flicked to Evelyn, and she could see the war inside him—his desire to keep her safe against his knowledge that she would never be okay with being fragile.

Finally, he sighed. "We'll see."

Chel smirked. "I'll take that as a yes."

Evelyn's chest burned with frustration. But she also felt relieved.

Because now she had something to look forward to.

Two weeks. Then she'd make sure no one saw her as weak ever again. She glanced at Remington and wondered if she should tell him about the thoughts of Alastor and the suffocating feeling that had woken her.

"Wait," Evelyn said. "How is Chel going to take me flying if you won't let me leave the castle grounds?"

Remm sighed and pinched the bridge of his nose. "No."

Chel grinned and winked at Evelyn.

Twenty-Three

Evelyn adjusted her hat, making sure it covered the bandages, before stepping into the hall. She had barely been in Hell for a week, and she was already restless. Her body still felt weak from surgery, but the idea of lying in bed doing nothing for two weeks was unbearable. She was used to working hard, not laying around. She looked at her hands, missing the work of writing notes and turning pages of old books in the library. She missed gearing up to search the mountain dig site for clues to history and the clash of mythologies.

Evelyn couldn't sit around for one more day, she had to do something—even if it just meant following Remington around like a stray.

She found him near the entrance of the castle, deep in conversation with a Hellion guard. He stood tall, exuding effortless authority, dressed in black with his dark hair curling at the nape of his neck. His presence commanded the space, a stark contrast to how he was on the Earthen plane. Evelyn was used to him trying to make himself invisible in the shadows. She was reminded of the first time she saw him, hiding in the shadowed corner of that campus party. He couldn't hide from her it seemed.

Evelyn also realized that here, he was not just Remington. He was the Shadow Heir. A term she'd heard Rue call him by. Rue had told Evelyn about their childhood and how Remington had been hidden from public and his true heritage. The more she watched him, she wondered if Shadow Heir had a different meaning.

The guard, a sharp-featured Hellion with dark red horns curling back over his head, stopped speaking when he noticed her. The dude clammed right up.

Evelyn felt the weight of his gaze and braced herself for whatever comment was coming.

But before he could say anything, Remington turned slightly and said, "You're supposed to be resting."

Evelyn crossed her arms. "You're not supposed to be so bossy, yet here we are."

The Hellion choked on what might have been a laugh but quickly masked it as a cough.

Remington shot him a glare before shifting his attention back to her. "You're supposed to be in bed."

"I'm fine," Evelyn insisted. "And I'm not going to sit in that room doing nothing for two weeks. So, I started exploring on my own."

"You can't wander this place alone," Remington reminded her.

"Then I'll follow you." She looked him up and down, reconsidering her plan with the way his gaze made her insides melt. "Or I can explore on my own."

Remington's eyes narrowed. He must have believed her,

because his jaw tensed in that way it did when he was irritated but unwilling to argue. She'd seen it too often this past week. Finally, he exhaled through his nose and muttered, "You will not explore on your own. But you may stay close to me at all times."

Evelyn grinned in victory.

The Hellion cleared his throat. "We had another Thrush sighting along the south ridge."

Remington stilled. His irritation at Evelyn faded, replaced with something much darker. "How recent?"

"Last night. The scouts reported movement near the caves but when they got close, it was gone." The Hellion motioned to his head. "They saw the white hair. He's the only thing in Hell with hair like that."

The Hellion glanced at Evelyn.

She absently had a piece of blonde hair wrapped around her finger.

Remington rubbed a hand over his face. "And the Black River issue?"

The guard hesitated. "The basilisks have begun their breeding cycle earlier than expected. It's causing problems with the livestock. Again."

Remington let out a low string of curses.

Evelyn, despite herself, asked, "Livestock?"

"The goat herds," the guard explained. "They've been disappearing."

Evelyn blinked. "Like... wandering off?"

Remington let out a humorless laugh. "No, being eaten. Whole. Completely gone."

Evelyn paled. "Oh."

"Basilisks are territorial," the Hellion continued.

"They're taking out anything that enters their nesting grounds. We've lost at least thirty goats in the last week."

"Thirty?" Remington's voice had a sharp edge.

The guard nodded. "And those are just the ones we've accounted for."

Remington muttered another curse. "I want an update by nightfall."

The Hellion inclined his head, paused, "You know, Prince, there is a way to tame the basilisk."

"I am aware." Remington grumbled.

The Hellion nodded then disappeared down the hall.

Evelyn waited until they were alone before saying, "Thirty goats?"

Remington sighed. "Welcome to Hell."

She wasn't sure if he meant the realm or the constant chaos he had to manage. Maybe both. But she wasn't going to sit back and do nothing while he dealt with it.

"How do you tame a basilisk?" Evelyn asked.

"You don't want to know the answer to that question."

———

Evelyn didn't like being left behind.

She understood that she wasn't at full strength—not even close—but sitting in a room with nothing to do while Remington handled whatever disasters Hell threw at him was not an option.

So when she overheard him planning to leave for the Black River, she confronted him.

"I'm coming with you."

Remington barely looked up from where he was noting

the ridiculous number of goats he'd be replacing to the mountain demons. And hoping his mother didn't give him hell for it when she returned.

"No, you're not." His voice was even.

Evelyn crossed her arms. "I'm not staying here alone with people I don't know."

"You won't be alone," he muttered. "Chel will keep an eye on you. I've ordered him to stay here with you."

"I don't want Chel to keep an eye on me. I want to go with you." She paused. "Or maybe I'll force him to take me flying while you're gone.

Remington finally turned to face her, his gaze sharp. "Evelyn, you just had surgery."

"I know but that was like a week ago." She clenched her jaw. "I'm not fragile, and I'm not helpless. I can watch you handle whatever needs handling. I won't slow you down."

His expression darkened, like he didn't believe her.

She took a step closer, looking up at him with innocent eyes. "Please."

Remington went still before he let out a long breath, raking a hand through his hair before muttering, "You're going to be the death of me."

Evelyn smirked. "Definitely not."

The Black River stretched like an endless, ink-dark vein through the mountains. Its waters were thick, unnervingly still at the moment, and they didn't reflect the sky.

Evelyn shivered, gripping her seatbelt as Remington

drove. She'd barely spoken the entire ride. She hadn't needed to.

Hell was loud in its silence.

The sky above them swirled in muted hues of sunlight; it looked like a storm was always threatening but never breaking. Every few miles, the land turned into a mix of jagged rock and ashen soil scattered with strange, twisting bone-like structures that jutted from the ground.

"That's from the war," Remington pointed out. "Those are the bones of Lucifer's basilisk."

"When you say war, you mean like a real war?" Evelyn asked, her voice low. "Like in the movies?"

"Yeah."

"And you fought in it?"

"Yes." He gripped the steering wheel of the Jeep harder. "We all did. We all chose a side."

"Rue said she wasn't there until it was over."

"That's because she was in the dungeon. She had been kidnapped." He glanced at her, his lips pressed into a thin line. "I probably shouldn't tell you all this, but now that you've been dragged this deep into our lives, you should know."

"So you were what, like fifteen and you fought in a war?"

Remington nodded. "With my family."

"And Thrush, you keep mentioning he's your cousin. Was he there?"

"We fought side by side."

"You were just kids." Evelyn sighed.

"If we didn't fight, we'd be dead." Remington cleared

his throat. "We came to the war to find Rue. Lucifer refused to release her. He brought an army, and we had our own. After my mother killed Lucifer, Dacre came out of the castle with Rue. She was unconscious. There was a healer with us, Teari, she woke Rue after the fighting was over."

Evelyn was staring at him.

Remington pointed to the river. "The basilisk played a big role in the war. If you tame a basilisk, it will be loyal to you. My mother had a family of them but Alastor killed all except one. The one basilisk that remained helped us win the war. The bones of the dead are sacrilegious. We won't touch them. They are reminders of Lucifer's oppression."

Evelyn was still watching him as he spoke. "So now your mother is breeding them?"

Remington nodded. "It's been a nightmare."

But the river itself unsettled Evelyn the most.

"There's something...wrong with it," she murmured, watching the unnatural black surface ripple as if something moved beneath it.

Remington's grip on the steering wheel tightened. "Yes."

"Has it always been like this?"

He hesitated. "No."

That sent another chill down her spine.

They arrived at a crumbling stone outpost, tucked against the side of a massive rock formation.

A demon stood waiting for them, tall and gaunt, with ashen skin and pupil-less black eyes. He wore tattered robes, and his long, clawed fingers twitched as he took them in.

Remington helped Evelyn out of the Jeep.

"Stay close to me," he warned. "Don't wander."

Two more SUVs pulled up and Hellions got out. They began unloading trailers with goats.

"Princeling," the demon greeted. "I see you got my message."

"Don't get used to these deliveries. They'll stop as soon as we–"

The demon's nostrils flared.

Evelyn's stomach knotted.

"She's human," the demon rasped, his gaze locking onto her.

Remington stepped forward immediately, his voice cold as death. "She's with me."

The demon's thin lips curled. "That is...unusual."

Evelyn held her ground, though every part of her was screaming not to look weak.

Remington wasted no time. "Your report."

The demon dragged his gaze from Evelyn—slowly. Almost reluctantly.

"The basilisks have nested deeper than before," he said. "They are larger. More aggressive."

"They're overbreeding," Remington muttered.

"Yes. And they have begun feeding outside of their designated grounds." The demon motioned toward a holding pen built from thick, enchanted steel bars. Inside, the remaining goats huddled, their eyes wide, their bodies trembling.

Evelyn counted less than a dozen.

"You've lost more since I last sent word," Remington said, voice low with irritation.

The demon dipped his head in a slow, deliberate nod. "Yes."

Remington exhaled sharply, pinching the bridge of his nose. "We'll need to cull some of the basilisk before they disrupt the food supply further."

The demon nodded, then flicked his gaze toward Evelyn again. "Shall I prepare a fresh meal for our... guest?"

Evelyn's stomach turned.

Remington stared him down. "She's not food."

The demon laughed softly, but it was not a pleasant sound.

Evelyn's hands tightened into fists. She knew Remington could handle this, but for the first time since arriving in Hell, she felt the weight of her humanity in a way that was impossible to ignore. And worse—so did everyone else. She didn't belong and it was a feeling she didn't like.

She searched the Hellions surrounding them until her gaze landed on Chel. He smirked at her as if to tell her, *I told you so*.

Twenty-Four

The drive back to the castle was quiet, the hum of the engine the only sound between them. Evelyn rested her head against the window, her fingers tracing idle patterns on the glass as the landscape of Hell rolled past— jagged peaks, sprawling pine forests, and the occasional distant flicker of something moving just beyond sight.

Remington glanced at her from the driver's seat. She looked exhausted, her color paler than usual. The trip to the Black River had clearly taken more out of her than she wanted to admit, but she had been stubborn about coming along.

Evelyn sighed dramatically. "I wish there was a coffee shop nearby. Every store we've passed looks closed."

"It's a habit of everyone who lives here. Lucifer would take and kill. All these years of my mother's reign and she hasn't been able to erase it."

"It's just all very... apocalyptic looking. Like we're driving through a movie set."

Remington raised an eyebrow. "This place is not exactly a hub for Earthen plane luxuries."

She shot him a dry look. "I'm just saying, if I'm going to survive here, I need caffeine. Lots of it." She sighed. "Maybe that's why I feel so moody. It's been a long time."

He smirked, amused. "You sound like Rue."

"I'll take that as a compliment." Evelyn sat up straighter, hopeful. "Do you even understand how many coffee breaks your sister has dragged me on? I'm completely addicted to the caffeine now. Wait—there *is* coffee somewhere, right?"

Remington hesitated. "Not quite the same as what you're used to."

"I'll take what I can get."

With a resigned sigh, Remington turned the wheel and maneuvered onto a less-traveled path. The road narrowed, winding through a rocky pass before opening into a small, dimly lit marketplace nestled between shadowy cliffs.

Evelyn sat up in her seat, eyes widening as she took in the unusual sight. The buildings were constructed into the stone, glowing lanterns illuminating the entrances. Strange, curling smoke wafted from chimneys, and creatures of all shapes and sizes meandered between open-air stalls. It smelled of roasted spices, something rich and earthy.

"What is this place?" she asked, voice hushed.

"One of the less chaotic trade hubs," Remington said, pulling the SUV to a stop. "It's where some of the more... civilized demons barter. And where you can find a cup of what they call coffee."

Evelyn stepped out of the car, stretching her legs. She felt eyes on her immediately—creatures watching from beneath hoods and masks, their gazes assessing. Remington was suddenly at her side, placing a possessive hand on the small of her back, guiding her toward a small, fire-lit shop at the edge of the market.

The Hellions parked behind them and got out, following at a distance.

Inside, the scent was overwhelming—dark, bitter, laced with something almost spicy. A demon behind the counter, short and round with curling horns and sharp, golden eyes gave a throaty chuckle as they approached.

"Well, well, well. Didn't expect the prince himself to darken my door. What brings you here, Remington?"

"My human wants coffee."

The demon's gaze flicked to Evelyn, his grin widening to reveal too many teeth. "Brave thing, bringing her to this place. Soul intact and all. Your human? Thought you didn't dabble in the skin trades."

Remington's hand on her back tensed. "Can you make it or not?"

The demon gave a low, rumbling laugh and turned to prepare the drink. Evelyn leaned toward Remington. "I feel like I'm in some kind of supernatural mafia movie now."

He smirked. "That's not far off."

A moment later, a steaming black cup was set before her. The demon watched with interest as she took a careful sip. It was stronger than anything she'd ever drank, bitter but oddly smooth, with an underlying spice she couldn't place. Maybe toasted cinnamon.

"Well?" Remington asked.

Evelyn considered. "It's... intense."

He huffed a laugh. "You'll get used to it."

She took another sip, then sighed. "Alright, Hell might not be *completely* terrible. Has Rue tried this?"

Remington smirked, ushering her toward the door. "I'll remind you of that next time you complain. And no. She left before the demon coffee trades kicked into gear."

Evelyn rolled her eyes but didn't argue. "Will you show me around?"

A look of confusion passed Remington's face. "You want to stay?"

Evelyn shrugged. "Why not? You've kept me locked up in that castle like Rapunzel for days."

The marketplace hummed with life, filled with the scent of smoldering incense, roasted meat, and something spiced that lingered on the air. Evelyn sipped at her coffee, still adjusting to its strength, as she and Remington wandered between the market stalls. The energy of the market was unlike anything she'd ever experienced—demon merchants bartering in growling tongues, creatures slinking in and out of shadowed corners, the low murmur of enchanted objects whispering to passersby.

Evelyn motioned for Remm to move closer to her. "What language are they speaking?" Evelyn whispered close to Remington's ear.

He shivered as he responded, "Hellspeak."

Remington kept close, his palm resting on the small of Evelyn's back or occasionally brushing against her arm. It was a quiet sort of possessiveness, a silent warning to anyone watching that she wasn't to be touched. She wasn't sure if she liked it or if it only made her more aware of how much she didn't belong. But his hand was warm and she was reminded of the night she met him, again. She liked it.

Evelyn peered into one of the stalls, where strange, iridescent stones pulsed softly beneath a layer of black velvet. She reached out toward one, but before she could touch it, Remington's fingers wrapped around her wrist.

"Careful," he murmured, voice close to her ear. "Some of these things will latch onto your energy if you're not paying attention. And you've toyed with enough magical stone." He gave her a knowing look.

"That wasn't on purpose." Evelyn glanced up at him, lips quirking. "And you couldn't have told me that *before* I almost grabbed one?"

His smirk was lazy, teasing. "Where's the fun in that? You seem to like the adrenaline rush of a near-death experience." He nodded to the shop owner before leading Evelyn away. "There is a lot of history that was lost with time. Lucifer kept the natural order of Hell under siege. There are customs, magic, and ... a lot of things that are just coming back to the surface."

She huffed and took another sip of her coffee, still letting him guide her through the winding paths between stalls.

"What about the people who die?" Evelyn suddenly asked.

"Their souls come here." Remington's response was frank. "Some turn into other creatures. Some stay suspended as the walking dead." He glanced at her, hesitant. "I don't want to scare you. This is something we don't typically discuss with humans."

Evelyn nodded. "There have been a lot of lost societies where I'm from. Part of what I love about my job is unearthing what was lost. What you're telling me is a bit strange, but mostly because it's real. And we've always been told this was something like fiction or fantasy."

They paused in front of a merchant selling dark, twisted jewelry. Another showcased knives carved from bone and obsidian, the edges glinting wickedly under the flickering torchlight.

"Anything catching your eye?" Remington asked, tilting his head.

Evelyn snorted. "Oh, sure. I've always wanted a cursed dagger."

He chuckled and steered her toward a quieter booth, this one filled with delicate trinkets—intricate metalwork, tiny glass vials filled with glowing liquid, and carved pendants that seemed to shift in color as she looked at them.

"Are these safe?" Evelyn joked.

One piece in particular caught her attention—a simple silver chain with a spherical green stone hanging from it, flecked with hints of red when the light hit it just right. It reminded her of Remington's eye color in the sunlight. Or... maybe it was more like Dacre's.

Remington followed her gaze and, he motioned for her to keep walking. "No. Not that."

"It looked kinda like an eye..." Evelyn felt her face pale.

Remington stopped at a clothing booth. Leather capes were hanging on hooks.

Evelyn touched a cape embossed with serpents and black flowers. "This is pretty."

Without hesitation, nodded to the vendor. "Ring it up."

Evelyn blinked. "Wait, what? No, I wasn't—"

"It suits you," he said simply, reaching into his jacket for a few coins she didn't recognize. The vendor accepted without question.

The merchant handed him the cape and a detailed metal clasp. Remington turned back to her, his fingers brushing against her neck as he fastened the cape around her throat and settled it against her shoulders until it fell correctly over her body.

Evelyn swallowed, pulse quickening. "You don't have to buy me anything, you know. I can pay for it." That was a true lie and Evelyn knew it. She was poorer than she'd ever been in her whole life right now.

"I know," he said, voice low. "But I like to."

His fingers lingered at the base of her throat for a beat too long before he finally stepped back.

Evelyn exhaled, wrapping her fingers around the material. It was warm against her skin, but there was something strangely comforting about being hidden underneath the thin leather. Back home people would think she was crazy walking around in a cloak like this, but here it was normal. She'd seen dozens of demons dressed similarly.

She smirked, trying to break the tension. "If you keep spoiling me like this, I might start thinking you actually like me."

Remington smirked, leaning in slightly. "And that would be a problem because...?"

Evelyn's breath hitched. He was too close. And she wasn't sure she wanted him to move away.

"Because," she managed, "I might start liking you back."

Remington's smirk softened into something more

thoughtful, his green eyes watching her closely. Then, with a slow, deliberate motion, he reached out and rubbed a few stray strands of hair between his fingers brushing against her jaw as he did.

"Would that be so bad?" he murmured.

Evelyn didn't have an answer for that. Or maybe she just wasn't ready to say it out loud. There was a flip-flopping feeling in the center of her stomach. Rue had forbidden it.

After a beat, Remm added, "I am not human. I am born of darkness." He glanced at her hesitantly. "I don't want to hurt you."

"Then don't." She focused on his lips, remembering...

Evelyn stepped back and looked away, took another sip of her coffee, hid the warmth creeping up her neck, and started walking again.

"Come on, prince of Hell. Show me what else this place has to offer." She smiled wide at him. "I'm feeling absolutely magical in this cloak."

Remington chuckled, falling into step beside her, his hand settled at the small of her back and Evelyn's body went warm.

Evelyn barely dragged herself out of the SUV; her vision swam, pain lancing through her skull so sharply it nearly drove her to her knees. She had pushed too hard. The small incision on her scalp burned and her head throbbed.

The moment she stepped foot on the castle grounds,

her balance tilted dangerously, her breath hitched at the crushing weight inside her skull.

Remington caught her before she fell.

"Dammit, Evelyn." His voice was sharp, threaded with anger and concern. "I asked you to wait before getting out."

"I'm fine," she whispered, though the words felt like a lie.

"You are absolutely not fine." He lifted her into his arms effortlessly, cradling her against his chest as he strode inside. "We shouldn't have spent so long at the market."

Evelyn should have protested—she hated feeling weak—but the moment his warmth wrapped around her, the pain dulled just a fraction and she let herself lean into him.

"I liked the market," Evelyn murmured, squeezing her eyes closed. The cloak he'd bought her felt like a warm blanket with the evening sun disappearing beyond the horizon.

By the time they reached her room, her headache had worsened.

The pressure pounded at the base of her skull, spreading forward like a storm behind her eyes. Her body felt too heavy, her limbs sluggish.

Remington kicked the door open with his boot, carrying her inside and setting her down gently on the edge of the bed.

He crouched in front of her, his hands framing her face, scanning her with fierce intensity.

"You should have told me you weren't feeling well."

"I *was* feeling fine." Her voice was barely a breath.

Remington's jaw ticked, frustration clear in the tight set

of his shoulders. But there was something else in his expression too—deep concern.

He exhaled through his nose, standing up and crossing the room in long, tense strides toward Evelyn's pill bottles on the dresser. He read the labels and shook each bottle. The steroid was too full.

"You haven't been taking your medicine?" he asked.

"I... um. I was trying to conserve it. In case the doctor wanted me to keep taking it."

"Christ. Evelyn," he turned to her. "How many times do I have to tell you that my family will pay for it? We dragged you into this mess. We will take care of you." He picked up the pain pill bottle and noticed it was still full. "Ev!" He turned to face her. "You've just been letting yourself suffer all this time?"

"It's not that bad." Evelyn was wringing her hands.

He brought the pill bottles to her and found a bottle of water on the small table near the balcony. "Take your medicine."

Evelyn took the vials and turned it between her fingers. "Okay. Okay. Bossy much."

"It'll help with the pain and healing."

She hesitated, but the ache in her skull was unbearable. Without another word, she twisted open the vials and shook out the medicine.

She took the bottle of water from Remington and swallowed the pills down.

Evelyn let out a slow breath.

Remington watched her closely, his gaze tracing every flicker of emotion across her face.

Then—

Without thinking, he reached up, unclasped her cloak, and pulled off her hat.

Evelyn sucked in a sharp breath, instinctively reaching up to grab it back—but he held it just out of reach.

Her heart pounded.

"I—"

Remington didn't say anything. He just looked at her, taking in the uneven patches of hair, the bandages still covering part of her scalp.

"You must care for the incision. It needs to be aired out." His throat worked as he swallowed. Then, softly—so softly it nearly broke her—he said, "And since you haven't been taking your medicine, I don't trust that you've taken care of the incision. The White Horse help me if it's infected." He gathered up the cloak and hung it across a nearby chair.

Tears pricked her eyes, and she hated how much his words affected her.

She turned her face away. "It's ugly."

"No." His voice was firm as he moved back to her. "It's you. And nothing about you is ugly."

The intensity in his gaze made her stomach tighten, heat rising to her cheeks.

He reached out, his fingers ghosting over her temple, careful not to touch where she was still healing. "I read your discharge instructions," he reminded her. "You were supposed to take these off days ago." He began gently peeling the bandages away.

Evelyn held her breath. "Maybe I should call the doctor and ask him."

He was so close now, his warmth wrapping around her; his presence a shield, a comfort. "Can't do that."

"Why?"

"I burned the paper with his number on it."

Evelyn's jaw dropped.

"I saw the way he was looking at you. Very inappropriate."

"He was just my doctor."

Remington frowned. "Sure. And I'm a fairy."

For the first time since waking from surgery, she didn't feel fragile. She felt seen.

Remington exhaled, brushing his thumb gently against her cheek. "What's bothering you the most?"

"My hair." She blinked up at him.

He sighed. "I know a healer who can fix it. Do you want that?"

Evelyn nodded. "Please."

"Okay." He lingered for a moment then kissed her forehead in a movement that warmed her body and made her heart ache.

TWENTY-FIVE

Remington sat slumped in the chair beside Evelyn's bed, arms crossed, head tilted slightly forward, his body heavy with exhaustion. He hadn't meant to fall asleep beside her. It was the middle of the night now.

The dim candlelight flickered, casting dancing shadows across the stone walls.

At some point in the night, she had shifted in her sleep, rolling slightly toward him. A strand of blonde hair had fallen across her face. She looked fragile like this. Too small, too human. And she was his responsibility now.

Having a human in Hell was far more work than he'd anticipated. He thought about the basilisk issues and the missing goats, and Thrush. That was just the tip of the iceberg. There were so many rebuilding projects that his parents had put on hold that he didn't even have the bandwidth to attempt to address.

The thought alone was enough to pull him from the last dregs of sleep. His muscles ached as he shifted, rolling his shoulders, and scrubbing a hand down his face.

Chel's voice broke the silence as the door creaked open. "Remington."

Remington's eyes flickered open fully. The Hellion stood near the doorway, his massive form almost blending into the darkness.

"A scout spotted Thrush again—this time further down the mountain."

Remington sat up straighter, his exhaustion momentarily forgotten. "And?"

"No sign of Alastor yet," Chel continued. "A team has been sent to track him, but he's slippery." His tone darkened. "And we're still losing goats. Something must be done about the basilisk. There's word that the herders are planning retaliation."

Remington exhaled sharply through his nose. Thrush sightings and basilisk. His hands tightened into fists as he thought of the creatures lurking by the Black River, growing bolder. Worse, his mother would put the fear of death in the herders if they killed her precious basilisk.

He still had the spring ball to plan. It was only a few weeks away. The Christmas ball had been successful at bringing high demons in to grow alliances against the skin trades.

He had too much to deal with already, and now— now he had *her*.

His gaze flickered back to Evelyn.

She hadn't stirred, her breath slow and even, her bandaged head barely peeking out from beneath the heavy blankets. The soft column of her neck was stretched out, pulsing veins visible. He licked his lips. The bite marks from Alastor had finally healed and the bruises were gone.

He wondered what it would feel like to press his lips there.

He closed his eyes and groaned. The humming noise was still in his head—distant but persistent, like a song playing from another room. But it was duller now.

It had been duller ever since he brought her here.

And that terrified him.

Remington left Evelyn's bedside without another word.

Chel followed him down the darkened corridors, their footsteps echoing off the stone.

He needed to feed.

By the time they reached the blood fridge, he felt the familiar gnawing hunger curling in his gut, the craving deepening, sharpening the moment he opened the heavy door.

The cold air rushed out, mist curling around his fingers as he reached inside.

Chel leaned against the doorway, arms crossed. His un-wavering gaze followed Remington as he pulled a bag of blood from the chilled shelves.

He tore it open with his teeth and drank like he hadn't had blood in a decade.

Chel didn't say anything at first.

Not until Remington reached for a second.

"I've noticed you've been drinking more lately."

Remington froze for half a heartbeat before taking another long pull from the blood bag.

"So?" he muttered. "Afraid I'm not going to leave any for you?"

Chel exhaled through his nose. "So, I also noticed that the humming sound in your head—" his eyes flickered toward the hall, where Evelyn still slept behind closed doors "—gets quieter when you're near her."

Remington's grip tightened around the blood bag.

He didn't want to talk about this.

"It's nothing."

Chel snorted. "Sure. You're just tearing through blood like a half-starved fledgling for no reason." His dark eyes gleamed under the dim torchlight. "And yet you refuse to feed from her."

Remington's jaw clenched.

The worst part? Chel was right.

The urge had been growing; the temptation to taste Evelyn's blood, to see if it would silence the hum completely.

But he wouldn't.

Couldn't.

Not when she was still healing. Not when she was so fragile already. Not after what Alastor did to her. Not when it would mean admitting that she was affecting him in ways he didn't understand.

Remington crushed the empty blood bag in his fist and tossed it aside.

"Get the reports on Thrush. I'll deal with it in the morning."

Chel didn't argue.

But as he turned to leave, his parting words lingered in the air—low and knowing:

"You won't be able to ignore this forever."

And Remington, for all his control, was starting to believe that too. He needed to change the subject.

"Teari is coming to see her."

The giant Hellion turned with a huge grin stretched across his face. "Oh, princeling, that's the best news I've heard all day."

Remington huffed out a laugh. The old Hellion was smitten with the Angel healer.

"I think she's out of your price range," Remington teased.

Chel rubbed his center, chest thick with muscle. "You can't put a price on this."

Remington made a gagging face before turning away from the Hellion and grabbing another bag of blood.

Twenty-Six

There was a knock on Evelyn's door.

"Come in," she called, closing a drawer after finally folding her clothing and putting them in the dresser.

"The healer will be here in a moment," Remington's voice was soft. "She wants to meet near the portal."

"Okay." Evelyn moved closer, grabbing her hat off the end of the bed, and moving to put it on.

"Leave it off," Remington ordered. "Have you seen these Hellions? They're ugly as sin. They don't care about your hair or the incision." He motioned for her to follow. "And then you won't have to carry it back."

"You're certain this healer is going to regrow my hair that fast? What if they refuse?"

"This healer once regrew my mother's hair six inches because she was mad at her." He smiled. "I think she'll help."

"Okay." Evelyn set the hat down and followed him out of the room.

It was true, what Remington had said. The Hellions

didn't even glance at her missing hair or the incision from surgery. They held the door open as she passed and stood guard.

As Remington led her closer to the portal in the nearby gardens, Evelyn noticed that there was only one Hellion standing guard close to them. She recognized Chel. He winked.

"Is that guy okay?" Evelyn asked.

"Chel? No, he's demented. And you're about to find out why."

The portal nearby shimmered as it was called into use.

There was a subtle shift in the air at first—a pressure change, like the moment before a thunderstorm breaks. Then came the light, a shimmer of gold and silver that cut through the ever-present gloom of the castle halls. A figure emerged from it, her presence so out of place in this realm of ochre light and shadow that Evelyn took a step back.

The woman—no, the angel—was unlike anything she had ever seen.

Teari was tall, her form wreathed in a soft, golden glow that flickered and pulsed with an ethereal energy. Her short blonde hair was cropped, her features chiseled and sharp, her piercing blue eyes settling on Evelyn with unreadable intensity. And her wings—massive, gleaming, impossibly white—extended slightly before folding neatly at her back.

Suddenly the light subdued as the portal went dark.

Evelyn swallowed hard, instinctively pressing closer to Remington's side.

"This is her?" Teari asked, her voice smooth but laced with something... wary. "The human?"

"Yes," Remington said simply. "This is Evelyn."

Teari's eyes narrowed as she studied Evelyn, her gaze flicking from Ev's scarred scalp to the dark circles beneath her eyes. Evelyn wasn't sure if she should speak or if doing so would somehow offend. She looked *too* perfect, too otherworldly.

"I can't believe you've brought a human into Hell," Teari said after a long pause.

Evelyn stiffened at her tone.

Remington exhaled, as if already anticipating the argument. "She's under my protection. She found a sacrifice stone on the Earthen plane and it brought Alastor to her door."

"A sacrifice stone? Haven't heard of one of those in a very long time." Teari tilted her head slightly. "And yet, your human is unwell."

"I'm fine," Evelyn interjected, though her voice didn't carry the conviction she wanted.

The angel's sharp gaze snapped to hers, and she immediately regretted speaking.

"You are not fine," Teari said.

Evelyn bristled but Remington stepped forward, his stance suddenly defensive. "She's stubborn. Like my mother. Remember?"

Teari held Remm's gaze for a long, tense moment then exhaled softly. Her wings shifted, feathers rustling, before her attention returned to Evelyn.

"It's a hard habit to break," she said finally. "Each time a human is brought here, chaos ensues." She nodded toward Remington. "The dark prince believes you should be healed."

Evelyn's breath caught. "Healed?"

Teari moved closer and lifted her hand. "Your body is weak. Your wounds, fresh. That is not ideal for someone living in this realm." Her eyes flickered toward Remington before settling on Evelyn again. "I can mend the incision. Restore what was lost. Tell me what happened."

Evelyn hesitated, her fingers twitching. "I... I had a tumor in my brain. It was giving me nosebleeds. The doctor removed the tumor but," she motioned to her head, "they shaved my hair. They cut into my scalp right here."

Teari motioned for Evelyn to sit on a nearby bench. "This won't hurt. But you may feel heat and tingling."

After, Teari rubbed her hands and held them on both sides of Evelyn's head.

Evelyn felt warmth.

"I'm just assessing," Teari's voice was soft.

Evelyn looked past the Angel and noticed Chel watching but... she realized, he was focused on Teari and *only* Teari.

"It seems they've removed all of the tumor. I can't sense any of it. The incision is healing slowly." She moved her hands and glanced down at Evelyn. "I can heal the scar and regrow the hair, if that's what you want."

Evelyn glanced up at Remington, uncertain.

"You don't have to," Teari said gently. "But if you want it... it's easy enough. I've healed worse wounds. Remington told me you're not taking the steroids as prescribed by the doctors. You won't need them when I'm done." Teari watched her with the patience of someone who already knew the answer.

Evelyn inhaled slowly. "Will it hurt?"

"No," Teari said. "You will feel warmth, nothing more."

"Do I need to pay you for this?" Evelyn asked. "I'm sure you don't take my crappy insurance."

"Certainly not." Teari smiled. "This is what I do. I don't take payment. Especially from humans."

Still, Evelyn hesitated—until Remington sat beside her and placed a reassuring hand on the small of her back. The simple touch grounded her, gave her the courage to nod.

"Then yes, please fix it," she said softly.

Teari lifted her hands, and Evelyn felt the warmth again as faint light came from Teari's palms. Light swirled toward her in ribbons of luminescent energy, wrapping around her head and shoulders like a whisper of fire. A rush of warmth flooded her scalp, tingling and weightless, and she gasped as something shifted—her skin smoothing, the tightness and itch of her incision disappearing, the familiar weight of hair cascading past her shoulders once more.

She lifted a trembling hand, fingers running through strands of silk-soft hair. It was all there as if nothing had ever happened.

Teari crouched, reaching forward to tuck strands of Evelyn's hair behind her ear. "There." Teari was searching Ev's eyes. "You're very pretty. Too pretty for a punk like Remington." She smirked and slid her eyes towards the offending prince.

Evelyn huffed out a laugh before her throat tightened. "I... I don't know what to say. Is thank you enough?"

Teari lowered her hands, the glow dimming. "Gratitude is not necessary." But her gaze sharpened as she added, "Hell is not kind to humans. If you stay... you may be forever changed."

Evelyn clenched her jaw. "How so?"

Teari's expression remained unreadable, but she gave the slightest tilt of her head before turning back to Remington. "You should not have brought her here. You know what happened to Shay."

"I'll handle it," Remington said. "She was not safe in her home. Alastor was feeding from her. He was ready to claim her forever."

Teari studied him for another long moment, then exhaled. "Perhaps it is best she is here then."

Remington nodded.

Heavy footsteps interrupted them. Chel was walking closer.

"Hey, Teari," Chel called, "I've got an injury, wondering if you could take a look at it."

Teari crossed her arms and smirked, knowingly. "I don't treat Hellions."

Chel's jaw dropped open as though he couldn't believe it. "Uh, what am I supposed to do then?" He rubbed his thigh. "It hurts really bad."

"Petition your royal family to find their own healer. It's been ages since they had a proper one." Teari's gaze narrowed on Remington.

"Why get another when you always come help us?" Chel was grinning like a fool.

Teari narrowed her eyes on the Hellion. "Also. You're lying. You're not injured. Not in the least bit." She crossed her arms. "Well, besides your brain is screwed up." Teari threw her head back and laughed.

"Hey, that's no way to treat an injured old man," Chel grumbled.

"You're perfectly fine."

Chel was standing directly in front of the Angel now. He lowered his voice, "I really just wanted to ask you to the spring ball." He tilted his head toward Remington. "Princeling here is organizing it with all of Hell's upper crust."

Teari laughed again. "You want to bring me as your plus one?"

"That's what I asked."

Teari touched Chel's arm and the Hellion's expression lit.

Remington bent to whisper to Evelyn, "We should probably leave these two alone. They're making me feel uncomfortable."

Evelyn giggled softly and nodded.

Evelyn exhaled a shaky breath as they walked away. "Well. That was... something."

Remington turned to her, his gaze softening as he reached out and ran his fingers through her newly restored hair. The touch sent shivers down her spine.

"Are you happy?" He asked quietly.

Evelyn's cheeks warmed, and for the first time in days, she truly smiled. "I feel like myself again."

"Good."

"So, Chel is infatuated with an angel?" Evelyn asked. "Seems kinda different."

"I told you. The guy is demented. A Hellion and an Angel." Remington laughed then stopped short.

"What?" Evelyn asked.

"Nothing." He cleared his throat.

Twenty-Seven

Remington leaned against the edge of his desk, fingers drumming idly on the wood as he waited for the call to connect. The weight of the past few days had settled into his bones; Evelyn's recovery, the Thrush sightings, the increasing number of missing goats, and the unsettling reports from the Black River. He needed answers. He needed guidance. He needed to talk to his parents and find out when they were returning from their holiday and taking all of this off his shoulders.

The line clicked.

"Well, well," came his mother's voice, rich with amusement. "To what do I owe the pleasure?"

Remington exhaled, glancing toward the heavy stone window. Beyond it, Hell stretched in endless evening shadows. "There's an issue at the Black River," he said. "The basilisk breeding program—there's something off about it. More of them are hatching than expected, and the demons living near there are losing more goats every day than we can replace."

Meg hummed, unconcerned. "And? Wait, wait. You replaced their goats?" Her tone increased in pitch.

"Yes, mother." Remington pinched the bridge of his nose. "And I'd rather not have a dozen basilisks tearing through the lower territories if this gets out of control."

She laughed; a sharp, wicked sound that sent a ripple of unease down his spine. "You're making this sound like a problem when it's an opportunity."

His jaw tightened. "An opportunity?"

"Claim one," she said simply.

Remington stilled.

"You have our blood," Meg continued, as if discussing something as trivial as dinner plans. "You're more than capable of controlling a basilisk. If the creatures are growing restless, it's because they recognize power when they sense it. Or worse–"

He scoffed. "I'm not about to waltz down there and grab a basilisk by the neck, Mother."

Meg sighed, as if he was being particularly dense. "You wouldn't have to. They submit to dominance. To darkness. I claimed a whole family of them before I had..." Her voice drifted and she never finished the thought. There was a pause then she added, almost too casually, "Don't be afraid to let your darkness out. If they are misbehaving, someone or something might already be claiming them."

The way she said it was unnerving—light, almost playful, like she was suggesting he indulge in a guilty pleasure. Not encouraging him to embrace the bloodline he spent years keeping at bay.

Remington clenched his jaw. He had spent his whole life balancing the weight of his lineage. He had always walked the line between control and chaos, never letting himself slip too far in either direction.

"You make it sound easy," he muttered.

"It is," Meg said. "You're the one making it difficult."

His fingers curled against his palm.

"If you don't handle it, someone else will," she continued. "And that someone might not have your restraint."

Remington exhaled slowly. He hated that she had a point. If the basilisk problem continued to escalate, others would get involved—others who wouldn't hesitate to use them for their own gain.

A thought was lingering in the back of his mind. Thrush.

He closed his eyes. "I'll take care of it."

"That's my boy." Meg's voice was warm, pleased. "Let me know how it goes."

The line went dead.

Remington lowered the phone, his grip tightening around it before he set it down.

Claim a basilisk.

It was reckless. Dangerous.

And yet, deep inside him, something dark curled at the thought.

TWENTY-EIGHT

THE SUV RUMBLED OVER UNEVEN GROUND, THE road to the Black River rougher than the last time they'd made the trek. Remington sat behind the wheel. Chel was in the passenger seat because he didn't fit in the back very well. Evelyn was holding onto anything she could grab, hoping to stave off a head injury with the way the SUV was jerking around.

Remington seemed a ball of nerves.

"It will be fine, princeling," Chel chuckled.

Remington grumbled as his fists tightened on the steering wheel.

"So," Chel drawled. "Did you ever hear how your mother claimed her basilisks?"

Remington didn't answer. He already knew.

Evelyn, on the other hand, shot Chel a wary glance. "I assume it was terrifying."

Chel chuckled. "Oh, you have no idea."

Evelyn looked between them. "I feel like I should prepare myself. Is it safe for Remington to do this?"

"He's a prince of Hell. Nearly everything is safe for him." Chel stretched his arms over his head, clearly enjoying himself. "Meg didn't just claim one basilisk—she claimed a whole family. And she did it the old way."

"The old way?" Evelyn echoed.

Remington sighed. "Chel—"

Chel ignored him, grinning. "She waded right into a nest; no weapons, no backup, just her and whatever lunatic confidence she was born with. Her Hellion was waiting on the shore, holding the basket."

Evelyn paled. "A *basket*?"

Chel smirked. "Big Basilisks don't submit to just anyone. You have to prove dominance. Meg outsmarted every ruler who'd ever tried. She didn't fight or harm them, she took their children." He shook his head, amused. "Your mother didn't just claim them—she *added* them to the family."

Evelyn looked mildly horrified. "I don't know how to feel."

Remington rolled his shoulders, eyes locked on the road ahead. He wasn't going to do it *that* way. He had no intention of tearing apart a basilisk with his bare hands. He had other ways to make them submit.

"Princeling is way bigger and stronger than his mother. He could pry their jaws open with his bare hands. That's what the others have done."

"Are you planning on ripping one in half, too?" Evelyn asked, her voice dry.

Remington huffed a quiet laugh. "No."

Chel snorted. "Yeah, no offense, but I don't think you've got your mother's lack of self-preservation."

Evelyn didn't look convinced. "And what's your plan, then?"

Remington didn't answer. Because truthfully, he wasn't sure yet.

The road sloped downward and the air grew colder as they neared the Black River. Remington parked the SUV near an alcove of Pine trees. A dense mist hovered over the water, curling around the banks like waiting fingers. Giant rocks dotted the shoreline.

Chel held the door open for Evelyn.

"Perhaps we should stay in the vehicle. It might be safer this way."

"I want to see," Evelyn said.

Remington walked closer, boots on the edge of the shoreline. He exhaled, steadying himself. Whatever happened next, he would handle it. He had no choice.

The Black River churned, dark and restless, the thick mist making it impossible to see more than a few feet ahead. The scent of damp stone and something reptilian filled the air, a fetid musk that clung to the back of Remington's throat.

He stood at the water's edge, boots sinking slightly into the wet earth and moss, scanning the rippling surface. Basilisks thrived in the cold river's depths, their serpentine bodies hidden beneath the black currents, waiting.

Chel leaned lazily against a nearby rock, arms crossed, watching. "You sure about this?" His tone was light, but his eyes were sharp. "It's not too late to give up."

Remington rolled his shoulders and flashed a wicked gaze to the Hellion. "Yes."

Evelyn stood a few feet behind them, clutching the edges of her jacket. "I don't like this," she muttered.

Remington stepped forward, the water lapping at his boots. He sensed it—*something* moving beneath, circling.

Then it struck.

A massive shape lunged from the river, scales glistening like polished obsidian, its jaws snapping inches from his face. Remington moved fast, twisting out of reach, his hands locking around the basilisk's thick, muscular neck.

The creature thrashed, its body whipping around with enough force to send water spraying in every direction. Remington tightened his grip, gritting his teeth as the basilisk coiled, trying to throw him off balance.

"Remm—" Evelyn's voice was edged with panic.

Chel reached out to silence her.

The basilisk surged forward, dragging Remington into the river. Cold water closed over his head, but he didn't let go. Instead, he adjusted his grip, shifted his weight, and hauled himself up, swinging one leg over the beast's back. And held on for dear life.

It bucked beneath him, furious. Its scaled fins flared, half-formed, still too small to carry its weight. Remington dug his knees in, wrapping his arms around its neck and forcing it down. The basilisk thrashed wildly, slamming his back against the rocks, but he held on.

Then, something shifted. The creature faltered. Its movements slowed. Its pupils—vertical slits of red—fixed on him, and Remington felt the connection snap into place.

Dominance.

It stilled beneath him, breathing heavy. Submission. Remington's head whipped back and he took a fresh breath of air.

Remington exhaled, soaked to the bone, victorious. And covered in basilisk slime.

Chel let out a sharp whistle from the bank. "That's *it*?"

Remington turned his head slowly, still catching his breath. "What?" He wiped his mouth and spit.

Chel grinned, his fangs glinting. "You're not gonna like this, but that thing's *tiny*."

Remington scowled. "It's a *medium*."

Chel shook his head, clearly enjoying himself. "Nah, that's a baby."

Evelyn, despite her earlier concern, stifled a laugh.

Remington clenched his jaw. "It's *loyal*."

Chel smirked. "Yeah, yeah. I just expected something... *bigger*."

Remington ignored him, patting the basilisk's slick scales. It growled low in its throat but didn't move to throw him off.

It was his now.

Size be damned.

Water streamed from Remington's dark clothing as he stepped out of the Black River, his breaths steady. The basilisk slithered behind him, its massive body parting the water with ease, its black scales gleaming in the eerie light. It obeyed him now, claimed, but there was a raw power in its coiled muscles—still a beast barely tamed.

Evelyn stood near the riverbank, arms wrapped around herself. She wasn't sure she'd ever get used to watching

Remm like this—commanding creatures from nightmares as if it was second nature. Maybe to him, it was. A shiver went up her spine as she stepped closer to Chel.

The water near them rippled. A low vibration thrummed through the ground beneath her feet.

Then—an eruption. Water sprayed.

A second basilisk surged from the river, larger than the first, its gaping jaw snapping in her direction. Evelyn's breath hitched as jagged fangs glistened.

It lunged.

She ran.

The ground was uneven, sharp rocks and twisted roots threatening to slow her, but fear propelled her forward. The basilisk's body crashed through the underbrush behind her, tearing through shrubs and knocking over a charred tree as it pursued.

She heard Chel and Remington shouting, heavy foot-steps echoing. She ran harder. Evelyn wasn't going to die by giant snake if she could help it. She couldn't battle one–she could only run as fast as humanly possible. She could hide. That was her only option. She scanned the forest. There was an outcropping of boulders. Yes. She could hide.

Evelyn barely made it behind a large boulder, heart hammering. Her hands pressed into the damp earth, breath coming in sharp bursts. She squeezed her eyes shut and covered her ears, waiting for the impact of those fangs—

Nothing.

Silence.

Slowly, she turned her head.

A figure stood in the distance.

Her stomach plummeted.

The man was taller than Remington, his long, ink-black coat shifting with the wind. His hair was a tangled mess of silver, and his piercing gaze locked onto her like she was prey.

Thrush.

Evelyn's body locked up, fear pressing against her chest. He was motionless, a specter against the gnarled trees, yet she could feel the weight of his presence, suffocating and ancient.

Then something shifted in the shadows behind her.

A second presence. No, not one—many.

Thrush's gaze flicked past her, and Evelyn followed his line of sight.

Figures emerged from the darkness, moving with unnatural jerks. Their eyes hollow, their mouths slack. A deathly moan vibrated through the trees.

The dead.

Evelyn swallowed hard. Remington had told her that they were nothing more than lost souls. They were part of Hell.

She looked to where Thrush had been. He was gone.

"Ev!" Remington's voice broke through.

"I'm here." Her voice broke as she stood, leaning against the boulder for support. "The dead are coming."

Remington's voice cut through the thick tension as he approached, his boots crunching against the ground. "Don't be afraid. They're just souls," he reminded her, but there was an edge of warning in his tone. "But they can still bite. And since you don't belong in this realm, avoid a bite."

The basilisk had slithered away, its predatory instincts

replaced with caution as it observed Thrush from the shadows. Evelyn wasn't sure if the creature feared him—or respected him.

Still catching her breath, she turned to Remington. "I thought I saw something... I thought I saw Thrush." She pointed in the distance where the pine trees were the thickest.

Remington's expression darkened, his patience thinning. "And what were you going to do about that?" His jaw clenched. "You can't take on Thrush. He'd probably kill you in a heartbeat."

Evelyn's jaw dropped open. She'd never seen Remington like this. Maybe he was afraid. Maybe he was vibing off the adrenaline of catching the basilisk but still, she didn't deserve it. She was just running for her life a few minutes ago.

Remington looked away. "This was a bad idea. I'm going to have to find another place for you."

Another place for you.

The words struck deep, and something inside Evelyn snapped. She wasn't sure what had just transpired between them but she was more confused than ever. And it made her angry.

"I'm not something you can just dispose of!" Her voice came out raw, shaking with fury and hurt. Tears burned her eyes.

Remington's face went slack, the heat in his expression draining in an instant. A flicker of regret crossed his features.

"I... I didn't mean it like that."

But Evelyn was already walking past him, jaw tight,

hands balled into fists. She didn't want to hear his half-apology, didn't want to be reminded how fragile her place here truly was.

Thrush had vanished, the dead lingering at the forest's edge, and Remington's basilisk watched her with its strange intelligence.

She had escaped one monster today. She was damned if she was going to add Remington to that list. His harsh words made her wonder if the real danger might have been standing right beside her all along. He was a prince with a sordid history and there were probably more reasons why Rue wanted him to stay away from Evelyn.

She stopped in front of Chel. "Take me back to the castle. I don't think I want to be near him right now."

Chel looked between the two before nodding and leading her toward another one of the Hellions SUVs that had followed them.

"He didn't mean it like you think," Chel said as he closed the driver's side door.

Evelyn buckled her seatbelt. "It doesn't matter."

"I think he was more scared of you getting injured than anything." Chel waved to the other Hellions as they drove away. "The dead are to be feared."

Evelyn cleared her throat then wiped her face with her hand. "My parents died during the dead outbreak on earth." She pressed a hand to her chin as it quivered, threatening a breakdown. "I was just a baby. When it was all over, my uncles took everything. They pillaged my parent's belongings and bank accounts. They left me with nothing when I turned eighteen. I was homeless. I was moneyless. I got through college on a scholarship but when the money ran out I had to go to work. Thank god I found Rue years ago. She's been the best friend I could ever ask for."

"Did you tell her?"

"Yes. And she was deceptively understanding about the horrors I lived through. Now I know why."

"Did you tell Remington?"

"No. I haven't told him. I don't think he cares much."

Chel slowed the SUV and turned to face her. "He cares, Evelyn. You might be a human but he has cared about you since the moment he met you."

Tears were sliding down Evelyn's cheeks. "I know to fear the dead. What he said to me was out of line."

"He is young. Give him time to sort out his thoughts. He'd just battled a basilisk."

Evelyn laughed a little. "He did."

"And then he almost saw you killed in front of his eyes."

Evelyn was nodding.

"And you said you saw Thrush. He has seen the worst of Thrush. He doesn't trust his cousin. I don't trust his cousin anywhere near you. That boy went to the dark side before any of us had a moment to recognize it and turn him away." Chel tapped the steering wheel. "But, strange things happen."

"Seems a daily issue here."

Chel took a deep breath and scratched his chin. "You lost your parents. So did Thrush." He turned to face her again. "Thrush's mother was killed during what we call the Fast-Zombie War. It was a shit show for all the realms. He was an infant, his mother was bitten as she held him. Thrush would have been next to die but Meg saved him."

"Rue's mother?"

Chel was nodding. "And, Thrush's father was already a ghost."

"Wait... What!"

"Welcome to *not* the Earthen plane. Weird shit can happen."

"So Thrush's parents are dead?"

"They were around him in their astral forms but very overprotective. He pushed them away. They felt it better to retreat to the Astral until he called them back."

Evelyn blinked. "What's the Astral?"

"Oh, it's another plane, like dreams and stars and stuff. Very impressionistic of life, more dreamlike than anything."

Evelyn rubbed her face. "My head is spinning."

"Thrush might sense a connection between you both. You were both orphaned. You might be able to help us reel him in. But you need to be careful. He's wild. He was trained with us as a child but never did his true time as a Hellion. And... he might be a little crazy because of it."

TWENTY-NINE

THE HOSPITAL SMELLED LIKE ANTISEPTIC AND stale coffee. Harsh fluorescent lights buzzed overhead. Evelyn sat on the padded exam table, her fingers gripping the edge, resisting the nervous habit of bouncing her knee. She wasn't expecting bad news but there was always that tiny sliver of doubt lingering in the back of her mind.

Also, she couldn't ignore that Remington was sitting across the room. Things had been uneasy between them since the incident at the Black River. Remington had yet to apologize. But Evelyn figured a prince of Hell wouldn't apologize for much, if ever. She couldn't hold eye contact with him for more than a second and their conversations had turned into simple yes and no. Every so often she'd hear him mumble in what he'd called Hellspeak at the shopping district.

Remington stood, leaning against the counter with his arms crossed, silent but present. He had barely left her side since bringing her back to the mortal realm for this appointment. The hospitals unsettled him. He said it was the smell.

She suspected it had more to do with the vulnerability of it all.

The door swung open, and Dr. Dane stepped in, smiling as he flipped through her chart. "Evelyn. You're looking well."

She let out a breath. "I feel better." The only issue was that she'd vomited again going through the portal. But she couldn't really tell the doctor that. He'd probably commit her for being nuts.

Remington made a low sound in his throat, and she shot him a look.

Dr. Dane sat on the rolling stool, spinning slightly as he reviewed her scans on the computer. "I'm guessing you haven't had any seizures since you never called me." He glanced at her quickly.

Evelyn shook her head, remembering how Remington said he'd burned the piece of paper with the doctor's phone number. Maybe she should ask for it again. That would really piss Remington off. But it would be worth it to watch.

"Everything looks great. No signs of regrowth or complications. Your incision healed beautifully, and you're in the clear to resume normal activity." He turned to her with an easy smile. "I want you to follow up in a year just to be safe, but otherwise, you're officially discharged." His expression changed just a bit.

"What?" Evelyn asked.

"Your hair grew back quickly." He stood and moved closer.

"My hair has always grown fast." Evelyn dismissed the

concern. How exactly could she tell him that an Angel healer made her hair grow back? "So, a year?"

"A year would be optimal." The doctor stood, offering his hand. "Take care of yourself, Evelyn. And try not to stress too much—you're young. Live your life."

She shook his hand, nodding. "I will."

As the doctor left the room she turned to Remington, expecting to see the usual sharp amusement in his expression. Instead, he was watching her, serious, assessing.

"What?" she asked.

His lips pressed together for a moment before he spoke. "It's good news."

She raised a brow. "You sound surprised."

"I'm not. Just..." He shook his head. "I'll meet you in the hallway."

Before she could question him, he was gone.

Frowning, Evelyn grabbed her coat and followed, stepping out into the corridor just in time to see him at the front desk. His broad shoulders squared, his presence enough to make the receptionist shift nervously as he slid a black credit card across the counter.

"I'd like to settle the bill," he said smoothly.

Evelyn froze.

The receptionist glanced at the screen, then back at him. "That's... quite a sum. Are you sure? We can bill the insurance."

Remington's expression didn't so much as flicker. "Run the card."

Evelyn stormed up to his side. "Remington—"

"It's handled," he said, not looking at her.

"Remm." She grabbed his arm, forcing him to turn. "You don't have to—"

He angled his head, eyes dark, unyielding. "I will."

The words sent a shiver down her spine.

The transaction processed, and the receptionist handed the card back. "All set."

Remington gave a sharp nod, pocketing his wallet before turning to Evelyn. "Ready to go?"

She stared at him, her pulse thrumming.

There were a dozen things she could say. A dozen ways she could argue. But looking at him, at the way he stood—so sure, so immovable—she knew it was pointless.

***

The restaurant Rue had picked was tucked into a quiet side street near Loyola campus, dimly lit with flickering lanterns and lined with old wooden beams that made the place feel timeless. The scent of roasted meat, fresh bread, and spiced wine filled the air.

Evelyn had barely stepped inside before Rue tackled her in a hug.

"You look amazing," Rue said, squeezing tight before pulling back to study her. "How are you feeling? Wait... Your hair grew back so fast."

"I'm better," Evelyn admitted, touched by the genuine concern in her friend's eyes. "No headaches, no dizziness, no nosebleeds." She tapped the side of her head. "And, thanks to Teari, I have my hair back."

Rue's voice dropped to a whisper. "Angels do come in

handy sometimes," she mused, leading Evelyn toward their table.

Dacre stood as they approached, nodding politely to Evelyn before clasping arms with Remington in greeting. The two men shared an easy, wordless exchange before Dacre's gaze landed on her. "I heard you had quite the adventure down there."

Evelyn sighed, settling into her seat. "Word travels fast between realms I guess."

Rue grinned, setting a stack of notebooks and books beside Evelyn's plate. "Which is why I brought you all of this. Research waits for no one, not even those recovering from brain surgery."

Evelyn's eyes widened as she picked up one of the old, worn books, flipping through the yellowed pages. "How did you get these out of the library?"

"I stole them." Rue smirked. "Actually, the librarian Layla helped me sneak them out. I'll bring them back as soon as you're done with them."

Remington rolled his eyes. "Are we really doing homework over dinner?"

"We are *discussing* important findings," Rue corrected, pulling out a folded map and spreading it across the table. Nearby diners started looking at them.

Dacre groaned and mumbled, "We should have reserved the private room if I had known this was going to turn into a research session."

"We think we've found a caved-in passageway that might lead to the healing waters you mentioned. There were some old texts describing the location, but we need to confirm it."

Rue dragged her finger over the map. "The opening isn't far from where we found the sacrifice stone. We've excavated most of the opening. I wish you could have been there," Rue said as she watched her friend. "You would have loved it."

Evelyn smiled sadly. "Hopefully next time."

"Definitely." Rue nodded.

Remington leaned in, scanning the map. "How deep is the collapse?"

Dacre answered, his deep voice even. "Significant. We'll need an excavation team. There are a lot of big boulders."

Evelyn glanced at the map, tracing her fingers over the markings. "So it's real?"

Rue nodded. "Yes. I want to be cautiously optimistic but everything is screaming that this is real." Rue leaned forward grasping Evelyn's hand. "All of our research for the last year... minds are going to be blown. Dr. Malcom has faced ridicule for years with his theories, but not us. Imagine the headlines when we get our research articles out."

"It's crazy," Evelyn said. "Some archeologists have worked their entire lives to find something like this."

The conversation shifted as food arrived—steaming plates of roasted lamb, fresh pasta, and warm bread with honey butter.

"So," Rue turned to her brother, wiggling her eyebrows. "Tell me about your *basilisk*."

Remington shot her a look. "It's fine."

Evelyn sipped from her wine. "He picked a tiny one according to Chel."

"It's *not* tiny," Remington shot back.

Evelyn smirked. "It's a little tiny." She shrugged. "Actually, it's terrifying. I don't know how big they can get but I hope to never see one again."

Rue burst out laughing. "I cannot believe you tamed a basilisk. How does it feel to have your own little murder snake?"

Remington muttered into his drink. "It's a *perfectly capable* murder snake."

Evelyn, feeling mischievous, turned to Dacre. "And how's Lucipurr?"

"I thought you'd never ask," Rue's grin turned devilish as she reached for her bag and peeked it open.

Green eyes looked back at Evelyn.

"Oh my gosh, the little void is here in the flesh!" She reached for Rue's bag. "Give him to me. I must have a snuggle."

Evelyn petted the kitten and snuck him pieces of lamb. "He is just the perfect little fur baby."

"He is," Rue agreed.

Dacre muttered something under his breath, but there was no mistaking the way his lips twitched in amusement.

After the plates were cleared and Remington left the table to settle the bill, Rue pushed the stack of books toward Dacre. "Can you help Ev get these to the truck? I need to speak with my brother for a second."

Evelyn's eyes were wide as she glanced at her friend.

"Actually, I need to use the restroom," Evelyn said as she stood. "I'll be back in a few minutes."

The scent of garlic and simmering tomatoes filled the air as Remington returned to his chair and leaned back, rolling his glass of whiskey between his fingers. The soft hum of conversation surrounded them, but his attention fixed on Rue. She sat across from him, arms crossed, her sharp green eyes narrowed in suspicion.

"What?" he asked.

"You're not telling me something," she said, her voice calm but firm. "Something's off with you. And with Evelyn."

Remington exhaled through his nose, glancing at the flickering candle between them. "She's fine. It's nothing."

Rue tilted her head, unconvinced. "She wasn't her usual self tonight. And I had another dream."

His grip on the glass tightened. "Oh?"

She ignored his irritation. "Evelyn and Alastor. I saw him with her. Again. Has he been snooping around the castle? That's the only thing I can think of."

Remington's jaw locked. "That will never happen. He ran off like a coward. If I ever see him again, I'll kill him. If the Hellions don't get to him first."

Rue studied him, searching for something in his face. "Then what else is wrong?"

He hesitated, debating how much to tell her. But Rue had never been one for tolerating withholding information. She'd find out and she'd be pissed. And, the longer he kept his mouth shut, the sharper her glare became.

Finally, he set his glass down. "She was nearly eaten by a basilisk. Then Thrush showed up."

Rue's eyes widened. "*What?*"

Dacre blew out a breath of disbelief.

"She's fine," Remm said quickly. "Shaken, but fine."

Rue's fingers curled against the tablecloth. "And?"

Remington exhaled, rubbing his temple. "I said something I shouldn't have."

Rue arched a brow.

"I told her this was a bad idea," he admitted. "That I needed to find another place for her."

Rue inhaled sharply. "Oh, Remm."

He looked away, jaw clenched.

Rue reached across the table, placing a hand over his. "You have to apologize."

"She screamed at me," he muttered. "Cried. Called me an asshole. She made Chel drive her home, er... back to the castle."

Rue snorted. "Well, you *were* an asshole."

He shot her a glare.

Rue softened. "Remm, Evelyn isn't like us. She's not a creature of Hell or Heaven. She's human. And her humanity—while wild and free—is sensitive to words like that. You *cannot* threaten her like she's one of our own. Or something different altogether."

"I didn't mean it as a threat."

"It doesn't matter," Rue said. "You need to fix it. Because if you break her trust, if you make her feel like she doesn't belong, she *will* leave. She could do something dangerous."

Remington swallowed hard, Rue's words hitting deeper than he cared to admit.

"She really likes you," Rue reminded him gently. "Don't make her regret it." She leaned forward. "Don't make me regret letting her go with you."

Dacre touched Rue's shoulder to calm her.

Remington sighed, rubbing a hand down his face. He already knew what he had to do. He'd felt like an ass all this time for not having taken care of what he'd done.

"Yeah," he muttered. "I'll fix it."

"Good," Rue said, glancing up. "Here she comes."

The night air was crisp, carrying the scent of old books and damp pavement as Evelyn adjusted the strap of her bag over her shoulder. The weight of the notebooks and photographs Rue had given her pressed into her ribs. Beside her, Remington carried a stack of books effortlessly, like they weighed nothing. Evelyn knew each book was about five pounds and Rue had loaded him up with ten of them that Evelyn needed.

The portal ahead was dark, tucked away in the shadows of the alleyway next to Peabody Library, an unassuming tear in reality that led back to Hell. Evelyn exhaled, trying not to think about the last time she'd stepped through it—how her stomach had twisted, how she'd emptied its contents the second they arrived on the other side. Stepping back into the Earthen plane was easy. She immediately felt at home.

Remington came to a stop just before they reached the portal. "Evelyn."

She turned, catching the way the golden glow of a streetlamp highlighted the sharper angles of his face, casting his dark hair in softer shadows. His expression wasn't his usual smirk or brooding scowl. It was something else— something hesitant.

"What's up?" she asked, shifting the bag on her shoulder.

His grip on the books tightened slightly. "I need to apologize."

She blinked. "For what?"

His jaw tensed, as if he was debating how to phrase it. "For saying I should find another place for you." His voice was quieter than usual, the edges rough. "For making you feel like you didn't belong."

Evelyn's chest pinched. She crossed her arms, watching him carefully. "You were a pretty big asshole about it."

He huffed a soft laugh. "I didn't mean it." His gaze dropped to the books in his hands, then back to her. "I don't want you to go anywhere, Ev. I *like* having you around."

The words lingered between them, warmer than the air, heavier than the books he held.

Evelyn's breath hitched slightly at the way he was looking at her. There was a pause—a shift in the air between them. His gaze flicked from her eyes to her lips.

She swallowed. "You're really laying on the charm tonight, aren't you?"

His lips twitched. "Is it working?" He licked his lips.

Her heartbeat stuttered. "Maybe." She signed. "I understand that you are under immense pressure, but please don't treat me like one of your minions."

Remington's smirk softened, and for a second, she thought he might close the space between them. She glanced down the alleyway to the shadowed figures of Rue and Dacre watching. Rue waved.

Remington reached out, gripped a lock of hair between his fingers and tugged gently. His fingers lingered for a fraction of a second longer than necessary before he pulled back.

Evelyn exhaled and tilted her head toward the portal. "Let's go before I say something wild that makes Rue worry." She flashed him a wide smile and winked. "Can't have her being mean to you again."

"Please. She's *so* mean to me." Remington chuckled, shifting the books under one arm so he could take her free hand. "Alright, try not to throw up this time."

Evelyn sighed. "I probably shouldn't be doing this on a full stomach."

He touched the portal, whispering the words that brought it shimmering to life.

She rolled her eyes. "Don't throw up. Don't throw up. I *won't* throw up."

And, miraculously, she didn't.

THIRTY

Evelyn drifted in the velvet depths of sleep, weightless and warm, lost in a dream that felt too vivid and too consuming. A hand brushed along the side of her neck, the touch featherlight but possessive.

"You feel it, don't you?"

The voice coiled around her, deep and amused, thick with want. She knew it. Recognized it immediately.

Alastor.

He was behind her, his breath ghosting over her bare shoulder, fingers tracing lazy circles against her skin. She shivered, caught in the space between fear and fascination.

"Come to me."

Evelyn's breath hitched. Heat licked up her spine, a pulse of something dark and heady wrapping around her like silk. The scent of nightshade and embers filled the air.

"You don't belong in his world. You belong in mine. You sacrificed yourself after all. And I was the only one to answer your call. I was the only one."

His lips barely grazed her ear, a whisper of contact that

sent her heart racing. A hand slid down her arm, curled around her wrist, tugging gently—guiding her forward, deeper into the haze of her dream.

She took a step.

And another.

The world shifted.

Evelyn's bare feet met cold stone. A distant sound—soft, echoing footsteps—pulled her further.

Then—

A sharp gasp tore from her throat as her eyes snapped open.

She wasn't in bed. She rubbed her eyes to clear the haze of sleep.

The chill of the hallway bit at her exposed skin, her nightshirt hanging loose over her body as she stood in the dim corridor of the castle. The air was cool, the strange night noises of Hell beyond the thick walls of the castle sent a shiver up her spine.

Her pulse pounded.

What the...?

She was standing outside her bedroom. No—past it. Nearly at the staircase leading deeper into the castle. The lingering ghost of the dream clung to her, that insistent pull to *go*, to *find him*, making her stomach turn. Something was wrong. She'd hated what Alastor had done to her, never wanted that creature to touch her again. How could a dream get her out of bed and make her feel like that? She shivered and rubbed her arms. She shouldn't be out here dressed in just a long T-shirt for sleeping.

Heart hammering, she turned on shaky legs and started back toward her room—

Remington's door was slightly ajar.

A sliver of candlelight flickered through the opening, casting a thin, golden glow into the hall.

Evelyn stilled.

She could hear movement inside. The rustle of fabric, the faint clink of glass against wood. A sigh, deep and exasperated.

She shifted closer.

"...you're drinking too much," Chel's voice, low and measured, carried through the crack in the door.

A pause.

Remington let out a slow exhale. "I'm fine. It's nothing."

"Are you?" Chel didn't sound convinced. "It seems like something. The other Hellions have noticed."

Evelyn bit her lip, heart knocking against her ribs. She shouldn't be listening. She *shouldn't*—

Remington spoke again, quieter this time. "The humming hasn't stopped."

Silence.

Chel's voice was softer when he spoke. "And does she stop it?"

A beat passed.

Remington's answer was barely above a whisper. "Yes. When we are close."

Evelyn's breath caught.

She stepped back, pulse erratic, guilt creeping up her spine. Whatever this was—whatever *he* was struggling with—wasn't meant for her to overhear.

Turning, she padded silently back to her room, shutting the door behind her.

Sleep was impossible now.

With a heavy sigh, she settled onto the couch, pulling the research materials Rue had given her onto her lap. If she couldn't rest, she might as well make use of the time.

Still, as she flipped through the old, thin pages, she couldn't shake the phantom touch of a dream that felt far too real.

Thirty-One

The grand ballroom of the castle gleamed under the golden glow of chandeliers, their enchanted flames flickering without source or smoke. The ceilings stretched impossibly high, adorned with tapestries that looked woven with stardust and blood. The polished black marble floors reflected the sparkle, making it look like the ballroom was set in the Astral plane. Music hummed through the air.

Remington stood near the bar, collecting a swallow of whiskey before greeting the attendees. His presence was commanding as he observed the growing crowd. The hall was filled with aristocrats and powerful creatures from both Hell and Heaven, mingling under the unspoken truce. There would be no warring tonight, no fighting. The realms had experienced more peace than ever before under the rule of Remington's parents. He wasn't going to let it all fall apart tonight.

He adjusted the cuffs of his suit—dark as Hellsky night,

it appeared lined with thread spun from shadows themselves. He checked the time. Again.

Evelyn was late.

His jaw tensed as he scanned the crowd, barely listening to the greetings of the noble families who passed through, bowing or curtsying before him. He nodded in acknowledgment, but his focus was elsewhere. The thrumming in his brain was loud as ever and he needed it to stop. *Where the hell was she?*

A heavy hand nudged his arm, and he turned to see Chel; dressed in leather, he arched a knowing brow. "Expecting someone?" A low growled echoed in his throat. "Unlike me."

Remington exhaled through his nose. "Evelyn should have been here by now."

"Patience, Princeling." Chel smirked. "A lady takes her time." He cleared his throat and searched the room. "Speaking of ladies, did you invite Teari? She didn't give me an answer."

"She was busy," Remington said. He muttered a curse in Hellspeak under his breath and turned to face Chel. The Hellion was leaning against one of the towering obsidian columns, looking as though he would rather be anywhere else now that he knew the Angel healer wouldn't be attending the party.

Remington caught his attention with a sharp nod. "Go find Evelyn."

Chel groaned, pushing off the wall. "What am I, her personal escort?"

"You're the only one I trust not to get distracted."

Chel snorted. "Fine, but if she's still getting ready, I'm not rushing her. You can suffer in your princely duties alone."

Remington waved him off, exhaling as he turned back to the line of guests he needed to greet. He had no choice but to keep moving, to keep nodding, to keep playing the part of the gracious prince. But no matter how many greetings he exchanged, his mind remained elsewhere, stuck in a whirlwind of frustration, curiosity, and something he wasn't quite ready to name.

A sudden lull in conversation caused Remington to look away from the demon he was currently speaking with.

Remington had prepared himself for many things—tedious conversations, political maneuvering—but nothing could have prepared him for *this*.

Evelyn stepped into the ballroom and for a moment, it was as if the entire room forgot how to breathe. There was an audible heartbeat of silence.

Remington had to try hard to hold his jaw in place. *Fuckin'-A.*

She looked like... he wasn't even sure how to explain it. Her blonde hair was twisted into an elegant updo, soft curls framing her face just so. But it was the dress that got him—the sleek black fabric clung to her, the hem landing just below her knees, sophisticated yet maddeningly enticing. The boat-neckline didn't dip low enough to reveal cleavage, but it bared both shoulders, leaving her neck exposed. Her whole neck from every angle.

All that delicate skin on display.

Remington licked his lips, feeling the sharp graze of his

own teeth against his tongue. His fingers twitched at his sides.

Then there were the heels—black with a bright red sole, dangerously high. Her every step was measured, elegant, and yet utterly sinful. She had the kind of effortless vintage glamour that turned heads and made men reconsider their priorities.

A Hellion stationed near the door immediately moved to her side. Chel was on her opposite side, his dark eyes finding Remington's immediately. He must've sensed what Remington did—the collaborative intake of breath from the crowd, the hard swallows of demons and angels alike, all eyes trained on Evelyn.

Remington clenched his jaw, possessiveness curling through his stomach like a slow-burning fire. He was halfway across the room before he even realized he was moving, cutting through the throng of guests with singular focus.

Evelyn spotted him then, her lips twitching at the corners. It was an innocent smile.

"Finally decided to show up?" he murmured as he reached her, offering his arm.

"I had a Hellion banging on my door, demanding I hurry." She looped her arm through his, fingers barely grazing his sleeve. "Did you send him?"

Remington didn't answer. Instead, his gaze swept over her once more, lingering at her throat–at the soft skin there, the pulse that fluttered just beneath the surface. *She had no idea what she was doing, showing up looking like that.*

"I take it you approve?" she teased, tilting her chin just slightly.

He exhaled sharply through his nose, forcing himself to keep his composure. "You're causing a problem."

Her brows lifted. "A problem?"

"Every creature in this room is thinking the same thing," he murmured, leading her further into the ballroom. "And I don't particularly like it. But you look nice. Very nice." His eyes traveled down her neck.

Evelyn laughed, a quiet, pleased sound. "Good."

Remington's fingers flexed at his side. *Oh, she was going to be trouble tonight.*

Evelyn was introduced to Demons and half-breed creatures that looked slightly human.

Remington's fingers twitched every time someone got too close to her. She was a sheep among wolves. He couldn't deny it. Every creature could sense that she was human.

A large Demon touched Remington's shoulder and they fell into a deep conversation about things Evelyn had never heard before. She was bored and eager to explore and meet new people. She slipped her hand out of the crook of Remington's elbow and wandered a few steps away.

The aristocrats of Hell were charming in their own dark way, but there was something... off. Their smiles lingered too long. Their pupils dilated when they looked at her. Even the ones who kept their distance did so not out of disinterest, but wariness.

And then came the more forward ones.

What Remington didn't know was that Lucifer's

bloodline was vast. His descendants might have only had a spec of the bloodline, but it was still there; latent, scattered throughout Hell. Tonight, some were here. And they were watching her.

A tall man with ink-black horns curling back through his dark hair, inhaled deeply as he passed. His expression sharpened in recognition. "Well, well... So *you're* the human the prince has been hosting."

Evelyn blinked. "I'm sorry?"

"Human. But a nice smelling one," he murmured, tilting his head as though listening to something. "Are you making that humming sound? I can't get it out of my head."

Evelyn's breath caught. "No," she whispered.

Suddenly, the attention on her sharpened, the air thickening with realization. She'd been a curiosity before, but now—now she was something more.

She wasn't just some human in Hell.

She was the sacrifice waiting a claimant.

Men began vying for her attention; a few stepped forward, offering their hands for a dance. Some were polite, but others were insistent and demanding.

"You must honor the tradition," one purred, reaching for her wrist. "Dance with me first." The demon pulled her into his arms and began a waltz-like dance that had Evelyn tripping over her own feet.

"I'm sorry. I haven't ever danced like this before." She pressed her hands against his hard chest and thought of shoving him away. He had a strange vibe and she didn't like it.

The demon grinned down at her before pausing. "We don't have to dance. I could take you for a walk outside."

"No, thank you. But no." Evelyn stepped back, pushing his hands away.

Another male, more brazen, grinned as he made to lift her from the floor. "Stay away from that one," the new halfling with gray hair took her hand, "he moves too quickly. No one should ever start the night with a waltz."

Evelyn let out a nervous laugh, trying to step back. She cast a quick, panicked glance toward Remington, but he was across the room, engaged in conversation with what looked like a high-ranking diplomat. His posture was stiff, like he wanted out of the conversation but he had royal duties to attend to.

Help me.

Evelyn twisted from another demon's grip, her stomach twisting. The moment had shifted—what had been a game of flirtation had turned into something else, something dangerous. They weren't asking for her favor anymore. They were testing her. Getting her further and further from Remington.

She searched the room, eyes landing on Chel. The crowd between them grew thicker and thicker.

More hands reached for her, voices overlapping—soft words, promises, commands.

Remington was still not moving but she noticed the way he rubbed the side of his head.

The further she got from him, the louder the humming would become in his head.

Evelyn's chest tightened. *Remm!*

It was Chel who made it to her first. The large Hellion

shouldered through the group, his deep voice cutting through the commotion. "Alright, that's enough. Get away from the human." He slapped hands and shoved bodies. "Get. I said let her go!"

Remington had finally gotten out of the conversation he'd been stuck in.

Chel's dark gaze flicked to Remington, sharp with warning. "Get her *out* of here."

At that moment, the room exploded into chaos.

"We want to see her."

"Let us try."

"She's sacrificed herself."

"She called us here!"

"This is ancient magic."

"Don't deny us a chance."

"She called the sacrifice."

"I want her."

"I want her."

"*I* want her!"

Evelyn was panicking, eyes wide and heart beating a million times a minute. She reached for Chel; his giant hand gripped her wrist and pulled her against his big body and growled at the surrounding demons vying for her.

More Hellions descended upon the party, their sudden appearance a clear signal—this ball was *over*. Guards pushed through the crowd, separating demons from their intended targets. Evelyn barely had time to react before a firm arm wrapped around her waist.

Remington.

His expression was thunderous, his shadows curling at the edges of his form, barely restrained. "Come with me."

Evelyn didn't argue. Her heart was beating so hard she didn't trust herself to decide about how to get out of the room. Her skin was crawling after having been manhandled by so many. They had demanded her attention. Touched her skin. Threatened to take her.

Remington squeezed her wrist. "Can you run in those heels?"

"I think so." Evelyn's eyes were wide with fear.

"Come now." Remington took off, his long stride too much for her to keep up with. She stumbled, tripped. Then she was lifted off her feet by Remm but something grabbed her leg.

Evelyn screamed.

Remington turned, clutching her to his side, baring teeth at the demon who'd grabbed her ankle.

"Release her now or die." Remington's voice was cold as ice. The space around them suddenly darkened, shadows drifting across the floor like smoke.

"Apologies." The curve-horned demon muttered. "But she is calling to all of us. You best claim her or someone else will. You should not have brought her around all of us with mixed blood. She is not safe like this. She never will be until someone takes her offering of sacrifice."

"Mind your business." Remington lifted Evelyn against his body and her heels fell off.

"Now that the others know, they'll come for her," the demon shouted. "Give her to me, I'll keep her safe."

"Fuck right off," Remington grumbled.

Evelyn wrapped her arms around Remington's neck and squeezed her eyes closed. She didn't want to see what was creating the strange noises in the ballroom. She heard

Hellions roar. There were bodies falling. Then, darkness. Silence.

Evelyn opened her eyes. It was so dark she couldn't see Remington's face. But he was still moving.

"Where are we?" she asked.

"My parents had hidden passageways constructed. We are somewhere safe. The Hellions will take care of the others." He slowed his pace before walking up stairs. He stopped and there was a faint light illuminating the small room he'd brought them to.

Remington released her legs and lowered her to her feet. He crowded Evelyn, pressing her against the wall. She could tell he was struggling with something. Maybe it was his control, or his words. She wasn't sure.

She sagged against the stone wall, her pulse still erratic. "What the heck was that?" she whispered.

"That rune stone you bled on was a sacrifice stone; it called everyone with even a spec of Lucifer's bloodline in their bones. You're a sacrifice, an unclaimed sacrifice."

"Oh." Evelyn looked up at him. "I'm not sure how I feel about being claimed or unclaimed or a sacrifice."

He was watching her closely. "Dressed like that–"

"Hey! I. Look. Stunning." She interrupted him in a moment of bravery. "And I shaved *everything*." A nervous laugh broke through.

He swallowed hard before continuing. "Alastor tried to claim you, but I interrupted him at the dig site." Remington was staring at her neck.

"I don't like what Alastor did." Evelyn was breathing heavy, her chest pressed against Remington. She rubbed the spot under her ear where he'd bitten her.

Remington tilted his head, slid the tip of his nose up her neck and then... she felt the edge of his tongue. Evelyn shivered.

"He should not have touched you. I'll kill him for it." Remington's hands were at her waist, sliding up, circling her ribs. There was something about his big hands pressing against her bones. He could crush her in a heartbeat. She knew it. She'd seen him with the basilisk.

Remington's chest was rising and falling with ragged breaths. He bent to lift her, his lips at her throat. Evelyn held her breath. For some reason, the idea of Remington pressing his teeth to her neck sounded better than anything ever in her life. She arched her neck.

Remington groaned a pained sound. "You are so soft and fragile," he murmured against her skin. He had wanted to possess her in front of everyone in the ballroom. Claim her for all to see but it wasn't right in the middle of all that chaos. She deserved better than the dark urges he'd been holding inside.

"I'm not that fragile," Evelyn whispered.

"Fuck. Have mercy, Ev. I want to bury myself deep and lose myself in you until you're ruined for any other man. But you're..."

"Human?" There was disappointment in her heart.

"No. Fragile. Small."

"I am none of those things."

"Compared to me you are." Sharp teeth scraped against her neck. "I want to drink from you while I fuck you slowly."

Evelyn whimpered. "It sounds like a good time." Her

whole body shivered at the thought. "If I beg please will you do it?"

He searched her eyes. "If I do, you'll be forever changed. You won't exactly be human any longer."

"It's okay. Sometimes being human sucks."

He chuckled softly. "Tell me to go away." He was pressing her against the stone wall and she felt every inch of him.

"I don't want you to go away. I want you to throw me over your shoulder and slap my ass and take me to my room like you did the night we first met."

Remington braced a hand beside her head, his own breaths uneven. His green eyes burned as they searched hers, as if still piecing together what had happened—what he nearly allowed to happen because he was trying to be polite and not piss off a higher level demon complaining about missing goats on his lands. These damned goats.

With voice low and jaw clenched he said, "Had I known the risk, I would have never let you come to the party."

Evelyn swallowed hard, her fingers still curled where she'd clutched the fabric of his coat earlier. She wasn't sure what rattled her more—the attention she had drawn, or the way the crowd had pulled them apart before he could intervene.

Or maybe... the way she had wanted him to risk losing her. It sure brought out a possessive side of him.

She exhaled, the sound shaking, and without thinking she reached for him. Just a touch, her fingers brushing the front of his jacket. "But you did see it," she murmured. "Eventually."

Remington didn't move away. If anything, his shoulders seemed to lose some of their tension.

"You were scared," he said softly. Not a question. "I didn't like that."

Evelyn let out a breathless laugh. "Of course I was scared. Those men, demons, whatever they were–they were demanding and touchy."

Remington's fingers lifted, hovering near her jaw before he finally closed the distance, brushing his knuckles against her skin. "I'm sorry I didn't intervene sooner. I hate that." His voice was rough, edged with something that sent a shiver down her spine. "I hate that they touched you."

Evelyn tilted her head slightly into his touch, her pulse betraying her. "You can make it up to me."

His gaze flicked to her lips. The way he stared made her lightheaded, her fingers curling against his chest without thinking.

"Yeah?" he murmured.

Evelyn nodded, lips parting, her heartbeat hammering for an entirely different reason.

He leaned in. Slow, deliberate, giving her time to pull away.

She didn't.

His lips brushed against hers. Not quite a kiss, just a breath away, just enough for the warmth of him to make her dizzy. He smelled like smoke and whiskey.

Evelyn swayed, her fingers digging into the lapels of his suitcoat to keep herself steady.

"Christ..." Remington groaned, fingertips brushing over her skin; the soft space under her ear, the column of her neck, her collarbone.

Evelyn felt ready to spontaneously combust.

There was a loud thud and footsteps echoed down the passageway they were in.

"Remm," Chel's voice called.

A throat cleared.

Loudly.

Remington went stone-still. "Fuck." Remington released Evelyn and settled her on her feet. He turned to face the Hellion, Evelyn hiding behind his back.

Mortification was quickly burning through Evelyn's dazed state.

"What do you want?" Remington snapped, his voice gravelly, thick with unspent tension.

Chel stood at the end of the corridor, looking thoroughly unimpressed. He held out something in his large hand. "The guests have gone home. The castle is cleared." He jiggled the item once for emphasis. "You forgot these."

Evelyn squinted, her brain struggling to catch up.

Her shoes.

Chel was holding her heels in his massive palm, like some Hellish fairy godmother who had the absolute worst timing.

Remington exhaled sharply and took them, stepping forward with an air of exasperated irritation.

Chel ignored him, his red eyes shifting to Evelyn instead. "Is she okay?" he asked.

"I'm fine," Evelyn managed, though her knees still felt like jelly. One hand went to her throat, rubbing the ghost of Remington's teeth and lips away. She cursed Chel inwardly for the interruption.

Chel's gaze flicked between them, then rolled his eyes. "Yeah. Sure."

He turned on his heel and strode off, muttering something about "bad decisions" and "could've waited two damn minutes."

Remington ran a hand down his face, exhaling a slow, long-suffering breath.

Evelyn, despite herself, laughed.

He shot her a look.

"What?" she teased. "You got us all hot and bothered only for the moment to get ruined?"

He growled under his breath and grabbed her hand, tugging her closer. "I don't need a moment," he murmured. "I need Chel to mind his own damn business. Who knows when I'll see you in that dress again?"

Evelyn smirked. "You like the dress."

Remington groaned, letting his forehead drop against hers for just a second. Then, still muttering, he slipped an arm around her waist and led her down the hall.

"Next time, I'll have to lock you in your room," Remington's voice was rough. "You do look stunning."

"Like Rapunzel?" Evelyn pouted. "But I like parties."

"Too bad. They're too dangerous. I think I'll lock you up like Sleeping Beauty. Put my basilisk outside the door too."

"Eww." Evelyn glanced up at Remington only to find him smirking down at her. "You're not funny."

"I'm hilarious," he argued.

"The most hilarious dark prince?" Evelyn didn't sound convinced. "I think not."

They returned to the ballroom. Destruction was everywhere. There were broken tables and chairs. Hellions and guards and servants were cleaning up the mess. Gore streaked the floor.

"Princeling," a familiar voice called and motioned to the door. "A guest waits for you."

Remington released Evelyn and signaled for Chel to get her.

"Duty calls," he muttered.

THIRTY-TWO

REMINGTON WATCHED AS EVELYN DISAPPEARED through the grand doors of the ballroom, flanked by a Hellion escort. The humming noise in his brain became louder the further she got from him. Even from across the room, he could see the way her shoulders tensed, the way her fingers trembled slightly as she smoothed her dress. She was still shaken. He should be the one walking her out. He should be the one at her side.

But his duties held him back.

Two Hellions were the only creatures remaining in the ballroom, waiting to see how the Prince of Hell would react to the chaos that had unfolded earlier. He clenched his jaw, smoothing his expression into something unreadable before turning away.

Outside the castle's grand entrance, the night was thick with mist rolling in from the mountains. A squat, broad-shouldered demon stood waiting near the gates, his molten eyes flashing with impatience.

Remington sighed. "Let me guess," he said, descending the steps. "You've come to complain about the basilisk."

The demon scoffed. "It's not a problem, it's a damn crisis. My herd is half of what it was and if you don't do something, we're taking care of it ourselves."

Remington's lip curled at the veiled threat. "You'll do no such thing."

The noble's nostrils flared. "And why not? These are *our* lands, our livestock, and our livelihoods. The basilisks may be yours to claim, but if you can't control them—"

Remington took a step forward, casting the demon in his shadow. "They *are* the Queen's," he said, voice low, dangerous. "And if you prefer her to return and handle your problem, I will beckon her."

The noble hesitated but didn't back down. "Do something. Or we'll have no choice but to hunt them."

Remington exhaled slowly, willing his temper to stay in check. "Your losses will be repaid," he said. "And the basilisk will be handled. But if I hear so much as a whisper of unauthorized hunts, I'll make sure you regret it."

The demon paled slightly but nodded. "Understood, Princeling." With a stiff bow, he turned and vanished into the night.

Remington stood there for a moment, the mist curling around his boots. His thoughts should have been on the basilisk issue, on the unrest brewing among the families near the Black River. But instead, his mind drifted to Evelyn—how she had looked tonight, how her breath had hitched when his teeth had grazed her throat.

Turning back toward the castle, he walked the quiet halls, heading toward his room.

As he passed by Evelyn's door he slowed, his hand clenching at his side. He could sense her behind the door, her presence humming at the edges of his awareness.

He could knock. He could quell the noise.

He could step inside, remind her of the way she had looked at him before Chel had interrupted. He could settle the distance between them before it widened again.

Instead, he sighed and kept walking.

There would be time for that after she recovered from the events in the ballroom, after they'd figured out what to do next with the effects of the sacrifice stone. Now that so many of Lucifer's bloodline knew about her, the threat was never greater. Remington rubbed his mouth and kicked open the door to his room.

THIRTY-THREE

THE NIGHT AIR WAS THICK WITH THE SCENT OF damp earth and the distant crackle of fire pits. A chill slithered down Evelyn's spine as she stood barefoot on the uneven ground outside the castle walls. The ochre glow of Hellmoon cast her skin in a ghastly haze. She blinked, disoriented, the cool wind biting at her skin. *How did I get here?*

Was she awake? Was she dreaming? The last thing she remembered was settling into bed, exhausted from a long day of research. Now she was outside, shivering in her nightclothes, the twisted pines of Hell's landscape looming around her.

Something rustled in the darkness.

A low growl echoed just beyond the dim torchlight.

Evelyn's heart pounded as she turned, her breath coming in sharp gasps. Shadows slithered between the jagged rocks, shifting, creeping closer. And then she saw it—something hunched and twisted, its red eyes locked onto her.

It moved. Fast.

A snarl ripped through the night as the creature lunged from the shadowline of the forest. Its eyes were red, body giant and rippled with muscle. It took a moment before Evelyn recognized the creature as one of the men she'd danced with at the party. Well, the dance wasn't necessarily willing since they'd grabbed at her arms and forced her in a waltz she didn't know. There was a pull, something else trying to drag her beyond the lunging creature. She was a statue, unsure of what to do or where to go. Evelyn had never been so still in her life as this moment. She wasn't sure if she was awake or dreaming. It all seemed so surreal.

The snarling creature was close, too close, she'd never escape it now. Her heart thundered in her chest. She barely had time to scream before a wall of darkness surged between them.

He moved like a force of nature, shadows bursting from his body fanning out like enormous wings. The air crackled with raw power, tendrils of black writhing around him as if they had a life of their own.

The creature yelped, twisting mid-air in a late attempt to escape, but it was too late.

He struck.

Then she heard the snap of bone, the wet squelch of flesh tearing—Evelyn flinched, hands flying to her mouth and covering her eyes.

It wasn't just that he killed. It was *how*.

The shadows swallowed the beast, consuming it in a rush of violent force. It shrieked once, then nothing—only the eerie quiet that followed. The darkness squeezed as the creature screamed and hissed, then burst into ash.

Evelyn's feet had never moved. Something was still calling to her from beyond the scene she'd just witnessed, something beyond the forests and the jagged mountains of Hell.

Come to me.

She saw a flash of white. Blinked. It was gone. Something was happening outside the castle grounds–a chaos that threatened to drag her in like a fish on a line. She felt her heart thump twice. Was that Thrush?

Come to me.

It was Alastor's voice in her head.

But then the creature that had nearly attacked her was neither. Evelyn was so confused.

Remington turned, his face half-lit by the ochre moonlight.

Evelyn blinked, remembering his hands on her body, his lips on her neck. She gasped.

His eyes were dark. Hollow. There was no green. Shadows still curled around him like living things clinging to his shoulders, his arms—his fingers twitched as if he were struggling to reign them back in.

He looked... *wrong*.

Like something *other*.

Evelyn took a step back, then another, her pulse wild.

He had saved her. But he had turned into something she didn't recognize. This was not the Remington that had kissed her sweetly in the hidden hallway of the castle.

Breath hitched in her throat.

Remington took a step forward, his voice rough. "Evelyn—"

The tugging in her center was strong, wanting her to go to the forest. She was so confused. She screamed.

Then she ran.

Her bare feet slammed against the stone path as she sprinted for the castle, her vision blurred with fear. The world spun, nausea roiling in her gut. Her body was weak, too weak, but she didn't stop, couldn't stop—

Remington's voice cut through the night. "I didn't want to kill him!"

Evelyn faltered but didn't turn back.

"I can't be killing like that," he yelled. "I will—to protect you. But I told you not to leave the grounds!"

She stumbled, panting, vision swimming. I didn't leave the grounds. I wasn't awake.

"I-I didn't know!" she cried, voice breaking as she backed toward the castle. This was like a bad dream. She blinked hard, trying to make it all make sense.

Remington's shadows receded, his expression twisted with something raw. "How many times should I tell you?"

Something inside her snapped.

"I don't know what's happening to me! Why are you being such a big asshole?" Her voice echoed off the castle walls and then she was running again, tears blurring her sight. She barely made it through the gates before her knees buckled.

Strong arms caught her.

Chel.

"Easy, girl. I won't hurt you." His deep voice rumbled as he steadied her, letting her cling to him for support. He didn't say anything about the way her body trembled, or how her breath hitched with barely contained sobs.

He just walked her back to her room, his presence grounding, his hand warm on her shoulder.

When they reached her door she hesitated, glancing back at the darkened halls.

Remington hadn't followed.

Chel sighed, watching her carefully. "He's not mad at you, you know."

Evelyn swallowed hard, her throat tight. "I don't—" She exhaled shakily. "I don't know what just happened."

Chel studied her, then gave a small nod.

"Get some rest," he said simply, before turning away. "There is a chaos in this realm that is difficult to explain."

Evelyn stepped inside her room and shut the door.

But sleep never came; only a few hot tears she hadn't wanted to let escape. Her fingers went to the scar on her head. "What am I doing?" she whispered to herself. "What is happening?" Her stomach twisted as she remembered what she'd seen. The demon... Remm had changed forms, he looked like a... *monster*.

Evelyn wasn't sure what she expected, she'd stepped away from everything she'd ever known. Heck, she was in a different realm that she never knew existed. She rubbed her head and wished for the carefree days of college with her best friend spent studying in the library and coffee and parties. Evelyn wiped at the tears streaming down her face. She couldn't go back in time, only forward. She couldn't make the strange sensation in her stomach go away. She sat on the bed and glanced around the room, gaze landing on her suitcase. Maybe she should just go home.

THIRTY-FOUR

Remington stood at the edge of the castle's outer walls, hands braced against the cold stone, shadows flickering around him like restless phantoms. His breathing was ragged, his mind a storm of frustration, guilt, and something darker—something clawing at his insides demanding *more*.

He shouldn't have lost control like that. He shouldn't have *terrified* her.

"Hell of a show back there," Chel's deep voice rumbled from behind him.

Remington exhaled sharply, but he didn't turn around. "Not in the mood."

Chel snorted. "Yeah? Well, I wasn't in the mood to chase after a sobbing human, but here we are."

Remington's grip on the stone tightened.

"Is she okay?" he asked after a moment.

"She's rattled." Chel leaned against the wall beside him, arms crossed. "I got her to her room. Didn't say much. Not that I blame her."

Remington pressed his knuckles to his forehead, trying to smother the infernal hum in his head. It had been building for weeks, growing louder, more insistent. It dulled when she was near, even in the slightest way...

His fangs ached at the memory of scraping her neck in the hallway earlier tonight. He'd rarely used them. He chose to drink from the bagged blood to prevent an unplanned blood bonding. The urge to use them on her was unbearable. Moreso since their time together in the hallway when she'd pressed against him and welcomed his dark desires.

"She doesn't remember walking outside," he muttered. "She doesn't know what's happening." Chel was quiet for a beat. "That's a problem. Right now, though? You need to get your shit together."

Remington barked out a hollow laugh. "You think I don't *know* that?"

Chel sighed, rubbing the back of his neck. "Listen. You can't keep doing this. She's human. Fragile. And you—you're barely keeping yourself in check." His golden eyes narrowed. "You're drinking more than usual. And it's not helping, is it?"

Remington didn't answer, only rubbed his mouth and pressed his tongue against his teeth.

Chel huffed. "You need to talk to your mother."

At that, Remington *did* turn, scowling. "You think my mother has the answer to *this*?"

"I think your mother has the answer to *everything*," Chel said dryly. "And you know it."

Remington clenched his jaw. He didn't want to admit it, but Chel was right. His mother had always known more than she let on. If anyone could help him understand what the hell was happening to him—

With a sharp exhale, he pulled out his phone.

Chel grinned, giving him a firm pat on the back. "Atta boy."

Remington shot him a glare before stepping away to make the call.

It rang twice before Meg's voice came through, warm and knowing.

"My sweet boy," she cooed. "I was wondering when you'd call."

Remington sighed, pinching the bridge of his nose. "Something's wrong with me."

Meg hummed. "No shit. Something's wrong because you keep denying yourself."

His chest tightened.

Meg continued, her voice deceptively light. "Let me guess. You're frustrated. Restless. Agitated. And I'd wager it has something to do with that lovely human you've been keeping close. I've met Evelyn a few times. She's a beautiful creature. Her aura is divine. Makes me want to bite her."

Remington stiffened. "I—"

"Don't you lie to me, my shadow heir."

He closed his eyes.

Meg's voice softened. "You're trying to fight what's natural. You're drawn to her. Her blood wants to soothe you, doesn't it? When she's near it dulls the noise?"

His grip on the phone tightened. "...Yes."

"Then stop denying yourself," she said simply. "If she's willing, take what you need. Claim what's already yours. Might be the best decision of your life."

There was a pause.

"You can ask your father how deep denial will take you." She whispered away from the phone and Remington recognized the sound of his father's deep voice.

"Do what she says, son," Sparrow's voice sounded.

Remington swallowed hard. His mother made it sound so *easy*.

Meg sighed, amused. "Oh, my dear boy. I've told you before. Don't be afraid to let your darkness out." Then, as if she were ordering dinner instead of urging him to give in to his instincts, she added, "But do try not to scare her to death in the process, will you?"

The line went dead.

Remington stood there for a long moment, staring at his phone.

Chel smirked. "Told you."

Remington exhaled, pocketing his phone. "Shut up, Chel."

Chel just chuckled. "So, what's the plan? Did you pick a day? I think Wednesday is a nice day to claim a pretty human forever."

Remington didn't answer right away. The Hellion's hearing was too good–he probably heard the entire phone conversation.

But in the back of his mind, his mother's words echoed against the constant hum.

"*Claim what's already yours.*"

THIRTY-FIVE

Evelyn stood in the castle's training courtyard, the air thick with the scent of stone and ash. Shadows stretched across the ground as the torches flickered against the looming walls. Chel stood in front of her, golden eyes gleaming with amusement.

"You sure about this, little human?" he drawled, tossing a short dagger from one hand to the other. "Shouldn't you be, I don't know, resting?"

Evelyn scowled. "I'm cleared for light activity. And that Angel woman, Teari, she said she healed me fully."

Chel arched a brow. "Self-defense isn't *light* activity."

"Flying then?"

Chel smirked. "That would cause princeling to anger."

Evelyn lifted her chin. "I need to be able to protect myself." Evelyn had a plan. She was going to learn to not need anyone, no protection. Then she wouldn't need to be in Hell, she could go home and protect herself. The confusion would be gone and she could let Remington go on with his life since she seemed to be interrupting so much for him. And then maybe he could go to therapy for his anger issues.

Chel studied her for a long moment before sighing. "Fine. But if you pass out, I'm throwing you over my shoulder and carrying you back inside. You'll be locked in your room with that damned basilisk."

"I'd like to see you try," she muttered.

Chel grinned. "Oh, I *like* you." He tipped his head to the side and Evelyn followed his gaze.

Remington's basilisk was there, in the distance, watching; scales glistening and body still. It looked like a giant snake in the grass.

Without warning, Chel lunged.

Evelyn barely had time to react before he was on her, moving impossibly fast. She yelped, stumbling backward, but Chel caught her wrist and twisted, pulling her off balance.

She hit the ground with a grunt.

"Lesson one," Chel said, standing over her. "You're *slow*."

Evelyn glared up at him. "No shit."

Chel offered his hand. She took it, and he hauled her to her feet effortlessly.

"Again," he ordered.

She braced herself as he came at her, this time managing to sidestep. Chel smirked but didn't let up, pressing forward, forcing her to react. She ducked, barely avoiding his grasp, but he was toying with her—she could see it in his expression.

Frustration burned in her chest.

Chel reached for her again, and this time, she *reacted*.

She swung her arm up, striking his wrist hard. He let go on instinct and she pivoted, kicking out. Her foot connected with his shin.

Chel grunted, stepping back.

Evelyn gasped, eyes wide. "Did I—?"

Chel grinned. "Not bad."

A flicker of pride swelled in her, but it was short-lived.

Chel moved faster than she could track, grabbing her and twisting her arm behind her back. He leaned in, his breath warm against her ear.

"Lesson two," he murmured. "If you hesitate, you lose." She was facing the forest. "I am a Hellion with ages of training. Those things out there, whatever is calling to you, they'll be chaotic and feral."

Evelyn struggled, but he held firm. "How do you know something is calling me?"

He squeezed her. "I can see the confusion in your eyes. And that night we found you out here you were not yourself. Half asleep and half awake."

Evelyn nodded.

"You're relying on human instincts," he continued. "That won't work here. You're in *Hell*, sweetheart. The things you'll face don't fight fair."

Evelyn swallowed hard. From the corner of her eye, it seemed the basilisk was closer.

Chel released her. "You need to stop thinking like prey."

She turned to face him, rubbing her wrist. "And how do I do that?"

Chel smirked. "By acting like a predator."

He tossed her the dagger. She caught it, barely. Fingers

fumbling, she gripped the hilt awkwardly. "I didn't go to college for this," she reminded him. "I'm usually deep in books and runes and rocks."

"That digging gave you muscle," he reminded her. "You're not starting from scratch."

Evelyn raised an arm, flexed exaggeratedly, and agreed. Slightly. There was some bicep that bulged.

"Let's try again," he urged.

This time, Evelyn didn't hesitate.

Evelyn sat in the garden courtyard, her back resting against the stone bench, twisting a vine between her fingers. The night air was cool against her skin, carrying the scent of damp earth and flowers. She pulled the cloak that Remington had bought her around her shoulders. Above her the sky stretched dark, pinpricked with the glow of distant stars. Somewhere beyond the hedges the sounds of the castle carried in muffled echoes—voices, the clink of goblets, the distant hum of a world she was still trying to understand.

But here, in the quiet, she could breathe. There were no judging eyes. No handsome dark princes to confuse her. Just her and the night and... the night was endless, it seemed. It went on forever and ever here, not like back home.

Evelyn shivered, felt it before she saw it—the weight of a gaze on her skin.

The basilisk.

Its presence was closer now, the rustle of scales against

stone just at the edge of the courtyard. It wasn't hiding. It was watching.

Evelyn's fingers stilled, the vine caught between them. She should have been afraid. A few weeks ago, she was terrified. She had run before, barely escaping the snapping jaws of another, but tonight, she vowed she wouldn't run again. She'd show Remington she was braver than before.

Evelyn plucked a small bouquet of Aster flowers and Black-eyed Susans, tying their stems together with a piece of vine. She set the bouquet in her lap and looked up.

Nothing moved.

Still, she felt it.

"You don't scare me," she murmured, testing the words on her tongue.

The basilisk didn't answer, but something in the air shifted. Not a threat. Not an attack. Just a lingering presence, like it was waiting. She wasn't sure what the damned thing might be waiting for. A pet on the head? She shivered. Hell to the no.

She exhaled, long and slow, and let herself relax against the stone. Her body was heavy with exhaustion from training with Chel, her muscles aching in a way that was almost soothing. The night wrapped around her like a thick blanket, and her eyelids grew heavy.

Just a moment, she told herself. She would just rest for a moment.

Her fingers loosened around the flowers. The world around her faded...

And then—

A voice.

Evelyn.

It was soft at first, curling around her like silk.

Come to me.

She stirred, but she did not wake.

The garden melted away, her consciousness caught somewhere between waking and sleep. A dream. But it didn't feel like one.

The air was different—warm and smoky with something rich, something intoxicating. The sensation of fingers grazing over her wrist sent a shiver through her body.

She felt him before she saw him.

Alastor.

His presence wrapped around her like a slow-moving tide, pulling her deeper. The dream sharpened. Her pulse fluttered.

You know where to find me.

Her body moved before her mind caught up. Still asleep, Evelyn stood.

The bouquet slipped from her lap, the flowers scattering across the stone. She turned toward the garden's edge, her bare feet ghosting over the cool earth.

She walked, drifting through the courtyard like a shadow, her path winding through the hedges and past the statues that lined the garden's perimeter. She stepped beyond the safety of the castle walls, past the heavy gates that had been left cracked open just enough.

No one noticed.

Not yet.

She moved deeper into the night, her steps silent, drawn by something unseen.

The forest loomed ahead, dark and waiting.

A figure stood at the edge of the trees.

Tall. Still.

A slow, knowing smile.

Arms, outstretched.

Evelyn walked straight into them.

"Welcome back, my sweet human."

Evelyn slumped against Alastor's body. He stretched one arm across her back, another under her knees and lifted her.

He smiled as he walked off into the night with Evelyn in his arms.

THIRTY-SIX

Remington stood in the office, arms crossed tightly over his chest, his patience wearing thin as the Hellion before him finished his report.

"Another sighting?" he muttered, rubbing a hand over his jaw.

"Yes, Your Highness," the Hellion said, shifting uncomfortably under his gaze. "Near the rock ridge. Just like before. He's getting closer."

Thrush was watching, waiting—but for what, Remington didn't know. Thrush never did anything for pure sport. There was something happening near the Black River that they hadn't realized.

And he didn't like it.

Remington exhaled sharply. "Double the patrols near the river. If anyone sees him again, I want to know immediately."

The Hellion bowed and left without another word.

Remington turned his gaze toward the dark window, his jaw tightening. He had other things to worry about, but this... this was a problem he couldn't ignore. Thrush was a problem, one he needed to solve quickly. The noise in his head suddenly got louder. Remington's mouth went dry and he moved toward the door; he needed blood.

A familiar voice interrupted his thoughts.

"Have you seen her?" Chel asked. His eyes narrowed as Remington rubbed the back of his head, the way he'd been doing when Evelyn was far from him and the noise in his head was becoming unbearable.

Remington turned. The Hellion's large form moved closer, but there was tension in his eyes.

Remington frowned. "What?"

Chel gave him a long, unimpressed look. "Don't be an idiot."

Evelyn.

Remington's stomach twisted, and he had to fight not to run. He hadn't seen her since the other day—since she had run from him, tears in her eyes, after he had lost his temper and killed the half-ling in the forest that had nearly attacked her. He'd let the darkness out, much more than ever before. Much more than he'd ever let anyone see.

After, he hadn't gone to her. He had wanted to, but something had kept him away. Guilt. Embarrassment. The memory of his own voice; too loud, too cruel. He needed to apologize. His sister would be disappointed to learn he'd waited this long. It was just... the way Evelyn had looked at him. Like he was something to be afraid of. Like he was a monster. Like he had disappointed her in the worst way. It was hard to grapple with human feelings.

His throat tightened. "She's in her room."

Chel's brows lowered. "No. She's not."

Remington stilled.

"She went to the courtyard after training," Chel said, glancing toward the gardens. "I figured she'd go rest afterwards, but when I checked just now, her room was empty." His expression darkened. "Something feels off."

Remington didn't wait to hear more.

He was already moving.

Chel followed, both of them striding through the long hallways of the castle, out the door and toward the stone archway and into the garden. It was dark, but the lanterns cast a soft golden glow over the cobbled paths and clusters of flowers.

She had been here.

Remington could feel it.

His gaze swept the area—and then he saw it. A small bouquet of flowers abandoned on the stone bench. The delicate petals had begun to wilt, the stems tangled with a thin piece of vine.

Something else caught his eye.

Her shoes.

Remington bent down, fingers brushing the cool leather. There was a pile of dark fabric. He lifted it and recognized the cape he'd bought her, embossed with snakes and flowers.

His stomach dropped.

"She was wearing those earlier," Chel said.

The basilisk was curled near the farthest edge of the courtyard, its massive body coiled, its unblinking gaze fixed on the tree line beyond the walls.

Watching.

Waiting.

Remington followed its stare. The realization struck him like ice down his spine.

"No," he whispered.

Chel stiffened beside him.

Hellions began collecting near them.

Remington's fingers clenched around Evelyn's abandoned shoes.

His heart thundered.

Darkness poured from his skin.

Evelyn was gone.

———

Remington stood in his room, methodically strapping his weapons into place. His blood burned beneath the surface, his teeth clenched so tight his jaw ached. The humming was deafening now; a rushing waterfall between his ears.

Chel stood near the doorway, arms crossed as he watched. He was already outfitted in his own battle gear, dark armor reinforced with infernal metal. His blade hung at his side. Concern was evident on his face.

"You're bringing that one?" Chel nodded toward the basilisk bone knife Remington had just secured at his belt.

"I used it in the war," Remington muttered, checking the fit. "It's never failed me."

Chel's eyes flickered with something unreadable, but he only grunted. He was there, he'd seen it. The blade was tipped with poison and would leave the stabbed paralyzed.

Remington tightened the strap and exhaled sharply. "Let's go. She's getting further from us with each passing minute."

They strode through the dim corridors of the castle, their footfalls heavy against the stone. The halls were quiet now. But the humming didn't care for silence. It was a drum in Remington's head, pulling him forward, leading him to her.

Chel cast him a sideways glance as they descended the staircase. "How exactly are we finding her?"

Remington didn't hesitate. "The noise."

Chel frowned. "The humming?"

"It's like a damn beacon," Remington said, adjusting his gloves. "Louder than it's ever been. I don't need a map. I just have to follow sound."

Chel nodded, but his face remained tense. Then, after a beat, he asked, "And what if someone claims her before you get there?"

Remington's gut twisted violently.

If that happened—if some other bastard got to her first, bound her to them before he could—

The humming would stop.

The bond would be sealed.

He'd kill them.

His grip tightened into fists. "That's not going to happen."

Chel arched a brow. "You sound awfully sure."

Remington scowled as they stepped outside, the cool night air greeting them. His basilisk lay coiled near the entrance, lifting its massive head as he approached.

"I'm sure," Remington growled.

"Should you eat something before you go?" Chel asked. "The blood?"

Remington shook his head. "I'm fine."

Chel was watching the dark prince closely. "You'll need the fuel."

Remington's phone was ringing in his pocket. He checked the screen. "Shit." He answered the call as he made his way to a nearby SUV and got behind the wheel.

"I had another dream," Rue's voice was panicked on the other end.

"Bad news," Remington grumbled as he slammed the driver side door closed. "She's missing."

"You have to find her!" Rue was nearly screaming.

"I'll find her."

"He has her." Dacre's voice was in the background. The phone clattered, sounded like it fell.

"Remm," Dacre's voice now. "She's having visions. Rapidly. You must find Evelyn."

"It's kinda hard when I'm on the phone." He threw the phone at Chel who was in the passenger seat and tore out of the driveway, into the night.

Thirty-Seven

Evelyn woke with a sharp breath.

The air smelled different—rich, spiced, laced with a metallic tinge. Her body felt heavy, as though she had slept too long. A chill crept over her skin as she sat up, her fingers pressing against the unfamiliar silk sheets beneath her.

This wasn't the castle.

Her pulse pounded in her ears. The room was dark, lit only by the flickering glow of candles. The walls were stone, smooth and polished so different from the fortress she'd come to know. The furniture was dark wood and deep velvet and there was an eerie stillness in the air.

Then, Evelyn saw him.

Alastor sat in a chair near the bed, legs crossed, watching her. His dark eyes gleamed in the candlelight and a lazy, satisfied smile curled his lips. In another life, he might be charming and devilishly handsome, but all that went to smoke the moment he tried to take Evelyn the first time.

Something on her wrist burned when she moved her arm.

Evelyn looked down, heart stuttering. Puncture marks, just like the ones that had healed beneath her ear. She touched it, a strange pulse thrumming beneath her fingertips.

Alastor sighed. "I'm trying to be gentle, but I couldn't help myself." He tilted his head, studying her. "Your blood tastes better than before."

Evelyn blinked, her mind sluggish, struggling to keep up. "I... I was sick."

"You're well now." His voice was smooth, like silk over steel. He shifted in his seat, his expression unreadable. "That's good. Very good."

Something cold coiled in her stomach.

Alastor leaned forward, resting his elbows on his knees. "I'm sorry I was so... forceful before. I didn't know what I was dealing with."

Evelyn's breath caught, her stomach twisted, and her skin prickled. Her last memory was of the garden. The flowers. The basilisk keeping its distance. She had sat down to rest—just for a moment. And then... Memories of the dream clawed their way to the surface—his touch, his voice calling her in the dark, the intoxicating pull, the way her body had moved without her permission like she had no choice.

She had no choice. Her eyes went wide. "Where am I?" Her hands curled into fists against the sheets.

A chair scraped softly across the floor.

She shoved the blankets off and stood abruptly, her legs trembling beneath her. "How did I get here?" She ignored the sinking feeling in the pit of her stomach.

Alastor's smile didn't falter, but there was something sharper beneath it now, something dangerous.

"You walked right into my arms, darling." He gestured toward the door. "Now, the question is... do you want to leave?" His brows rose. "I don't think you want to leave. I'll keep you safe. I'll keep you..." He licked his lips, contemplating his last words. "I will keep you."

And deep down, something whispered that she might already know the answer. Things were definitely stressed with Remington; so much was forbidden. There was so much she didn't know about this world.

The unfamiliar room was dim, flickering candlelight casting shadows across the dark stone walls. The sheets pooled around her feet, rich and silken, but they might as well have been chains. She closed her eyes and took a deep breath, the teeth marks on her wrist burning a sensation that sent a sickening dread curling in her stomach. No, this wasn't right. He was doing something to her. His voice was hypnotic.

She pressed her hands to her temples. "No," she whispered. "No, I—I was in the garden." Evelyn's pulse pounded. "Leave me alone." She forced herself to take a step away from him, ignoring the dizziness that followed.

He tilted his head, watching her as if she were something rare, something breakable. "Having some fight in you is good." He shifted, crossing his legs. "You came to me," he repeated, his lips curving as if amused by a private joke.

"No," she whispered. "That's not possible." Evelyn swallowed hard. The mark on her wrist pulsed again.

His dark eyes gleamed. "Isn't it?" he said simply, stepping closer. "I called and you came. Willingly." He reached out, but she jerked away. His smirk didn't falter.

"I wouldn't—"

He moved fast, closing the distance between them and caught her chin between his fingers, forcing her to look up at him. His touch was deceptively gentle but she could feel the power beneath it, coiling and waiting.

"You will again," he murmured, his breath ghosting over her skin. "Even now, you hear me, don't you? That little hum in the back of your mind, the pull in your chest. You might try to fight it, but your body knows the truth."

Evelyn shuddered, her breath uneven.

"You started this. You called me and never stopped." His lips brushed against her temple as he whispered, "No matter where you go, I will find you. And when you sleep, I will call you back to me."

Evelyn couldn't move. She was more confused than ever.

She took a step toward the door, then another, eyes locked on his. He didn't stop her. She reached for the handle, expecting resistance, but it turned easily in her grasp.

Evelyn hesitated.

"You can go," Alastor said, stretching back in his chair, his hands folding in his lap. "If you truly want to."

Her heart thundered. This felt too easy. She wrenched open the door, her bare feet moving swiftly across the cold floor. The corridor beyond was long, twisting, bathed in the same candlelit glow. She ran, taking turns at random, searching for anything familiar.

But the halls stretched endlessly, shifting in ways that made her question her own steps.

She stopped, panting, her palms pressed against the cool stone wall. The air was thick with something strange. Something that tugged at her chest, whispered in her ear, lulled her into a strange, dangerous calm.

"Where are you going?" Alastor's voice drifted toward her, though he was nowhere in sight.

Evelyn turned sharply, eyes darting between the empty halls. She could still feel his presence. He was everywhere, thick and suffocating, curling around her like smoke.

She forced herself forward, picking up speed, willing herself to ignore the pull in her gut. *Keep moving. Keep moving.*

The corridor suddenly opened into a vast room with towering windows, moonlight casting a pale glow over the polished floor. A door stood at the far end—massive, iron-wrought. *That's it. That has to be the way out.*

She sprinted for it.

Alastor materialized beside her in a whisper of movement. One second, she was alone. The next, his presence was at her back, an unseen force, a warmth curling over her shoulder.

"You can run," he murmured, his breath just ghosting over her ear. "But I'll always find you again. And you'll want me to."

Her fingers brushed the handle.

"You'll dream of me."

She flinched, shoving the door open, her heart hammering.

"You'll beg me to call to you," he said, his voice as soft as silk. "And you'll come back to me."

She stumbled into the cold night air, her feet pressing against damp grass. A shudder ran through her as she turned, expecting to see him standing in the doorway, smirking at her panic.

But the door was gone.

The entire structure—the hallways, the massive windows, the stone walls—had vanished, swallowed by... she was back in the bedroom.

Evelyn's breath shook as she looked at the furnishings surrounding her. Had she ever left the room? Her arms trembled as she looked down at the bite mark on her wrist.

A shiver crept down her spine.

"Even if you got out, you'd come back to me." Alastor touched her hair.

He sounded so sure.

Thirty-Eight

Evelyn stood before a gilded mirror, fists clenched at her sides as she stared at her reflection. The dress Alastor had given her was draped across her body like a second skin—deep crimson, the fabric shifting like liquid when she moved. It was beautiful but it felt wrong, like a costume meant to parade her around rather than clothe her. The neckline dipped lower than she would've liked, and the delicate golden chains woven through the bodice gave the impression of something binding.

Alastor appeared behind her in the reflection, his presence coiling around her like smolder from an ember. His dark eyes flicked over her, approval evident in his smirk. "You look perfect," he murmured.

Evelyn swallowed hard, refusing to meet his gaze. "Where are we going?"

"You'll see soon enough."

She clenched her fists; arguing felt pointless. Every time she pushed, he pulled, and somehow she ended up right where he wanted her anyway. Speaking with him was an endless riddle and escape was an endless maze.

A vehicle waited outside–sleek, and dark. Evelyn climbed in without another word, her stomach twisting.

The journey was quiet except for the rhythmic clatter of tires against loose stone. She tried to ignore the way Alastor watched her, the way his gaze lingered too long as if he were memorizing every inch of her.

She spent too many days with him and had learned that the look meant he'd be asking for her wrist soon enough. And she'd watch him bite and lick and attempt to seduce her. She shivered at the memories. She hated them.

The Black Mansion loomed ahead. Gas lamps flickered along the entrance, their glow barely penetrating the thick mist curling around the estate.

The vehicle stopped at the steps and Alastor helped her out, like a gentleman. His touch made her tremble.

The moment she stepped inside the mansion, Evelyn felt the air buzzing with tension. Murmurs filled the vast hall and as she lifted her gaze, her stomach dropped.

She recognized the creatures and half-lings.

The men from the spring ball.

These were the ones who had forced her into their arms, spinning her around like she was nothing more than an amusement, a temporary possession to be admired and then discarded. And yet, their eyes now held something darker.

Recognition.

Understanding.

Desire.

Alastor had something dark planned for her.

"No, Evelyn whispered. "I don't want to be here."

"You called us. This is fate." Alastor's hand pressed lightly against the small of her back, guiding her forward. She wanted to shove him away and bolt, but she held herself still, refusing to show fear. She took a shallow breath.

A man stepped into her path, his lips curling in a knowing smirk. "Didn't think we'd see you again so soon," he murmured, his breath fanning across her cheek.

Evelyn's body tensed, disgust curling in her gut. "Get away from me."

He chuckled, tilting his head. "You don't understand, do you?" His fingers brushed against her wrist, grazing the faint mark Alastor had left. "And now we know exactly what you are." He was looking her up and down. "And I can't wait to taste you for the first time now that the Dark Prince has abandoned you."

Evelyn yanked her hand back, heat rising to her cheeks. Before she could stop herself, she lifted her palm and slapped him hard across the face. The sound echoed through the hall, sharp and final.

The murmurs stopped.

The man touched his cheek, stunned for only a second before his expression darkened. "You're going to regret that."

Alastor's chuckle slithered through the silence. "Careful," he said lazily. "She's still mine. She's merchandise. And a fragile human. Don't mark her."

Evelyn's breath hitched. Mine.

A cage. A claim.

She shot a desperate glance at the doors, at the

windows, at the unfamiliar faces watching her with hungry eyes. No way out.

Her heart pounded as she prayed, silently, desperately.

Remington, please find me.

Alastor tugged her along and into a large room. The demons around the grand chamber sat in a semi-circle of velvet-draped chairs, their expressions a mix of hunger, amusement, and vicious anticipation.

Evelyn stood at the center of it all, barely breathing. She felt like an animal being led to slaughter, a rare prize displayed for the highest bidder. The weight of their gazes pressed down on her, suffocating and sharp, and no matter how hard she willed herself to stay strong, fear coiled deep in her chest.

A voice rang out, smooth and cruel.

"Shall we start the bidding?"

Evelyn flinched at Alastor's words, at the casual way he addressed the gathered demons. His fingers brushed the small of her back, light as a whisper, but the touch burned like a brand. She forced herself not to recoil, not to let them see the way her hands trembled at her sides. She looked up at him, eyes wide. If Remington wasn't going to come for her, then Alastor was her only hope. The man was barely hanging on, all the words he'd whispered to her in that bedroom as he drank from her wrist were truth. He wanted her.

The first bid came almost instantly.

"Five thousand soul shards."

"Seven."

"Ten."

"Fifty."

"Two hundred."

The numbers rose quickly, too quickly. Evelyn's stomach twisted, her breath catching as she scanned the crowd. Their eyes glowed with dark fire, their faces eager, expectant. Some she recognized and some were strangers entirely—demons and half-breeds of old bloodlines, all drawn to her by something she couldn't control.

The sacrifice stone.

She swallowed hard.

One demon stood from his chair, smirking. "Two hundred and twenty thousand soul shards." He licked his lips. "And I'll make it worth her while."

A sickening wave of laughter rippled through the room. Evelyn's fingers curled into fists. She thought for a moment then grabbed Alastor's free hand.

"Let me stay with you," she whispered under her breath, eyes pleading. She used every spec of innocence and charm left in her body. "Don't let them take me. I'm worth more than whatever they'll give you." She glanced up at him, eyes wide. "A lifetime of fresh blood. A lifetime together."

Alastor swallowed hard and reached forward, fingers touching her neck. "I missed feeding from here."

Evelyn nodded in feigned agreement. Before another bid could be called—

Alastor let out a slow, exaggerated sigh and clapped his hands together once. "Actually..." he drawled, "I've changed my mind."

Silence fell.

Evelyn's heart lurched as the words settled in the air.

One of the demons stood sharply, his chair scraping

against the floor. "You *what*?" His sharp horns gleamed under the chandelier's dim light. "You called this auction, *Alastor*. You don't get to—"

"Ah," Alastor cut in smoothly, "but I *do*." His lips curled into a slow, cruel smirk. "Because I've changed my mind. She is mine. The sacrifice is nearly claimed between us."

The room erupted into shouts.

Alastor ignored them all, grabbing Evelyn by the wrist and dragging her toward the exit.

"Wait—" she struggled, but his grip was iron.

A clawed hand shot out, grabbing Alastor's shoulder. "You're betraying us," the demon snarled, his teeth bared. "You called us here for nothing but a tease—"

Alastor turned so quickly that Evelyn barely registered the movement. His free hand shot out, claws raking across the demon's throat in a single, effortless motion.

Blood sprayed the marble floor.

The demon choked, stumbling back, gurgling.

Evelyn barely bit back a scream.

"Anyone else?" Alastor asked, lazily shaking the blood from his fingers.

No one moved.

"Good."

And with that, he yanked Evelyn through the doors and into the night.

***

The moment they arrived back at his estate Alastor dragged her inside, his grip still tight on her wrist.

He didn't speak. He didn't acknowledge her frantic heartbeat or the way she stumbled in her heels to keep up with his pace. He didn't let go of her until they reached the room he'd kept her in, where he finally shoved her forward.

Evelyn caught herself against the edge of a dark wooden table, her pulse hammering. "What the fuck was that?" she spat.

"Now don't play games, little human." Alastor only smirked. "I heard your begging, little sacrifice. The whole room heard you beg me."

"Don't call me that."

He stepped forward, eyes gleaming. "I like calling you that. And you just admitted that you want me. That you'd rather stay with me."

Evelyn clenched her teeth, willing herself not to step back. "Why did you stop the auction?"

"Because I decided I didn't want to share."

Her breath hitched.

Alastor reached out, trailing a single finger along the mark on her wrist—the one he'd left there. "You're right, a lifetime of fresh blood is worth more than a million souls for a creature like me."

Evelyn swallowed hard. She glanced at the door, wishing Remington's face would appear.

Thirty-Nine

The road stretched endlessly before Remington, shrouded in twilight as he gripped the wheel of the SUV, its engine growling like a beast. The tires kicked up dust from the cracked asphalt.

Chel sat in the passenger seat, arms crossed, his hulking form barely fitting comfortably in the confined space. His sharp eyes remained fixed ahead.

For a long while, there was nothing but the rhythmic hum of the tires and the noise inside Remington's head—a persistent, low vibration like a distant song only he could hear. It had been guiding him, drawing him toward Evelyn like an invisible tether, but... it was getting weaker.

Remington clenched his jaw, his fingers tightening on the steering wheel. He exhaled sharply through his nose; trying to focus, trying to push past the gnawing sense of unease slithering up his spine.

Then the hum flickered, like a candle about to go out. He sucked in a breath.

Remington's foot pressed harder on the gas. "Something's wrong."

Chel turned his head slightly. "What?"

"The humming noise that led me to her before is fading." Remington's voice was low, controlled, but the tension in his shoulders betrayed his growing anxiety.

Chel straightened. "This is not good."

"No, it's not."

A moment passed. Remington didn't want to think about what it meant, but he knew. If the call was fading it meant someone else was trying to claim her.

Chel shifted, cracking his knuckles. "How bad?"

Remington ground his teeth together. "Bad."

The humming pulsed again—one final whisper in his skull—then... vanished.

Remington jerked the car to the side of the road, throwing it into park. His breath hitched and he sat in absolute stillness, waiting for the hum to return. It didn't. He gripped the sides of his head and sucked in a breath.

"No."

His pulse thundered in his ears.

Chel exhaled through his nose, rubbing his chin. "Talk to me, Princeling."

Remington swallowed, his throat dry. "It stopped. Someone claimed her or..."

Chel let out a slow, measured breath. "She's dead."

The words hit like a punch to the ribs. Remington's fingers curled into fists against the steering wheel, his claws digging into the leather. A growl rumbled in his chest, but it wasn't anger—it was something far worse.

Regret.

He had waited too long. Let his own damn hesitation put her in more danger. He should have claimed her before anyone else had the chance. He should have done what his mother told him to do.

Now, she was in someone else's hands.

Chel watched him carefully. "Remm... Hit that gas pedal or I'll toss you out of the driver's seat and do it myself."

Remington slammed his palm against the wheel, the entire car shaking with the force of it. "I waited too long." His voice was raw, thick with frustration.

Chel didn't argue. Instead, he reached over and gripped Remington's shoulder, steady and firm. "Then let's get her back. Pedal to the metal, boy."

Remington exhaled sharply through his nose, then nodded.

He threw the car into drive, and the engine roared as he sped forward into the dark.

FORTY

"I've been doing some digging," Alastor murmured. "The sacrifice stone hasn't been activated in ages, but I figured out what needs to be done."

Evelyn's stomach turned. "What... what do you mean?"

His smile widened. "I have to *drain* you, little sacrifice. Nearly all of your blood. Then give you some of my blood and only then, will the ritual be complete. We'll be bonded forever. You'll never leave me."

A cold sweat broke out along Evelyn's back.

She was unsure of what to say to him. This game had gone on too long. She closed her eyes, realizing there was no hope of escape. She could barely breathe with the thought of being bound to Alastor for the rest of her life. She'd never see her friends again, never spend hours in the library researching with Rue. She'd never have a real family. Her eyes burned with tears.

Alastor tsked. "Now, now. Don't fret. This is what you asked for. This is what you wanted."

Before she could react, before she could lunge for the

door or claw at him, hands wrapped around her wrists, tugging her arms behind her back.

Panic flared, sharp and instant. "Alastor—"

"Shh," he cooed. "This will take some time. But don't worry, I'll keep you comfortable."

Her body trembled.

No. No, no, no—

Alastor tilted his head, watching her with a gaze that was almost affectionate. "Don't look so scared, Evelyn. I told you before you can't run from me. Even if you tried, I'd only find you again. You'd return to my side, begging for this."

He leaned in close, whispering, "Just like before."

Evelyn's breath hitched.

His lips grazed the shell of her ear. "Go on, fight it. Try to resist. But we both know how this ends."

Darkness swam at the edges of her vision, exhaustion settling into her bones.

Her body wasn't her own.

It hadn't been for some time now.

And as the grip tightened around her wrists, as Alastor traced a finger along the pulsing vein in her throat, she realized one thing with terrifying clarity... she wasn't strong enough to escape him.

FORTY-ONE

THE ESTATE WAS NESTLED DEEP WITHIN THE withered trees, a structure of dark stone and ancient wood, barely more than a ruin. The air here was thick, stagnant, tainted with the scent of damp earth and something sharper—something metallic. Blood.

Remington's fists clenched as he stalked forward, his eyes narrowing on the dim glow seeping from the cracks in the boarded-up windows. The humming had never returned, but his instincts, sharper than any magic, had led him here.

Chel moved beside him, his steps unnaturally quiet for his size. "There's no way he's keeping her in a place like this without some kind of protection." His voice was low, wary.

"I don't care," Remington growled.

They reached the outer wall, pressing into the shadows. The wind rattled the trees, whispering through the skeletal branches like a warning.

Chel tilted his head, scanning the perimeter. "There's a back entrance, but I guarantee it's warded."

Remington ignored him. His gaze had locked onto something else. A window—partially covered, just enough for him to see inside.

His stomach dropped.

Evelyn.

She was laying on a bed; she looked so pale, so small. Her head lolled to the side, golden hair tangled around her whitish face, and her chest barely moved with each shallow breath. Her shirt and jeans were torn, her skin marred with the faint remnants of dried blood.

A handprint stained her wrist, dark and unnatural.

Remington's blood turned to fire.

He didn't think. He moved.

With a snarl, he launched forward, driving his shoulder into the door. The wood splintered on impact, shattering inward as he barreled through.

Alastor stepped from the shadows of the room, his mouth curled into a smirk that barely hid his surprise. "Well, well. You're interrupting."

Remington didn't answer. He lunged.

Their bodies collided, the force shaking the foundation. Alastor twisted, dodging the first blow, but Remington was faster—he drove a fist into Alastor's ribs, hearing the satisfying crack of bone.

Alastor staggered but recovered quickly, his claws flashing as he swiped for Remington's throat.

Remington ducked, pivoting sharply, and slammed Alastor against the wall. The impact sent dust raining from the ceiling, the stones groaning beneath the force.

"You took what wasn't yours," Remington growled, his voice dark and full of venom.

Alastor grinned, blood trickling from the corner of his mouth. "You hesitated. I pounced on opportunity. You're slow, just like your fucking parents."

Rage surged through Remington. He grabbed Alastor by the throat and squeezed, forcing him down.

"You don't get to touch her," he snarled. Dark shadows escaped his shoulders in tendrils, wrapping around Alastor like a snake.

Alastor choked out a laugh. "You think you've won? Look at her." His eyes flicked toward Evelyn. "You're too late, Prince. She's mine. Forever."

Remington's gut twisted, but he didn't loosen his grip. He didn't look at Evelyn. He wasn't going to risk distraction ever again.

Behind him, Chel moved swiftly, cutting Evelyn's restraints with a blade. She slumped forward, barely conscious, and Chel caught her, his large hands gentle as he checked her pulse.

Remington saw the movement in his periphery and made his decision.

He drove his fist into Alastor's face.

The impact sent the demon sprawling, his body hitting the ground in a crumpled heap. He wasn't dead—not yet.

He would be soon.

Alastor laughed as he stood. "Your father tried this once before. Your mother too." Blood was dripping out of his nose.

"I am not my parents," Remington seethed. "I am something much worse."

Don't be afraid to let your darkness out. His mother's words echoed through his mind.

As the room darkened, Chel gave him space and let him do the honors.

Dark tendrils wrapped around Alastor and kept him still.

Remington gripped his basilisk blade and in one swift movement, cut a crescent across Alastor's throat. Blood spilled down the Demon's chest and his eyes went wide.

"You will never threaten our family again," Remington spat as the life drained from Alastor's body.

Alastor dropped to the ground. Remington's shadows followed, wrapping around him like a sheet, squeezing every last molecule of air and blood from his body until the creature turned to dust.

He turned, his breath still ragged, and strode toward Evelyn.

Chel was already lifting her into his arms, her body limp against his chest.

"We need to get her out of here," Chel said, his voice steady despite the tension in his stance. "I'll hold her until you're calm."

Remington nodded, his eyes lingering on Evelyn's face. His entire body felt like it was on fire. He waited for the hum to return, the call of sacrifice stone but it didn't come, which could only mean she was dead.

"The healing cave on the Earthen plane." Remington headed to the SUV. "Come on. I have to get her there as fast as possible."

Without another word, they turned and carried her into the night.

FORTY-TWO

The tires screeched against the dark road, kicking up dust and gravel as Remington pressed the gas pedal to the floor. The SUV's engine roared, but it wasn't fast enough. Remington sighed with relief as the hum in his head returned, though faint, but it wasn't guiding him—it was warning him. Evelyn was closer to slipping away for good in the back seat and with every second that passed, she faded further.

Chel sat in the back, his massive frame crammed into the seat as he held Evelyn close, his hands pressing against the worst of her wounds. Bitemarks—too many—leaked blood that soaked through her clothing, her skin pale as moonlight. Her breath came in shallow, uneven gasps.

"Stay with us, Evelyn," Chel muttered, adjusting his grip, his hands practically shaking. He pulled his phone from his pocket, dialing Rue and Dacre with one hand while keeping Evelyn steady with the other.

The call connected. "Chel?" Rue's voice came through, sharp with concern.

"Meet us at the research caves. Now," Chel ordered. "She's in bad shape."

"What happened?" Dacre's voice cut in.

"I had a vision of this." Rue's voice broke with a whimper. "I told you."

"No time," Chel snapped. "Get there." He ended the call before they could ask anything else. Next, he called the nearest Hellion outpost and instructed them to fire up the portal, setting it to connect in the mountains where Rue and Evelyn had dug up the sacrifice stone.

Remington's hands tightened around the steering wheel, his knuckles bone-white. His mind was a storm, rage and fear clashing in violent bursts. He should've claimed her. He should've stopped this before it even started. The thought burned through him like fire.

The Hellion portal loomed ahead, a shimmering tear in reality itself. It flickered between the worlds near a Hellion outpost. Dark shadows lurked nearby as he approached.

The SUV skidded to a violent stop. Before the dust could settle, Remington was already out, yanking the back door open. He reached for Evelyn, lifting her into his arms. She barely reacted—her head lolled against his chest, her fingers twitching weakly against his jacket.

Chel stepped out after him but hesitated, watching Remington warily. His energy was wrong—dark, unstable. The same eerie, consuming force that had erupted from him when he'd lost control the other day now radiated off him in waves. Shadows coiled tighter around his body, creeping toward Evelyn, as if they wanted to claim her for themselves.

"Princeling," Chel said carefully, stepping forward. "Are you—"

Remington's glare cut to him, sharp enough to make even a Hellion pause. "I'm not losing her." His voice was raw, guttural, like he was barely keeping himself together. "I'm fine. I won't hurt her."

Chel exhaled sharply but nodded. He wouldn't get in the way. Not now.

Without another word, Remington stepped into the portal.

The shift between realms was immediate—a pull deep in the chest, a snap of pressure that normally made Evelyn sick. But this time, she didn't stir. She didn't gag or sway. She didn't even move.

And that terrified him.

Remington's boots hit solid ground on the other side, the crisp night air of the Earthen plane cutting against his overheated skin. The distant, looming silhouette of the mountains stretched ahead and nestled among them, the research site—the only place that held a chance at saving her.

He adjusted his grip on her, pressing a kiss to her forehead.

"Just hold on, Evelyn," he murmured. "We're almost there."

The hum returned to Remington's brain. But it was stuttering, flickering, static sound. Almost as if it was dying with her.

FORTY-THREE

Remington's boots crunched against loose rock as he adjusted Evelyn's weight in his arms, holding her closer.

He made his way down the abandoned road he'd driven months ago when he didn't know where the humming in the back of his mind was taking him. It all seemed too strange now. Whatever this location was ages ago was starting to come into focus. A portal at the mountain peak, caves with runes and history that had been abandoned and forgotten, and the healing waters of the cave pool was clearly a connection between realms. Which meant there must've been a time when the Earthen plane was very aware of the close connection of Hell.

Remington didn't feel the burn in his legs as he ran, carrying Evelyn. He veered to the left, toward the opening in the forest canopy where he'd found Evelyn alone at the dig site months ago. He noticed Dacre and Rue's SUV.

Ahead, the entrance to the cave yawned wide, a gaping wound in the mountainside. And waiting at its mouth, Rue and Dacre stood with anxious expressions, their figures illuminated by the soft glow of lanterns.

The second Rue caught sight of Evelyn she gasped, one hand flying to her mouth. Tears spilled down her cheeks before she even spoke. "Oh, no—Remington, what happened?"

Remington didn't stop moving. He couldn't. "Alastor," he gritted out. "Where's the water?"

Dacre shot Rue a glance before stepping forward, gesturing toward the darkened cave behind them. "This way," he said, his usual smooth tone edged with concern.

Rue sniffled, wiping her face as she fell in step beside them. "The runes," she said, voice unsteady. "They say that only the sacrifice and the claimant can enter the water."

Remington's stomach tightened. "What do they say, exactly?"

Dacre ran a hand through his hair. "That the waters were meant for the ill and their guardian. No one else can pass beyond the threshold." His gaze flickered to Evelyn's limp form.

"Stay close then." Remington's voice was rough, almost bitter. But now wasn't the time for that. Not when she was still bleeding out in his arms and on the edge of death.

Rue took a shaky breath. "Just... be careful. And Remington?"

He looked at her.

She reached out, her fingers brushing Evelyn's cold hand. "Bring her back. Whatever it takes. She's always liked you since the moment you two met. Maybe this has always been your destiny, together."

Remington gave a sharp nod and pushed forward into the cave.

Inside, the air grew thick with the scent of old stone and lingering magic. The walls were slick with condensation, carved with ancient runes that pulsed faintly. Shadows stretched long and deep, curling along the uneven ground like reaching fingers.

The hum in his head, the one that had guided him through Hell and the Earthen plane, was deafening now. It gave him hope that she would live.

Evelyn stirred weakly in his arms, her breath barely a whisper against his collar. "Almost there," he murmured, more to himself than to her.

Following the tunnel, he finally stepped into a cavern that stretched high above him, its ceiling lost to the darkness. And there, in the center, lay the pool.

It wasn't large—only about twenty feet across—but the water glowed with an eerie, silvery-blue light, shimmering as though stars had been trapped beneath its surface. The air here was heavier, thick with old, forgotten power.

Remington swallowed hard. The White Horse had said this place hadn't been used in ages, maybe longer. Would it still work? Would it be enough?

There was only one way to find out.

He kicked his boots off and walked forward.

Remington stepped into the pool, his breath hitching as the water lapped against his legs, then his waist. It was warmer than he expected, thick with ancient magic that sent a shiver up his spine. The glow from the water cast eerie reflections on the cavern walls, illuminating the neglected runes carved into the stone. He recognized some of them.

Evelyn lay limp in his arms; her skin cold, her lips pale. The deep crimson of her wounds had smeared against his shirt, the sight twisting something primal inside of him.

"Come back." He dipped lower, submerging her body except for her face; watching, waiting. The water swirled around her as if testing, tasting. He felt the magic tremble, uncertain, as if the pool itself had forgotten its purpose after being untouched for so long.

"Come back. Come back. *Come back to me.*" His voice was a strained whisper, begging. "I'm not well without you." He touched her chin. "I cannot *do this.*"

Remington's throat tightened as he cradled her closer, pressing his forehead against hers, the damp strands of her hair clinging to his skin. The scent of her blood was still thick in the air, but beneath it, he swore he could still catch the faintest trace of her—something sweet, something alive. Something like sunshine.

"My fingertips will remember every curve. Every touch. Forever." He swallowed hard, his voice breaking. "I... I cannot live like this without you. *Please.* Ev. Come back to me."

Beyond the cavern entrance, Rue stood motionless, her breath caught in her throat. She had heard him—every raw, vulnerable word.

Dacre gently pulled her away, shaking his head and pressing a finger to his lips.

Rue blinked up at him, realization dawning. This was private. A confession Remington hadn't meant for anyone to hear. No man would willingly bear his soul like this with witnesses.

And yet, as she glanced one last time at the shadowed figures in the water, she knew.

He loved Evelyn.

And if she didn't wake up soon, she wasn't sure what would become of him.

Remington's hands trembled as he brushed wet strands of hair from Evelyn's face. The bruises along her neck stood out against her pale skin; deep bruises marring the delicate column of her throat. He forced himself to breathe, to shove the rage aside, but it burned in his chest like a slow-building fire. Shadows threatened to escape his body and crush something into ash.

"What happened to you? What did Alastor do?" His voice was lower now; raw, controlled only by sheer will. He hated himself for avoiding her for that single day. He should have apologized for shouting at her and kept her by his side all day long. He should have leaned into her touch and smiled at her laugh. He'd felt bare without her there asking questions and listening to the needs and wants of the local demons. She was a light at his side, one he didn't know he needed.

Evelyn made a small noise, something between a sigh and a whimper, and tipped her face away.

His grip tightened around her, not to hold her captive, but to anchor her—to remind her that she wasn't alone anymore. When he tipped her chin slightly, guiding her to look at him, she didn't resist. But she also didn't meet his gaze. Her eyes were dull.

Remington swallowed hard. *She was different.*

The Evelyn he knew—the one who had stubbornly refused to be intimidated by Hell's dangers, who teased him with mischievous smiles and quick wit—was gone. He could see it in her eyes, or rather, in how she refused to look at him.

So much had happened in the days she'd been gone. He could feel the weight of it pressing against her shoulders, curling her in on herself. She had given up. Her light had shattered.

He remembered what Rue had said about humans. Words had meaning.

He sank further into the water, making himself smaller so he wasn't looming over her. "Ev, look at me."

She hesitated but finally let her gaze flick up to meet his. There it was—the dull sheen of exhaustion, of hurt. The sheen of unshed tears.

Her lips parted slightly, and when she spoke, her voice was so soft he almost didn't catch the words. "I really liked you, Remington."

He stiffened.

"But your sister told us no... and I have to move on. You were never coming back. And you were so mad. I made you so angry. Just let me go."

The words cut deeper than he expected.

Rue had told her no. She'd told both of them no, but she'd changed her mind.

Evelyn had *wanted* him, too. Maybe not in the same all-consuming, maddening way he had wanted her, but still... it had been there. She'd begged him to use his teeth on her, completely disregarding the fact that she'd lose her humanity. And he had avoided her.

His jaw tightened. He had left her unclaimed in Hell.

And Alastor had been waiting.

The realization made his rage rise like a tide, but he forced himself to push it down. None of that mattered now.

Only one thing did.

"I'm here now. And I'm never leaving. I'll never let you out of my sight again. Never."

She gave a soft, humorless laugh, but it wasn't the kind he liked—the teasing, playful sound she used when she was pushing his buttons. This one was hollow, lifeless.

Remington reached out, brushing his knuckles against her cheek. The second she flinched, his stomach dropped.

He yanked his hand back as if burned. In such a short time, Alastor had hurt her enough to make her scared of touch.

His teeth clenched so hard he could feel the sharp points digging into his tongue.

He took a slow breath, then softened his tone. "Close your eyes. You're safe now."

Evelyn hesitated for a moment, but then her lashes fluttered shut. "Just let me go..." she whispered. A tear fell from the corner of her eye and into the water.

Remington held her against his chest as the cave glowed

softly around them, his grip tightening protectively. He'd hold her like this for as long as she needed. Forever even. He'd never let her go.

Remington felt the shift before he saw it.

A pulse of energy rippled through the water, spreading from the ancient stone walls of the cave and moving over his skin like a whisper of fire.

The runes tattooed along his arms and chest began to glow, a soft golden light threading through the inked markings. He sucked in a sharp breath, watching as the glow from the walls resonated with his own markings, like two forces recognizing each other. His Uncle Jed had given him the tattoos as a teenager, runes of protection and strength. It was old Nephilim magic. He looked from his skin to the stone walls; there was definitely a connection between realms here. Without a doubt.

And then—Evelyn stirred.

The bruises along her throat, the ghostly pallor of her skin, the shallow rise and fall of her chest—it all began to change. Her skin took on a warm, healthy glow, the water around them shimmering as if responding to the shift.

Remington tightened his grip around her. "Ev?"

Her lashes fluttered. A deep inhale shuddered through her as her eyes blinked open, dazed but finally clear.

She looked at him, blinking against the dim silvery light that surrounded them. Her brows knit together in confusion. "What happened?"

Relief hit him so hard he nearly crushed her to his

chest. Instead he let out a ragged breath, his forehead resting against hers for a fraction of a second.

"You almost died."

She stared at him, her expression unreadable. Then she let out a slow exhale, her lips curving in a wry smile. "Seems to be a habit of mine, especially since I met your family."

Remington huffed out a breath, his grip on her tightening. "Not one I intend to let you keep."

She looked down, frowning at the water lapping around them. "The water... it healed me?"

"Not just the water." Remington let his hand drift to her wrist, where the faintest shimmer of Alastor's bitemark had disappeared.

Evelyn's fingers brushed over it absently, curiosity flashing in her eyes. "You're glowing."

Remington shifted slightly, adjusting her in his arms. "It's the sacrifice stone." His voice was lower now, strained. Remington swallowed. "And... it's changed everything. You've been claimed now, officially."

"About time, princeling." Her lips parted, waiting for him to continue.

His fingers trailed up her arm, barely a whisper of touch, but the connection between them *burned*. He could feel the pulse of her blood—*his* blood now, too— beating in rhythm with his own. The hunger in his chest was not just physical. It was deeper, older than he could name.

He hesitated, then finally admitted, "I need your blood." His throat bobbed as he forced the words out. "I need *you*. And you need me. I will *not* let you go."

Evelyn didn't flinch. She didn't shrink away.

The water lapped around them, warm and charged with the energy still pulsing from the glowing runes.

Remington's eyes were bright green, but dark with something deeper than hunger.

"Evelyn." His voice was raw, his hands steady but tense as they held her. "If we do this... if I bite you, if you take my blood... there's no undoing it. The bond will be permanent."

She didn't hesitate. "I know."

"You'll be forever changed." His fingers flexed around her waist, muscles taut as if bracing himself. "You're not afraid?"

Evelyn shook her head, lips curving into a small, knowing smile. "Not of you. Not of being with you."

Something in him cracked, his grip tightening. "You should be. Your safety will always be at risk."

But she wasn't. Not when he looked at her like that, as though she was the only thing in existence.

Her hands slid up his chest, over the glowing runes that marked his skin, and she felt his sharp inhale at her touch. "Do it, Remington. I'm ready. I don't want anyone else."

A curse rumbled in his throat before he surged forward, his lips crashing against hers.

It wasn't gentle. It wasn't soft. It was heat and desperation, fire and need.

His hands tangled in her damp hair, his kiss devouring as if he'd been holding himself back for too long. Evelyn moaned into his mouth, pressing closer, feeling the way his body trembled beneath her touch.

"Tell me to stop," he rasped against her lips, his breath uneven, his restraint thinning to a thread.

She met his gaze, her fingers tracing down his chest, nails lightly scraping over heated skin. "No. Never stop. Don't you dare."

A growl tore from his throat.

Remington gripped her hips and pulled her tighter against him, water splashing between them as he pressed open-mouthed kisses down her jaw, her throat, her collarbone. He paused where her pulse beat wildly beneath her skin.

"Last chance." His fangs grazed her neck, a silent warning.

Evelyn only tilted her head, exposing more to him. "I'm yours, Remington."

The moment the words left her lips, his control snapped.

He sank his fangs into her flesh, deep and claiming.

Evelyn gasped, pleasure and pain blurring into something intoxicating. Her fingers dug into his back as heat coiled low in her stomach, spreading like wildfire.

Remington groaned against her skin, pulling her blood into his mouth, into himself, and fuck—she tasted like power. Like life. Like something he could never give up.

She whimpered his name, and the sound shattered him.

He wrenched back, his lips stained red, pupils blown wide with need. Before she could think, before she could catch her breath, he bit into his own wrist and stretched it toward her lips.

"Drink," he commanded, voice hoarse with desire. "Finish the ritual."

"Is that what this is? A ritual?" Evelyn teased.

"I'm not sure what the fuck anything is anymore. But something deep within me says that we have to do this."

Evelyn hesitated only a second before wrapping her fingers around his arm, bringing his bleeding wrist to her mouth.

The first drop of his blood hit her tongue, and fire exploded inside her veins.

A gasp tore from her throat, her body arching against his as the bond snapped into place, an invisible tether pulling them impossibly closer.

Remington let out a guttural groan, his hands yanking at the thin, soaked fabric still clinging to her body. Evelyn did the same, her fingers fumbling with his clothing, desperate to feel his skin against hers.

There was no patience left between them, no hesitation. Fabric tore. Skin met skin. This was the blood lust.

Remington's lips found hers again, his kiss deeper, hungrier. His hands mapped every inch of her, memorizing, claiming. Evelyn moaned into his mouth, her nails dragging down his back, urging him on.

"You're mine now," he murmured, voice wrecked as he lifted her, settling her apex against him. "Forever." The muscles of his shoulders and chest flexed as he moved her to him.

She gasped as he thrust into her, the bond between them burning hotter, brighter. She felt a pinch on her shoulder, glanced down to find Remm's mouth there. Blood dripped.

Evelyn clung to him, wrapping her legs around his waist to take him deeper as the water rippled and crashed around them. He moved with purpose, with need, with devotion, each stroke branding her as his.

Evelyn moaned into his kisses. She had never felt like this. And as they shattered together, as the bond locked into place like a force of nature, Evelyn knew—there was no turning back. She didn't want to go back. Never.

Forty-Four

Evelyn blinked against the dim light filtering into the cave, her body still buzzing, still adjusting. The water had washed away every trace of her injuries, the bruises, the blood, the bitemarks, the exhaustion. She felt... different. Lighter. Whole in a way she hadn't been before.

Remington's hand was wrapped tightly around hers as they stepped out of the cavern. The cool mountain air hit her skin, and she shivered. They were both still drenched with nothing to wear but wet clothes.

Rue stood by her SUV and uncrossed her arms, a towel already extended. "You two look... better."

Remington let out a dry laugh. "She's alive, so I'd say that's better."

Evelyn rolled her eyes but took the towel gratefully, rubbing it over her hair.

Dacre leaned against the hood of the SUV, watching them with an unreadable expression before pushing off and tossing Remington a look and a nod.

"So, what now?" Rue asked, her sharp gaze flicking

between the two of them. "You want to stay here for a while, or are you going back?"

Remington didn't hesitate. "We're going home." His grip on Evelyn's hand tightened, as if he was afraid to let her go now. "There's too much unfinished business I need to deal with it before our parents return. The basilisk breeding, the missing goats, and Thrush."

Rue huffed. "Of course. Better you than me."

Dacre pulled open the driver's side door.

Remington gave a short nod and guided Evelyn toward the SUV. She climbed into the backseat, pulling the towel around her shoulders and as soon as Remington slid in beside her, his fingers found her thigh, resting there possessively.

She glanced at him, raising a brow. "Do you always get handsy after a life-threatening experience?"

He smirked but said nothing.

Evelyn didn't push because the truth was, she felt it too; this overwhelming need to be close, to touch, to drown in him. The bond was new, burning, and it was only getting stronger.

The drive was silent except for the hum of the engine, the tires crunching over gravel. And when they finally reached the portal at the peak of the mountain, Evelyn exhaled slowly.

She stepped out, adjusting the towel, but before she could do or say anything, Remington's hand was on her back, guiding her forward.

"I'll call you," Rue shouted as Remington led Evelyn away.

Ev glanced back and smiled with a short wave.

They stepped through the portal, and the moment the magic swept over her, Evelyn felt it—the shift. The difference.

Hell welcomed her back, but it wasn't like before. This time, the atmosphere wasn't suffocating. She exhaled, surprised by how *right* it felt.

Remington didn't stop walking. His fingers laced tightly with hers as he marched toward the castle, his jaw tight, his pace quick.

Evelyn stumbled, trying to keep up. "Remm—slow down—"

"No."

She groaned. "I just got my legs working again!"

He let out a rough exhale before suddenly grabbing her and hoisting her over his shoulder like she weighed nothing.

Evelyn gasped. "What the hell?! Put me down!"

"Can't." His grip on her thighs tightened as he strode forward. "I have to get you inside."

Evelyn tried to twist to look at him. "What do you mean?"

His voice was low, growled against her jeans. "Didn't think the blood lust would be this strong."

A deep flush crept up her neck.

He was moving faster now, his breathing heavier.

Chel appeared at the entrance of the castle, blinking at them. "Uh—Remington?"

"Shove off, Chel."

Chel lifted a brow but wisely stepped aside. "I take it Evelyn is well?"

Evelyn lifted her head and waved. "I'm good now."

Evelyn let out an indignant noise as Remington carried

her straight past him, straight through the halls, and up the stairs; moving with a purposeful, single-minded focus.

They reached his bedroom and he slammed the door closed.

Finally, he set her down.

She barely had a second to breathe before he was herding her toward the bathroom, stripping off his wet clothing as he went.

The bathroom was already warm and steam curled in the air as Remington turned on the shower.

Evelyn swallowed, still catching up as though her mind was moving in slow motion.

She turned to say something—only to be met with his burning gaze.

"Come here," he murmured. "You're soaking wet."

Evelyn licked her lips, pulse spiking as she stepped closer. He tore at her soaked clothing.

"Never wear these again," he muttered.

"Okay. Sure," she agreed.

Her fingers trembled as she reached for the shower door, stepping beneath the water's spray. The heat hit her skin, relaxing her muscles, but then—Remington was there, stepping in behind her, crowding her against the tile. He'd disposed of his clothing rather quickly.

Hands slid down her arms, gripped her wrists and pinned them above her head, his nose brushing along her throat.

"I didn't know it would be like this." His voice was gravel; husky and dark. "I want to touch and taste every inch of you. Forever."

She shivered, her breaths coming quicker. "I'm cool

with that." She glanced down his frame; he was so much bigger than her, tall and muscled.

A low, satisfied noise rumbled from him. "Don't fight it."

And then—his mouth crashed against hers.

Heat. Fire. *Possession.*

Evelyn arched into him, hands twisting in his grasp as he kissed her like he was starving.

His lips left hers only to trace down her neck, over the space where he'd bitten her before. She gasped when his fangs scraped over it, her knees going weak.

Remington released her hands only to slide his fingers down her soaked skin, gripping her waist and pressing her against the slick tile as he lifted her and settled between her thighs.

His breath was ragged as he dragged his lips over her shoulder, along the curve of her collarbone. "I need you."

Evelyn's fingers curled into his wet hair. "Then take me."

His growl was the only warning she got before he moved, lifting her thigh just so then pressing her hard against the tile as he sank into her.

A cry left her throat, swallowed by his mouth.

The water rained down around them, steam curling, skin sliding against skin.

And as Remington moved, claiming her, branding her, binding them even deeper than blood—

Evelyn knew that nothing would ever match this. She'd gladly give up everything on the Earthen plane to be with him. When she felt the scrape of his teeth against her neck, she arched closer to him, willing him to take.

"I can't get enough of you," Remington whispered against her skin.

She was watching him closely.

Remm went still. "There's something I have to say." His fingers tilted her chin up. "I'm sorry."

"For what?"

"For losing my temper that night you wandered into the forest. For letting the darkness out." He closed his eyes, pressed deeper into her, and released a breath. "For not apologizing right away like I should have. Forgive me."

"Forgive the dark prince." Evelyn smirked as her hands raked down his muscled chest. She tightened her legs, pulling his hips closer, sighing at the burn and the stretch of him inside her. "I'll forgive you."

"I'll be better," he promised.

She smiled, pressed her lips to his shoulder and nipped him with her teeth. "You already are."

FORTY-FIVE

"W**HY DO SOME PEOPLE CALL YOU THE SHADOW** heir?" Evelyn asked, tracing her fingertip over the tattooed runes on Remington's chest. She didn't realize he had so many.

Remington tucked a hand behind his head and glanced down at her. "I was kind of a surprise."

Evelyn glanced up at his face. "How so?"

"My mother didn't realize she was pregnant with twins. And things weren't always stable between the realms. Before the war our parents were at odds. Enemies really. A daughter was innocent enough but a son was risk. No one knew I was her son. No one knew I was the son of a King from the Seven Kingdoms of Heaven either. She kept me in the shadows until I was old enough to protect myself."

"When did that happen?"

"Right before the war. My parents reconnected and resolved their differences. My father didn't know we were his children until then."

"This is some high quality family drama," Evelyn muttered.

Remm chuckled, the sound vibrating against her side. "The stories I could tell you…"

"Tell me." Her fingers traced a rune over his collarbone. "And then tell me about these. I've always seen them but never understood what they were."

"They're runes, various spells." Remington pointed to the rune near his shoulder. "This one is for strength." He moved his finger. "This one is for protection. This one is to dim my aura."

Evelyn moved up on her elbow, scowling. "Why would anyone want to do that?"

"Just before the war, my mother hid us on the Earthen plane but she didn't know that me and Rue being together in a realm we didn't belong in would cause our auras to surge and light up the sky. It brought a lot of trouble." He pressed his finger to another marking. "Our uncle Jed gave us these. Rue has some also."

"She must keep them well hidden because I've never seen them."

"It's a spell so she doesn't stand out on the Earthen plane. There's a lot of archaic magic that we are just beginning to understand."

"Like the sacrifice stone."

"Yes, that."

"So," she murmured, dragging her nail along the curve of one glowing rune, watching it pulse in response, "I'm a vampire now?"

Remington stilled beneath her, then huffed a quiet laugh. "What?"

"You heard me," she said, grinning against his bare shoulder. "You bit me. I drank your blood. We bonded. Isn't that, like, Vampire 101?"

He turned his head, giving her an unimpressed look. "You think I'm some sparkly, brooding bloodsucker?"

Evelyn snorted. "Oh, no, you're definitely broody." She tapped his chest. "And you do bite." She tilted her head, exposing the fresh mark on her throat, teasing. "But you don't sparkle. Major disappointment, honestly. I need to find me some glitter."

Remington growled, flipping them so he was on top of her, caging her in beneath his weight. "You really want to test my patience? I'll cover my body in fucking sparkles and you'll be scraping them off your skin for years." He smirked.

She let out a breathless laugh, but it faded when his sharp teeth grazed the already-sensitive skin of her neck. A delicious shiver ran through her.

"I could make you regret that little joke, Ev," he warned, voice dark and lazy, but his hands were slow and gentle as they skimmed down her sides, thumbs grazing her ribcage.

Evelyn tilted her chin up, her smirk widening. "Oh no," she deadpanned. "Not more biting. Whatever will I do?"

Remington cursed under his breath before crashing his mouth against hers, effectively cutting off her laughter. He kissed her slow and deep, as if he had all the time in the world, as if he meant to remind her—again and again—that she was his, just as much as he was hers.

When he finally pulled back, he brushed his thumb over her swollen lips, his expression softer now. "You're not a vampire like in your Earthen plane movies, troublemaker."

Evelyn sighed dramatically. "Damn. And here I was, ready to start dressing in all black and lurking ominously in corners."

Remington chuckled, resting his forehead against hers. "You already do that."

She gasped. "I do not—"

"Yes, you do." He kissed her temple. "You're also very dramatic." Another kiss, this time at the curve of her jaw. "And reckless." His lips moved lower, skimming her throat.

Evelyn shivered but grinned. "And yet, you're obsessed with me."

Remington sighed, feigning defeat, but his eyes glowed with something fierce and adoring when he looked at her. "Yeah," he admitted, lips brushing against her skin. "I really am. From the moment I saw you." Remington squeezed her closer. "Are you gonna be okay with this?"

"What?" She flattened her hand on his stomach and felt his muscles flex. "Being with you? I've been dreaming of it since I saw you standing in the shadows at that party." She bit her lip.

Remington smiled. "Being a semi-human in Hell."

Evelyn shrugged. "The Earthen plane, as you call it, isn't all that wonderful. What family I have left betrayed me the moment they stole my inheritance and tossed me out on my ass when I turned eighteen." She sat up, goosebumps spreading over her back and shoulders. She shivered. "This might be Hell, but some of the creatures here have treated me better than family."

Remington rubbed his hand up her spine. "They're your family now." He sat up and curled an arm around her waist. "You'll never go without."

"Don't promise that." She closed her eyes.

"I'm gonna promise that." He tugged her closer. "And much more." He went quiet for a heartbeat.

"What?" Evelyn could tell there was something wrong immediately.

"Will you stay here or will you want to go back to the Earthen plane?" He gripped her chin between his fingers and tilted her face up. "I don't want to spend a moment of my life without you by my side, but I understand how important your research is to you and my sister."

She swallowed hard, lost in his gaze. "I do enjoy our work."

"My parents should return from holiday soon. They'll take over the major responsibilities of the throne. We could figure something out. A way to split our time between realms."

Evelyn thought about the books and files in her room. The urge to complete the project they'd been working on surged.

Remington's expression changed, as though he'd felt her thoughts. "I want to show you something." He moved to get out of the bed.

Evelyn held her breath as she watched him get dressed. Muscles flexed as he pulled on a black T-shirt that made his eyes stand out and a pair of old jeans. He brought her a blanket and wrapped it around her shoulders. "Do you want to walk across the hall to get some clothing, or should I carry you?"

"I'm not a child," Evelyn teased as she stood.

"Definitely not." A growl echoed in his throat. "But you're still small."

She wrapped the blanket around her and walked across the hallway to her room, Remington close behind her.

After she'd dug through her clothing and found jeans and a sweatshirt, she grabbed a hair-tie off the dresser and twisted her hair up in a messy bun.

Remington sighed from the doorway, eyes glued to her.

"What?" Evelyn asked.

"Come on." He held out his hand and she crossed the room to him.

Remington led Evelyn down the hall and to the winding staircase. They went down to the main floor, then through a few more hallways and Evelyn realized even though she'd been here for weeks, she'd barely seen a quarter of the castle.

Remington stopped in front of an ornate wooden door. "This was supposed to be a surprise for Rue." He pushed the door open. "But I think she could share it with you."

Evelyn gasped. "Oh my..."

They stepped into a giant library. Shelves lined the walls and went to the two story ceiling. A shuffling noise echoed from the back of the room and Evelyn realized the shelves were half empty.

"What is this?" she asked.

"Rue loves libraries so I had this built for her. I was hoping that one day she'd come back to us and I wanted her to finally feel at home."

Evelyn's hand went to her mouth. "She is going to love it."

Remington raked a hand through his hair. "It's not complete. We've been digging through the ruins of the collapsed castle to gather as many of the old books and scrolls we could find." He motioned to a shelf that was nearly full. "There is a shop owner at the market I brought you to who has been helping find rare books of Hell."

Evelyn walked closer to a bookshelf. She squinted, trying to read the text on the spine. "What language is this in? It's like nothing I've ever seen before."

"Hellspeak." He said something strange and guttural. "I know a little. We need to learn more."

"Why are you showing me this?" Evelyn asked. "I mean... I love it. It's wonderful, but if this is for your sister, why show me?"

"Because I think it could help your research. There's ancient text here." He reached for a book. "This is where we found information on the sacrifice stone. And the White Horse had some knowledge. Rue is already uncovering the connection between Hell and the Earthen plane; I think this could help."

Evelyn was nodding. "You're right. And she's going to love this." She took a leather bound book off the shelf and carefully flipped through it. "This is... gosh." Evelyn bit her lip as a million thoughts ran through her mind. "We could discover so much. Dr. Malcom would kill to see this place. After all the negativity he's endured over the years. For him to finally know that he was right. And that our research really means something..." She shook her head. At the same time, curiosity surged inside Evelyn's chest. She wanted to touch and read every piece of paper in this library. She wanted to move the table from her bedroom down here and spread out all of the books and papers and files and lose herself in the magic of discovery.

Evelyn sighed, tears collecting in the corners of her eyes.

"What's wrong?" Remington asked.

She set the book back and hurried toward him, jumping a little to throw her arms around his neck. "It's just the best thing anyone could do for their sister. She's gonna love it–"

A violent crash echoed through the castle, shaking the walls, and sending vibrations through the stone floors. Books shifted on the library shelves, dust trembling in the air.

Evelyn went stiff in Remington's arms, her fingers tightening against his shirt. "What was that?" she whispered.

Remington was already setting her on her feet, his body tense as he turned toward the library doors. His shadows, always restrained but never truly absent, coiled at his feet like wary serpents waiting for his command.

"Someone is here," he said, his voice sharp with authority.

Evelyn took a step back, hesitating. "Should I—should I go?"

He shot her a quick glance, his golden eyes flashing. "No. The Hellions are collecting. Come with me." Then, softer, but firm, he added, "But don't be afraid."

She swallowed, steadying her breath. Right. She was not some fragile thing—not anymore. She followed him as he strode out of the library and into the grand hall where Hellions were already assembling at the castle entrance.

The main doors had been blown open, heavy iron and wood splintered outward. Smoke curled in the air, the scent of sulfur thick and acrid.

Remington stepped forward first, shielding Evelyn as they approached the wreckage. The Hellions had already begun searching for threats, weapons drawn.

At the foot of the shattered doors lay a crude wooden crate, broken open from the force of the explosion. Something had been thrown against the castle entrance with enough power to rattle its foundations.

Evelyn's breath caught in her throat when she saw what lay within the remains of the crate.

A goat skull.

The flesh had been stripped away, the bones scorched black, and dark words were carved into the surface. Blood still clung to the base of its horns. The sight made her stomach twist.

One of the Hellions crouched beside it, sniffing the air before looking up at Remington. "Mountain demons." His voice was gravelly. "The scent is fresh."

Remington exhaled slowly, nostrils flaring. "I'm guessing the basilisk ate more goats."

"Appears so," Chel added grimly, walking closer.

Evelyn knelt beside the skull. "What do they want?" she murmured.

Remington's jaw clenched. "The basilisk keep eating their goats near the Black River." He lifted his gaze to the broken doors, then to the darkened horizon beyond. "The mountain demons relied on those herds. They warned me they'd retaliate."

Evelyn stood, brushing her hands against her thighs. "Are we going to bring them more? Like last time?"

Remington turned to her sharply. "We?"

She met his eyes, unwavering. "Yes, we."

His expression darkened, but she didn't back down.

One of the Hellions nearby cleared his throat. "They sent another message." He lifted a scrap of parchment that had been nailed to the crate with a rusted iron spike. He handed it to Remington, who read the words aloud.

"Come with an offering, Prince of Shadows. Bring flesh to replace what was stolen, or we take flesh from you."

Evelyn exhaled. "Friendly."

Remington muttered a curse under his breath and crumpled the note in his fist.

Chel approached from the hall, arms crossed. "If we're going to fix this, we need to move quickly. The basilisks will be restless if there's no more food. And the mountain demons? They don't wait long before turning to war."

"Fuck. I do not have time for this." Remington cursed again. He turned to Evelyn, expression hard. "Fine. We go. But stay close to me."

She lifted her chin. "I'll try my best."

Remington let out a rough sigh before turning to Chel. "Gather the Hellions. We ride for the Black River."

Chel nodded and disappeared into the castle.

Evelyn shivered slightly, staring at the skull. The Black River. The basilisks. The mountain demons. And there was something else... She'd seen Thrush in those forests. They'd been chasing him for months.

FORTY-SIX

THE SUV RUMBLED ALONG THE JAGGED MOUNTAIN path, the heavy tires kicking up dust and loose gravel as they neared the Black River. Remington's basilisk followed, slither-floating down the road behind them. The drive had been quiet, tense. Evelyn sat in the passenger seat beside Remington, her fingers curling around the edge of her seat. Behind them, Chel and the other Hellions drove in separate vehicles. A convoy of sorts.

Outside, the peaks of Hell's mountains stretched like jagged teeth against the ochre-colored sky. The Black River slithered through the valley below; a dark, shimmering thing that had always looked unnatural. The last time they'd been here, the water churned and pulsed, hiding the monstrous shapes of the basilisks beneath its surface.

But now, as they neared the river's edge, something was... wrong.

The river was still. Too still. Almost serene.

The usual eerie undulations of the current had ceased, the obsidian surface reflecting the dull light of the sky like polished glass. Evelyn shivered. Even the air here felt different—too heavy, too expectant.

Remington noticed. His hands tightened on the wheel as he pulled the SUV to a stop near the gathering of mountain demons waiting at the riverbank. The Hellions stepped out first, moving with caution. Evelyn followed, swallowing the unease creeping up her spine.

The mountain demons were already agitated, their sharp features twisted into scowls. Their long, wiry hair was tangled with beads and bone charms, and they gripped their crude weapons like they expected a fight.

"You took too long," Barok growled, stepping forward. He was broader than the others, his horns curving back in thick, ridged arcs. His yellow eyes burned with fury. "We sent our warning, and you delayed."

"We brought the goats," Remington said coolly, nodding toward the back of the SUV where the animals were penned in. "Your herds will recover."

Barok spat onto the ground. "This isn't just about the damn goats. This is our livelihood."

Another herder stepped forward, his expression grim. "Something else is happening here." He gestured to the water. "The river has never been this quiet. It waits for something."

Evelyn frowned. She glanced toward Remington, but he was already scanning the surroundings, green eyes sharp. His basilisk slithered down from the rocks above, its massive, sinewy body coiling beside him, forked tongue flicking at the air. It let out a low, guttural hiss, the spines along its back bristling.

The Hellions braced themselves, waiting to reveal the trailer of goats they'd brought.

And then, without warning, the Black River exploded.

The water shattered apart, sending black droplets flying through the air. The stillness was broken in an instant as massive forms surged up from below—basilisks, their obsidian scales gleaming, their forked tongues lashing the air.

The mountain demons scattered, screaming curses as the creatures lunged forward, their long bodies twisting through the air.

"Evelyn!" Remington shouted, reaching for her.

She stumbled back as one of the basilisks snapped its jaws where she'd just been standing. Another barreled into the group, slamming a Hellion to the ground with a sickening crunch.

Chaos erupted.

Remington's basilisk roared in challenge, launching itself at the others, sinking its fangs into the nearest threat. The beasts clashed, their screeches rattling Evelyn's skull. The ground thundered underneath her feet as creatures writhed and fell and fought.

But as the fight escalated, she slowly realized something else was happening—she was being herded.

Another basilisk lunged at her, not to kill, but to drive her back. Her feet scrambled against the loose rocks as the creatures closed in, forcing her away from the others. Separating her.

"Remington!" she called, but the roar of battle swallowed her voice.

She caught a glance of his dark hair flying, the glint of

his weapon. "Ev!" his call was cut off by a huge basilisk whipping its tail in front of her.

Her heart pounded as she staggered backward. Then to the side. She noticed she was headed toward the forest's edge, the twisted trees offering little comfort. But she wasn't alone.

Remington's basilisk slithered after her, positioning itself between her and the threat. Its long body curled protectively around her, head raised, tongue flicking furiously.

The fighting behind them raged on, but Evelyn's breath hitched for an entirely new reason.

Because someone else was there.

A figure moved between the trees, his tall, muscular form blending into the shadows. She recognized him instantly.

Thrush.

He stepped forward, the strange, almost spectral glow of his eyes locked onto her. His lips parted in a sharp grin, revealing too-white teeth.

"You don't belong here," he murmured, his voice like the wind whispering through dead leaves.

Evelyn swallowed hard. Her pulse hammered as he moved closer; his gait was slow, unhurried, like a predator indulging curiosity.

"You smell wrong," he continued, his nostrils flaring as he inhaled deeply. "Not like them. Not like Hell."

She took a step back, her breath catching as his long fingers reached toward her.

Before he could touch her, Remington's basilisk lunged, a guttural hiss ripping from its throat.

Thrush didn't flinch. Instead, his gaze slid to the beast, something dark passing through his expression. Then he hissed back, sharp and animalistic, his fangs flashing.

For the first time, Evelyn saw true anger flicker in his eerie eyes.

"You," Thrush spat, taking a step toward the basilisk. "You killed mine."

The basilisk reared back, its body tensing, ready to strike.

Thrush's expression twisted with something almost like grief—then rage. He took another step forward, ignoring Evelyn entirely now, his fingers curling into fists. "I should skin you alive for that. I should sear you on a rock and eat you for dinner."

The basilisk didn't back down. It let out another low hiss, muscles coiling, waiting.

Evelyn's breath came short and fast. Thrush was furious. Remington was still back at the river, fighting.

And she was caught between a grieving crazed man and the monster. She had no idea how to escape.

Evelyn took a slow, steadying breath, forcing her hands to remain at her sides even as every instinct screamed at her to run. Thrush loomed close, too close. He didn't look like he belonged; he looked wild, dirt clung to his face. Evelyn watched him and he looked like the boy next door–handsome, athletic. His blue eyes shifted in the dim light–they seemed to change color. Light filtered through the twisted trees. His eerie gaze flickered between her and the basilisk, still coiled and ready to strike.

"You're with Remington?" he asked, his voice a rasping

whisper, almost amused. "I heard others speaking of claiming you."

Evelyn hesitated, unsure if answering truthfully was the right move. But lying to Thrush felt dangerous—like he'd see right through her anyway.

She nodded.

A flicker of something unreadable passed through his expression. "Hmm." His long fingers twitched at his sides. He moved even closer, his sharp gaze tracing over her like he was trying to solve a puzzle.

"Evelyn," he started, his tone more careful now, "how have you been... since coming to Hell? You'll make this your home now?"

She glanced up at him, surprised by the question. "You mean, besides the near-death experiences?" she tried to joke, but his sharp look told her he wasn't in the mood. She sighed. "It's... different."

His eyes searched hers. "Different how?"

Evelyn exhaled. "It's hard to explain. I feel like I belong here, but also like I don't. Like something's changing inside me, and I don't fully understand it yet."

Thrush's expression darkened slightly, but he nodded. "And the Earthen plane? Do you miss it?"

Evelyn was quiet for a long moment. Did she? The human world felt so distant now, like a dream she'd woken up from. But there were parts of it she still longed for. She missed spending time with Rue. She missed Loyola campus and the comforts of her apartment. She missed the constant chase of her research.

"Sometimes," she admitted. "But... I don't think I

could ever go back and live there again. Not after everything. I don't want to leave Remington."

Evelyn forced herself to stand her ground. "Thrush..." she started, keeping her voice steady, though her pulse pounded. "I don't want anyone else to get hurt."

Thrush tilted his head, considering. "And?"

She swallowed. "Do you know how to stop the basilisks from attacking? Can you—can you call them off?"

He laughed. The soft, rasping sound sent a chill through her bones. "You think I control them?"

Evelyn clenched her fists. "I think you're the only one here who might be able to do something about them. I didn't exactly walk over here to you unassisted. They herded me like a cattle dog. They brought me straight to *you*."

Thrush hummed in thought, his gaze flicking toward the river then back to her. His fingers curled lazily, and before Evelyn could even process what he was doing, he snapped them.

The effect was instant.

The basilisks hissed once in protest before one by one, they slithered away, their massive, scaled bodies retreating into the Black River. Within seconds, the water was still again as if the creatures had never surfaced.

Evelyn let out a slow, shaky breath. "Thank you."

The wild man nodded once.

"Evelyn!" Remington's voice, rough and desperate, cut through the quiet. Her heart clenched at the sheer urgency in it.

Thrush smiled. "Your dark prince comes."

Evelyn ignored him, turning toward the sound. "I'm

here!" she called back. She looked to Thrush once more. "Tell the basilisk to stop eating the goats."

"What would you rather have them eat?" Thrush's lips quirked up in a half smile.

"Fish."

Thrush bit his thumbnail as he contemplated. "Not many fish here."

"Then have the basilisk fish in other waters," she suggested.

"Sounds so easy when you say it like that." There was a glint of humor in Thrush's eyes.

Through the trees, Remington's green gaze locked onto hers, relief flashing across his face as he pushed through the underbrush. His shirt was torn, blood smeared along his arm, but he didn't seem to care. His gaze snapped to Thrush, his lips pressing into a straight line.

"Thrush," Remington called, "don't run."

Thrush looked at Evelyn then back at Remington. "Why not? I like running. You're all so slow."

"Come home, Thrush," Remington said. "You've been out here alone for too long."

Shadows curled around Remington's body, protectively spreading toward Evelyn.

"You've found yourself a human," Thrush sneered. "Of all people. You—"

"Rue has someone too," Remington interrupted. "She misses you. We *all* miss you." Remington held out a hand. "Come back with us."

Thrush's arms twitched as though his body was preparing to flee and he was making a conscious decision to keep every muscle in place.

"It's starting, isn't it?" Remington asked. "You didn't do your time as a Hellion and the curse is coming for you."

"A curse?" Evelyn asked.

Remington explained their family was cursed on the Angel side. Each had to do their time as a Hellion. To know good, they must know evil. To rule with peace they must know chaos. They must know darkness. A long time ago, Sparrow's father never did his time and it cursed his children, turning them senile. Sparrow cured his bloodline by doing his time as a Hellion. Remington was spared because he did his time as a Hellion. But Thrush hadn't.

Evelyn stared at Remington. "So you trained as a Hellion." She glanced at Chel in the distance. "You were one of those?"

"Yes," Remington replied. "I also trained with the Angel Legion in Heaven."

"Sounds well-rounded," Evelyn muttered.

Thrush growled.

"Is it happening already?" Remington asked. "You should have done your time as a Hellion years ago. We could have done it together."

Thrush growled again, then... his head ticked to the side and his shoulders twitched.

"Is that it?" Remington pointed. "It's starting. You will only get worse."

Thrush was curling his hands into fists. "I don't want to relive those memories. Going back will bring it all to the forefront."

"It's different now. We've rebuilt the castle. The war is over. It's been over for years." Remington stepped closer. "Come *home*. Please. Brother."

"I am not your brother."

"Close enough," Remington replied. "We were closer than most."

Thrush nodded his chin just once. "True."

"Come. Get clean clothing. Sleep in a bed." Remington glanced at Thrush from head to toe. "Take a hot shower."

"I have a hot shower," Thrush snapped.

"But do you use it?" Evelyn asked. "There's a lot of dirt on your skin."

"Watch your human mouth." Thrush stepped closer, intimidating.

"No." Remington stepped in front of Evelyn. Shadows crept from his shoulders and boots. "She's off limits. She. Is. Mine."

Evelyn gasped, afraid that he'd lose control and turn into the monster of shadow and smoke and crush his cousin to dust.

"New tricks, prince?" Thrush smiled. "I have some tricks of my own."

"Show me." Remington tipped his chin.

But Thrush merely smiled, stepping back into the darkness. "Another time," he murmured, before his form melted into the shadows of the forest, disappearing entirely.

Remington spun to face Evelyn, his hands gripping her arms, checking her for injuries. "Are you hurt?"

She shook her head. "I'm fine."

His jaw clenched. He let out a sharp breath before pulling her against him for a brief, crushing moment. Then, he stepped back, scanning her face. "What the hell happened? How did you end up over here?"

"The basilisk chased me." Evelyn hesitated, glancing

toward where Thrush had vanished. "I—" She exhaled. "I talked him down."

Remington narrowed his eyes. "You *talked* him down?"

"He stopped the basilisks," she murmured. "I asked him to."

His brows furrowed, suspicion flickering in his gaze. But before he could press further, he glanced back toward the river where the Hellions were regathering.

They started walking back toward the others, Remington keeping her close at his side. His voice softened, but there was still tension in his frame.

He reached up, brushing a strand of hair from her face. "You're sure you're not hurt?"

She smiled faintly. "Not even a scratch."

Remington exhaled slowly, his gaze lingering on her for a beat too long before he turned, guiding her back toward the others. "Come on, then. We're going home."

"What about Thrush?" Evelyn asked.

Remington's jaw tightened, as if he already knew that answer but didn't like hearing it aloud. "I can't force him. He will come home when he's ready."

FORTY-SEVEN

The courtyard was warm under the midday Hellsky, the scent of crushed lavender and wild rose clinging to the air. Evelyn knelt in the grass, carefully threading together a small bouquet of blue asters and black-eyed Susans. They'd become her favorite flowers, mostly because they looked so out of place in Hell. Her fingers moved absently, her mind drifting as she considered the work ahead—more research, more digging through ancient texts, more attempts to understand the mystery of the runes and caves she and Rue and Dr. Malcom had discovered.

A sudden rustle beyond the stone wall caught her attention. She stilled, tightening her grip on the small knife Remington had all but forced her to carry at all times. Her heart gave a single hard thump against her ribs as she rose to her feet, stepping quietly toward the edge of the courtyard. The garden's stone wall was four feet tall, covered in creeping vines that swayed lightly in the breeze. She could see over the top and beyond it—someone was watching her.

She moved closer, her fingers firm on the knife's hilt. "Who's there?"

A shadow shifted on the other side. Then, a voice—deep, unhurried, laced with amusement. "Are you always this suspicious, or only when you're picking flowers?"

Evelyn exhaled, relaxing slightly. "Thrush."

The man leaned casually against the wall, peering over with a smirk. His white-blonde hair was unkempt, wild like the rest of him. His piercing blue eyes studied her with sharp, unreadable interest. It had been nearly a week since he'd disappeared on them near the Black River.

"We've been wondering if you'd come." Evelyn smiled.

"You talk about me often, little human?" he asked. "I'm flattered."

She rolled her eyes but didn't deny it. Thrush had become an unexpected presence in her mind since their last encounter. His strange balance between raw violence and sharp wit made him an anomaly even among Hell's creatures. And then there was the way Remington talked about him, like he'd lost his best friend. Like he'd lost his brother.

Thrush glanced up at the castle beyond her, his smirk fading into something contemplative. "So, this is where the dark prince lives." His gaze returned to her. "Do you like it here?"

Evelyn hesitated, then nodded. "I do."

Thrush hummed, noncommittal. "I think I'd hate it."

She didn't argue—Hell wasn't for everyone. Especially not for someone like Thrush, who was barely leashed as it was. Evelyn didn't know a lot about the guy, but he had a dark edge and she'd heard the way Remington talked about his cousin. Evelyn wondered if Thrush truly knew where he belonged. Or if he belonged anywhere at all.

His eyes flickered back to her, playful again. "Be honest. Do I look scary?"

Evelyn raised a brow, taking him in—the sharp cut of his cheekbones, the way his body seemed perpetually coiled for a fight, the untamed gleam in his blue-shifting eyes and the dirt smeared across his cheek and clothing.

"You look like trouble," she said, tucking her knife away. "But scary? No. I've met worse. Much worse. Bad vibes for days kinda creeps. You don't have that." She tapped a finger on her chin. "But you have a bit of a *darker* kinda prince kinda vibe going on."

Thrush laughed under his breath. "That's the nicest thing anyone's ever said to me." Then, tilting his head, he asked, "You got any single friends?"

Evelyn snorted. "Why? Thinking about settling down?"

"I like options," he said with a smirk. "And Remm seems happy for the first time in years. I've been watching him."

"Mm." She crossed her arms, narrowing her eyes. "You should see Rue. Are you going to do your time, or are you just going to wander around making bad jokes? I'd hate to watch you slowly go crazy—we just met, after all."

Thrush's grin faded. He stared at her, unreadable, his jaw ticking slightly as if considering something.

Evelyn didn't back down. Instead, she took a step closer and held out her hand. "I'll help you. Someone told me... you lost your parents. I lost mine too. And... I might have a friend I'd consider letting you meet, but not if you're bat-shit crazy."

His gaze flicked down to her offered hand, then back to her face. A slow, amused smile crept onto his lips. "You're not qualified for the kind of help I need."

Evelyn shrugged. "Try me, wild boy. None of us grew up in a perfect world." She shrugged. "Or at least I didn't."

Thrush exhaled through his nose, something like reluctant amusement in his eyes. Then, after a beat, his giant hand landed in hers, his grip firm but not crushing.

"Don't tell your boyfriend I let you boss me around," he murmured, his voice low, teasing.

Evelyn smirked. "My boyfriend will be thrilled to see you here. Don't forget he begged you to come here the other day and you blew him off."

With an easy, almost lazy movement, Thrush leapt over the stone wall like it was nothing, landing beside her in the courtyard. He stretched, cracking his neck, then looked down at her.

"Well then, little human," he said, "lead the way."

Forty-Eight

The scent of old parchment filled the air as the dim, flickering light from the chandeliers cast long shadows across the dark stone floors. The space finally had a reverence that had been absent for too long.

Rue stood at the entrance, eyes wide as she took in the sight before her. "You did this," she breathed, stepping forward slowly.

Remington smirked, arms crossed over his chest. "It was supposed to be a big surprise."

Evelyn glanced up from where she was seated at a long wooden table, her research materials sprawled across the surface. "He even helped organize the texts," she added with an amused smile.

Rue spun on her heel, eyes narrowing at Remington. "You?"

Remington snorted from behind her. "It was mostly Evelyn. I just did the heavy lifting."

Rue let out a small laugh, running her fingers along the spines of several old books. "This is incredible. It won't convince me to move back, but I'll admit..." She sighed wistfully. "I love this library."

"You never know," Remington teased, nudging her shoulder as he walked past.

Rue scoffed. "I have too much research to do on the Earthen plane."

Evelyn leaned back in her chair. "Speaking of research, what did you bring me?"

At that, Rue straightened, suddenly serious. She motioned to Dacre, who carried a large bundle wrapped tightly in several layers of thick blankets. He set it carefully on the table, his usual amused expression replaced with something more somber.

Evelyn's breath caught as she reached for the bundle. "Is this—?"

Rue nodded. "The sacrifice stone."

A heavy silence settled over the room. The weight of what had happened—what had nearly happened—lingered between them.

"I didn't want it falling into the wrong hands," Rue murmured. "Or worse, someone else triggering it the way you did." She glanced at Evelyn, worry flickering in her gaze. "I still don't understand why it was just discarded in the dirt for all this time. So many people could have been saved with this ancient magic."

Evelyn placed a hand over the stone, feeling its cold surface beneath the fabric. "I didn't walk away unscathed. I gave up some things." She glanced up at Remm. "But I'm perfectly fine with that."

Remington exhaled sharply. "You realize you're likely going to find more of these, right?" He gave Rue a knowing look. "Artifacts with just as much power. Maybe worse. Maybe stronger. Calling on creatures and magic we've never seen before. Just from flipping through a few of these books it seems there is a lot of ancient magic and connections lost between the realms."

Rue lifted her chin. "That's the point. So much has been hidden, buried. I want to rediscover what was lost. I want answers. For our family."

Dacre nodded, stepping beside her.

Rue continued, "The connections between giants and angels, the artifacts left behind—you've only scratched the surface." She looked to Evelyn. "We've been focusing on fifteenth-century Nephilim in the Alleghany Mountains, how they influenced modern mythology. If we're both right, it could change everything we know about their role in history."

Evelyn's fingers tightened over the wrapped stone. "They left behind more than just myths. I'm just wondering why so much of it was buried and abandoned."

Rue's expression was resolute. "Maybe they left behind *proof.* They didn't destroy it all so we could uncover it."

A slow smile spread across Evelyn's lips. "Then let's discover it."

Dacre groaned. "Great. More digging in the dirt."

Rue smirked. "You'd better get used to it. History doesn't unearth itself."

Dacre wrapped his arms around her and pressed a kiss to her cheek. "Okay, fine. But only because it's you. If anyone else asked, I'd tell them to go fly a kite."

"As it should be." Rue kissed him until Remington and Evelyn made puking noises, then she pulled away laughing.

A small meow interrupted and a little black kitten jumped up onto the table, sniffing the books Evelyn had left open.

"Oh you brought the little baby!" Evelyn made her way back to the table and pet Lucipurr. "The dark void likes to read." She scooped up the kitten and snuggled him, pressing her face into his fur. "Why does he always smell like freshly baked biscuits?"

Lucipurr meowed as though to say it was his signature scent.

Remington leaned against the edge of the long wooden table, arms crossed as he watched Rue carefully. The library felt smaller now, the weight of what he was about to say thickening the air between them. Evelyn sat beside the sacrifice stone and released Lucipurr, running her fingers along the fabric-wrapped edges.

Dacre, ever watchful, stood just behind Rue, his expression unreadable. "Please don't bleed on that again."

Evelyn folded the fabric over the stone. "Nope. Nope."

Finally, Remington exhaled. "Thrush is back."

Rue froze. Her hands, which had been idly flipping through a brittle parchment, went still. Slowly, she lifted her gaze to meet Remington's. "He's home?"

Remington nodded once. "Very much so."

Something flashed in Rue's expression—relief, excitement, and something deeper, something guarded. "I want to see him."

"No," Remington said firmly.

Rue scowled. "What do you mean *no*?"

Remington pushed off the table, running a hand through his hair. "I mean wait. He's... different." He hesitated, searching for the right words. "The transition back to Hellion has been rough on him. He's not the same as you remember."

Rue's jaw tightened. "None of us are."

"I know that." His voice was gentler this time. "But you need to understand—whatever he was before, whatever you thought you knew... it's changed."

Rue's fingers curled around the edge of the table, her knuckles whitening. "Where is he?"

"He's keeping his distance," Remington admitted. "For now."

"Why?"

"He waited too long to do his time," Remington answered.

Rue inhaled deeply, trying to steady herself. "The curse."

Remington shook his head. "It's mild but he seems to be recovering. He still has moments where he's lacking recognition."

Rue gritted her teeth but didn't argue. Instead she turned away, rubbing her arms as if trying to shake off a chill that had settled deep in her bones. "I guess I should tell you..."

Remington moved closer.

"I had a vision of him."

"Of Thrush?" Remington asked.

"It was just the other night," Dacre said, "she woke up screaming in the middle of the night. Good thing we moved to that big lot near the forest so the neighbors didn't hear."

"Tell me," Remington said.

Rue was nodding and pacing. "I didn't see a lot, it was just of him fighting; he looked like he was losing his mind and in a dungeon. Do you have him locked up, Remm?"

"No." Remington shook his head. "I'm not a barbarian."

"Okay. Good. I don't think that would help him at all. He needs space, a lot of space. And maybe some therapy." Rue was staring.

Evelyn, silent until now, leaned forward. "Do you think he's dangerous?"

Remington met her gaze. "I think he's close to losing himself."

For a long moment, the only sound in the room was the crackling fire and the distant echo of the castle settling. Evelyn reached across the table, her fingers brushing against his in silent support. Rue chewed on her lip, clearly still troubled.

Remington exhaled. "I'll talk to him." He ran his hand through his hair. "We won't let what happened to our parents happen to him."

Rue nodded. "No. We can't do that."

FORTY-NINE

REMINGTON STRODE THROUGH THE CASTLE HALLS, rubbing his temples. He was late. Late because Evelyn—his wicked, wonderful, maddening Evelyn—had told him she needed his help with *something important* and now she was nowhere to be found.

The Hellions were waiting for him. He was supposed to be at some dull meeting about security measures in the southern territories, but instead he was here, wandering the corridors like a lost fool.

He paused outside the ballroom, catching the faint sound of music seeping from beneath the heavy double doors. His brow furrowed. The ballroom hadn't been used since the Spring Ball. Why the hell was it—

Suddenly the door cracked open; a small hand gripped his wrist and pulled him inside.

"You tricked me," he said, voice low, knowing exactly who was behind this.

Evelyn leaned against the closed doors, grinning. The cape he'd bought her was clasped tightly around her neck.

"Dark prince," she murmured. "You made me wait." She reached up, slowly, and flicked the clasp. The cape fell.

Remington's breath caught.

She was wearing the dress. *That* dress.

The wide-necked black gown from the Spring Ball, the one that had nearly driven him insane with how it bared the delicate slope of her shoulders and throat, how it clung to her curves like it was painted on. But unlike the first time she wore it there was no crowd, no leering demons, no threat looming over them. Just her. Just him. He had time to appreciate it.

Evelyn stepped toward him, slowly. "We never got to dance," she said softly.

The music was playing on the far side of the room—a slow, sensual rhythm.

Remington's fingers twitched at his sides. His whole body felt coiled, hungry. "Evelyn," he warned.

She tilted her head, her exposed throat teasing him with its vulnerability. "What's wrong, my dark prince? Can't focus?"

His throat went dry. *Fucking hell.*

Evelyn took a step toward him, her bare shoulders gleaming under the candlelight. Her lips curled in amusement as she noticed the way his gaze fixated on her neck.

Remington let out a harsh breath, running a hand through his hair. "The Hellions are going to be annoyed that I'm late."

Evelyn made a soft, exaggerated gasp. "Oh, my poor baby." She reached up, gripping his face between her hands and pressing a teasing kiss to his lips. "How dare anyone boss you around, you sweet, wicked thing."

She kissed him again. And again. Then a dozen more times; each one featherlight, playful, igniting something wild inside him.

"They're so mean and serious all the time," Evelyn whispered between kisses, her lips trailing along his jaw.

Remington growled low in his throat. "Fuck. You're going to be the death of me." He gripped her waist and, with no hesitation, tossed her over his shoulder.

Evelyn yelped, laughing as he stalked toward the door.

"I'm taking you to bed," he muttered, determined to get them both out of this room before he lost the last shred of his control.

"Wait," she squealed, kicking her feet. "I wanted to dance with you."

Remington stopped mid-stride, groaning. He smacked a hand over his face. "Shit." He bit his lip, thinking. "Shit. I don't like waiting. I actually despise waiting. I'm an instant gratification kinda guy."

Evelyn wriggled in his grasp, and he let her slide down his tall, lean body. She pressed close, her hands smoothing over his chest. "Then stop waiting. Dance with me." She draped her arms over his shoulders, threading her fingers into the hair at the back of his head. She swayed, closed her eyes, and let the music guide her movements.

They danced for about ten seconds. Then his restraint snapped.

Remington grabbed her by the waist and spun her, pressing her back against the nearest wall. His mouth crashed onto hers, all teeth and heat and desperation.

She moaned against him, her hands tangling in his hair,

nails raking against his scalp. He bit her bottom lip, drinking in the little gasp she made.

"Tell me you're mine," he growled against her mouth.

Evelyn's breath hitched. "I've always been yours."

That was it. That was all he needed.

His fangs elongated, his pupils blown wide with hunger. He ducked his head, his lips brushing against her throat. *Soft. Warm. Perfect.*

"I need to taste you," he murmured, voice rough.

"Please do." Evelyn tilted her head, granting him full access. "I like it when you bite me."

Remington let out a shaky breath. He pressed a final, reverent kiss to her skin before sinking his fangs deep into her flesh.

She gasped, her fingers tightening around his shoulders, her body pressing closer. Pleasure, sharp and electric, shot through both of them, binding them together in a way that was more than physical. Their bond ignited, deepened, *solidified.*

His hands roamed her body, gathering the fabric of her dress, desperate to feel her. She arched against him, her hands just as frantic, tugging at his shirt, at his belt. His cool fingers slid up her leg to her core and pressed, lightly at first, then deeper...

"Am I supposed to feel like this?" Evelyn asked. "All hot and angsty and... absolutely desperate?"

Remington pushed the neck of her dress down her arm, revealing creamy white skin. His only response was a growl of satisfaction.

Evelyn shivered, the remnants of patience vanishing completely.

The music played on, forgotten. The ballroom stood silent witness as Remington pressed her against the wall, hips pressed tight against her core.

"Remm," Evelyn whispered, feeling his hardened length nudge her open. "Tell me it will always be like this." She sighed as he pressed fully inside her body.

"Always," he murmured against her jaw before kissing her again. "Fuck." He groaned, gripping her tighter.

As they clung to each other, their bodies tangled, their bond thrumming with new life, and Remington knew—there was no throne, no title, no war that would ever mean more than this.

More than her.

More than *them*.

His dark heart was hers. *Forever.*

Footsteps echoed outside the door.

Remington went still. Evelyn shifted her hips, unfulfilled and heedless.

"Shh," Remington pressed a hand over her mouth.

Voices echoed. Male and female.

"Someone is here," he warned her.

Her smirk softened. "I'm not afraid. Fuck me and feed from me. You promised to ruin me."

Something inside him snapped.

Remington cupped the back of Evelyn's neck, his thumb skimming her jaw. He felt her pulse race beneath his fingertips, heard the soft hitch in her breath as he began moving inside her again.

"Then neither am I," he murmured, his voice low and rough.

She shivered against him, fingers tightening in his hair,

her body arching into his as his mouth captured hers. The ballroom was dimly lit, the golden glow of the chandeliers casting long shadows across the polished floors. The music played on, an elegant melody at odds with the sinful things he was doing to her.

Evelyn panted. His lips trailed down the slope of her neck, fangs grazing teasingly. She let out a soft, breathless laugh.

"If you bite me every time we dance, I'm going to start thinking you have a thing for ballrooms," she teased.

"I have a thing for *you*," Remington corrected, his voice like velvet and sin. He kissed her deeply, his hands skimming over the fabric of her dress, bunching it higher—

Footsteps.

Remington froze. Evelyn did, too, her nails digging into his shoulders as they both turned toward the grand ballroom doors. The sound of boots echoing in the hallway grew louder.

"Who the fuck—" Remington started, lowering Evelyn just enough so she could stand.

Before they could scramble to fix themselves—

BAM!

The double doors to the ballroom burst open, slamming against the walls with a deafening crack.

"Ah, hell," Remington muttered.

Evelyn yelped and tried to shove him away, frantically smoothing down the skirt of her dress, but it was too late.

There, standing in the doorway, were two very familiar figures.

His mother, Meg, dressed in all black with a fur-lined coat draped over her shoulders, looked between them with raised brows, unimpressed but highly entertained. His father, Sparrow, stood beside her, eyes narrowing as he took in the scene.

Evelyn, half pinned to the wall with her dress askew. Remington; shirt unbuttoned, hair a mess, eyes still burning with lust. Pants half-zipped.

Meg tsked. "Well, well, my boy. I see we've returned *just* in time."

Evelyn groaned and buried her face in her hands. "Oh my god."

Sparrow sighed heavily, rubbing his temples. "Remington."

"Father," Remington said smoothly, straightening his shirt like he hadn't just been caught about to defile Evelyn further in the middle of a damn ballroom.

Sparrow's gaze flicked between them, his frown deepening. "If you're going to act like a rutting beast, at least have the decency to do it behind closed doors."

"The door *was* closed," Remington growled.

"Oh, my child," Meg mocked, throwing her hands up in exaggerated distress. "Were you not expecting us?"

Remington shot her a flat look. "You weren't due back for another week."

"Yes, well, plans change," she said, stepping further into the room. She gave Evelyn a once-over, eyes gleaming with interest. "Evelyn, you're looking quite... ravished." She winked. "It looks good on you. All rosy cheeks and red lips." Meg glanced back at Sparrow. "I remember those days."

Sparrow's lips tipped up.

Evelyn made a strangled noise, cheeks flaming.

Meg smirked, focusing on the two of them again. "I approve."

"Can we not do this right now?" Remington ground out, adjusting the cuffs of his sleeves, trying to collect what little dignity remained.

Sparrow gave him an unimpressed look. "We *will* talk later." He turned on his heel and strode from the ballroom, muttering something about *irresponsible princelings.*

Meg, however, lingered. She leaned in close to Evelyn, voice just loud enough for them both to hear. "Next time, lock the doors." She winked and followed after Sparrow, laughing under her breath.

The moment they were gone, Evelyn let out a shaky breath, hands still pressed against her burning face. "I want to die. Right now. Just—melt into the floor."

Remington sighed, pinching the bridge of his nose. "That... was *not* how I wanted them to meet you officially."

Evelyn peeked at him between her fingers. "*Officially?* They don't know?"

"Oh, we know!" Meg shouted from the hallway. "The whole fucking realm knows."

His parents were laughing as they walked away.

Remington let out a rough laugh, stepping closer and pulling her hands away from her face. "They'll get over it," he assured, pressing a kiss to her palm. "Eventually."

Evelyn groaned again, resting her forehead against his chest. "I don't think I will."

Remington smirked, wrapping an arm around her waist. "Well, if you're traumatized anyway, we might as well finish what we started."

Epilogue

The scent of roasted coffee beans and cinnamon filled the air as Evelyn settled into her seat at *The Coffee Connection*, her fingers wrapped around a steaming mug. Across from her Remington lounged in his chair, long legs stretched out, looking entirely too at ease for a prince of Hell on the Earthen plane and out for a cup of coffee with friends. However, he didn't have any coffee. He'd settled for a raspberry smoothie. Beside him, Dacre sipped his espresso, eyes flicking to Rue, who was scanning the coffee shop's entrance with mild impatience.

"You're fidgeting," Dacre murmured, reaching out to still her hand.

Rue huffed. "I'm not fidgeting. I just really want a pumpkin spice latte. I can't believe it's on backorder."

Evelyn smirked. "You're definitely fidgeting."

Rue rolled her eyes before shifting her attention back to Evelyn. "Anyway, you'll like what we found—"

"Speaking of that," Evelyn interjected, raising a brow, "where are the books?"

Rue grimaced. "They're coming."

Evelyn narrowed her eyes. "What do you mean *coming*?"

"Layla's sneaking them out of the library." Rue tapped her fingers against the table. "She'll be here soon."

"Sneaking?" Remington's voice was dry with amusement. "Should I be concerned? I didn't bring extra protection detail if you get arrested for stealing books."

"She *works* there," Rue muttered. "I just don't want the old man at the counter to ask too many questions. He was hovering around the circulation desk this morning and I couldn't get the books out. Which is annoying because they were borrows from Harvard."

Before Evelyn could press further, a presence shifted behind them. The air thickened slightly—just enough for her to notice.

Remington glanced over his shoulder. "Thrush still in the bathroom?"

Dacre snorted into his coffee. "He said he needed a moment of silence."

Evelyn tilted her head. "At least he's wearing clean clothes and doesn't have dirt on his face."

"You saw him on the drive over," Rue muttered. "He almost jumped out of the car when a truck honked."

Remington sighed. "He's adjusting. It takes time." He watched the hallway entrance where Thrush had disappeared to nearly fifteen minutes ago.

Evelyn tapped a nail against her cup. "How is it that chaos hasn't erupted with you two in this tiny coffee shop?" Her eyes narrowed on Rue and Remington. "The fluorescent lighting isn't even that bright here."

Rue nodded toward the carved doorframe. "The runes. Keeps us from causing a disturbance."

Evelyn traced the rim of her cup. "I saw Thrush adding more when we got here."

Rue's lips quirked. "He has some magic of his own. Subtle, but strong." She glanced at her brother. "We learned some but it can't be forced. I think Thrush's came from his father."

The bell above the door jingled, and Layla strode inside, a canvas tote slung over her shoulder. She looked flushed but determined as she scanned the coffee shop. Spotting them, she hurried over, her gaze flicking toward Rue.

"Oh my gosh," she announced, plopping the bag onto the table. "Never ask me to do that again. Lugging this sack of books over here was hell." She shook her arms out. "I'm not gonna be able to lift a book for a week. Those were heavy."

Rue grinned. "You're the best, Layla. I'll make it up to you."

Layla smiled, but before she could respond, the door to the hallway leading to the restrooms swung open. Thrush stepped through, his posture stiff, his sharp gaze scanning the room as if preparing for an ambush. He had to duck so his head didn't scrape the doorframe.

Then, he stopped.

Layla turned.

Their eyes met.

The air in the coffee shop seemed to *shift*.

And then Rue's body jerked.

Her pupils vanished, her eyes going stark white. The coffee shop went silent as everyone watched Dacre catch

Rue as she convulsed slightly before going eerily still. He held her close, arms wrapped protectively around her small frame.

"She's having a vision," Dacre warned. "She'll be okay." He pressed his lips to her temple and whispered something no one else could hear.

A small meow came from beside Rue, it was muffled and coming from her bag.

"You brought the baby?" Evelyn reached for Rue's tote bag. "Why didn't you tell me sooner?" She pulled the kitten from the bag and snuggled him. "Do you want me to get you some milk while your momma takes a glimpse into the future?"

Lucipurr meowed once.

After a long, tense moment, Rue gasped and blinked rapidly, her fingers gripping the edge of the table.

She turned, looking between Layla and Thrush.

Then she exhaled a single word.

"Shit."

Lucipurr said, "*Meow*." As if to echo her.

PREVIEW OF: THE SHADOWS ARE DARKEST

*This is ***unedited rough draft***.

The Shadows are Darkest is another book in the next generation Veil of Shadows world.

This is a companion to The Sky is Starless and The Night is Endless.

The Shadows are Darkest

By M. R. Pritchard

CHAPTER ONE

Layla reached up on her tiptoes and pressed a book into place. Reshelving was a bitch without her step-stool. But those were the new rules from the manager, James, who'd just taken over Loyola Library. Layla used to have freedom in her work, now she found herself avoiding the sniffling man at the front desk. He always had something negative to say. She was too slow, spoke too long to guests, took too long reshelving. He blamed the step-stool she dragged around with her and forbid her from using it any longer. Well joke was on him because at five-foot one, Layla couldn't reach much on the top shelves, and climbing the bookshelves resulted in her slipping and scraping her shins. Her arms ached from reaching up so high. She set the big book back on the cart and brushed curls out of her face. She was going to walk this cart back to James and let him know she wasn't going to risk her life climbing the bookshelves to reshelve.

Layla marched back to the front desk, short, blonde curls bouncing right along with her irritation. She wanted to give the guy a piece of her mind. But, she didn't want to lose her job. There weren't many libraries left in Baltimore, Maryland. She thought about the abandoned Peabody Library downtown and wished she'd been able to work there before it was shuttered.

Layla turned the corner and slowed to control her cart. James was at the front desk, typing on the computer and ignoring the girl standing there. Layla recognized the girl who'd requested an interlibrary loan on a fifteenth-century art book. Layla's heartbeat picked up, she didn't like that James was ignoring the girl. She pushed the cart into place and went to the counter.

"Here to get your loaned book?" she asked the girl.

"Yeah. I thought it would never come in." She checked the time. "Is it right here? I've been waiting a while. I have class starting in a few minutes."

The girl glared at James.

"It's right here. One sec." Layla went to the hold-shelf and grabbed the book. She scanned everything and passed it to the girl. "Enjoy."

"Thanks." The girl was putting the book into her back-pack when James turned.

"Make sure you return that by the due date." He turned to Layla. "Where have you been?"

"Reshelving." Layla was logging out of the computer.

"Then why are there still books on the cart?" James pressed a finger to the glasses sliding down the bridge of his nose.

"I can't reach the top shelves. That's what my step-stool was for and you took it away." Layla's heart was beating a mile a minute, she was angry and annoyed.

James looked her up and down like she could do some-thing about her height before rounding the counter and walking off with the book cart.

Layla sighed. A notification dinged from the computer. She turned and saw a message from Rue, one of the Arche-ology doctorate students. Layla and Rue had an under-standing, many of the ancient books Rue had been requesting weren't supposed to leave the library, but Layla had been sneaking them out. They were books no one had touched in ages.

She squinted at the request Rue had sent. The title was in another language that looked like Latin and strange symbols.

"What the heck..." Layla printed the request and found that the book was at Loyola, but it was in storage in the basement. She shivered. The basement was super creepy.

The lighting was bad and the old books held a strange energy that she couldn't place. If it weren't for Rue, she'd make James go down there.

"You are gonna owe me one-hundred coffees," Layla muttered as she folded Rue's request and put it in her pocket.

CHAPTER TWO

The training yard beside Hell's castle sweltered with heat and magic, the air thick with the scent of scorched rock and blood. Thrush's breath came ragged as he squared off against another Hellion, a bigger one this time. Still wasn't bigger than him. The weight of his blade was steady in his grip. His opponent lunged, but Thrush was faster, twisting out of the way and bringing his blade down in a brutal arc. Sparks flew where steel met steel.

Thrush should have had control. Should have been able to stop at the right moment. But the anger boiled beneath his skin like molten lava. Something inside him twisted harder, dark and volatile. A shadow unfurled in his chest, spreading through his veins. The Hellion in front of him stumbled back, eyes widening in horror as sparks flew around Thrush's fingers. The air crackled.

"Thrush, back down." Remington's voice cut through the space, firm and unyielding.

Thrush gritted his teeth, but the magic didn't stop. It surged outward in a violent wave toward the Hellion he had been battling. The creature lunged to the side just in time.

A scream rang out—Evelyn.

The sparks lashed toward her like a gasoline fueled fire. She scrambled backward, but it was too fast. Before the rush of magic could touch her, a massive scaled body surged between them. Remington's basilisk slammed its tail into the ground, sending up a cloud of dust as it herded Evelyn away, its coiled body a shield.

Remington moved just as fast, shadows unfurled as he stepped into the storm of Thrush's magic. The dark tendrils pushed against the streak of magic, crackling in defiance.

"Stand. Down." Remington warned again.

Thrush sucked in a sharp breath, but the magic wouldn't settle. His pulse hammered. His hands trembled.

"I can't," he ground out.

The magic rippled, sparks flew from his fingertips, desperate to consume, to destroy—

And then Remington was in front of him, gripping the front of his shirt, shaking him hard enough to snap him back to reality. The darkness in Remington's eyes burned, his fury barely leashed.

"You almost killed her," Remington seethed.

Thrush tore free, breathing hard. "I didn't mean to—"

"Doesn't matter. Your magic doesn't give a damn about your intentions. If you can't control it, you're a danger to everyone here." Remington was searching Thrush's face. "It wasn't like this before. What is happening to you?"

Thrush ran a shaking hand through his sweat-drenched white hair. He could still feel it, coiling at the edges of his consciousness, waiting. "I don't know." His voice was raw. "I can feel it slipping. Every day, I feel like I'm losing control." He glanced at Evelyn. "I'm sorry. I didn't mean to hurt you."

Evelyn moved behind Remington. "I know. But you need to be more, wild boy."

For a long moment, there was silence between them. The basilisk still stood protectively near Evelyn, its tongue flicking, watching Thrush as though deciding whether or not to strike.

Thrush ran a hand through his hair. "You said the curse was going to clear when I took my turn as a Hellion. Your parents told me that."

Remington was watching him for a moment before he let out a slow breath and took a step back. "We need to fix it."

Thrush swallowed hard, the weight of his own power pressing down on him. He wasn't sure if it could be fixed.

But if he didn't find a way to control it, someone was going to die. And next time, there wouldn't be a basilisk to save them.

Thrush squeezed his eyes closed and held in a tik. His jaw clenched and unclenched, his shoulder quivered.

Author Note

Dear Reader,

I have been writing in the Veil of Shadows world for so long (since 2014) that I'm finding it hard to leave. Thus, I have at least 6 books planned for 2025 from the Veil of Shadows world. These will be next generation, focusing on Meg and Sparrow's children and side characters that we have loved throughout the years. AND Nero & the White Horse.

Thank you for diving headfirst into this world of angels, demons, vampires, zombies, Heaven and Hell. It's been a wild ride. Buckle up, there's plenty more on the way! I cannot wait to continue on this adventure with you.

A special *Thank you* to my husband who has listened to me type away for all of these years and also tapes all of the book boxes for me and the readers.

Another *Thank You* to my editor, Kristy. Look at all these books we've worked on! Here's to many more!

Another *Thank You* to my readers, I can't do this without your support and enthusiasm!

A final *Thank you* to Booktok! I have met so many wonderful readers and gained new fans. Long-live Book-Tok! Thank you for all of your excitement and enthusiasm for my books, for coming to my Livestreams and hanging out while I pack orders, and for being genuinely awesome and supporting.

About the Author

M. R. Pritchard delves into the profound clash between good and evil, the mystical realms of gods and monsters, and the intricate transformations of ordinary people into beings of immense power. Her gripping narratives often unfold within the haunting backdrop of apocalyptic or post-apocalyptic landscapes, offering a unique blend of suspense and wonder.

M. R. Pritchard is a two-time Kindle Scout winning author, her short story "Glitch" has been featured in the 2017 winter edition of THE FIRST LINE literary journal. Her short story "Moon Lord" has been featured in Chronicle Worlds: Half Way Home (Part of the Future Chronicles) and will be time capsuled on the moon on the Lunar Codex in 2024.

Visit her website MRPritchard.com and Subscribe. You'll get subscriber only content, deleted scenes, updates, special previews of new projects, and book deals.

ALSO BY M. R. PRITCHARD

Other Books by M. R. Pritchard

Science Fiction/post-apocalyptic:
The Phoenix Project
The Reformation
Revelation
Inception
Origins
Resurrection
The Phoenix Project Compendium Edition
The Safest City on Earth
The Man Who Fell to Earth
Heartbeat

Asteroid Riders Series
Moon Lord
Collector of Space Junk and Rebellious Dreams

Steampunk:
Tick of a Clockwork Heart

Dark Fantasy:

Veil of Shadows Series:

Sparrow Man

Nightingale Girl

Scarecrow

Raven King

Nightjar

Night Owl

Etched in Darkness

Embrace the Night

Shadows of Destiny

Midnight Serenade

Echoes of Treachery

Temptations of Fate

Omens of Darkness

Temptations of Fate

Veil of Shadows Omnibus 1

Veil of Shadows Omnibus 2

Veil of Shadows Omnibus 3

Veil of Shadows Omnibus 4

The Sky is Starless

The Night is Endless (2025)

The Shadows are Darkest (2025)

Standalone Fantasy

Thread the Bone

<u>Fantasy/Fairy Tale Love Story/Romance:</u>

Muse

Forgotten Princess Duology

Midsummer Night's Dream: A Game of Thrones

<u>Poetry/Short Stories</u>

Consequence of Gravity

www.ingramcontent.com/pod-product-compliance
Lightning Source LLC
Chambersburg PA
CBHW061543190726

48289CB00004B/1149